Forever Love
BOOK 2

USA TODAY BESTSELLING AUTHOR
SIOBHAN DAVIS

Copyright © Siobhan Davis 2019. Siobhan Davis asserts the moral right to be identified as the author of this work. All rights reserved under International and Pan-American Copyright Conventions.

This is a work of fiction. Names, characters, places, incidents and dialogues are products of the author's imagination or are used fictitiously. Any resemblance to actual people, living or dead, or events is entirely coincidental.

This book is sold subject to the condition that it shall not, by way of trade or otherwise be lent, resold, hired out, or otherwise circulated without the prior written consent of the author. No part of this publication may be reproduced, transmitted, decompiled, or stored in or introduced into any information storage and retrieval system, in any form or by any means, whether electronic or mechanical, including photocopying, without the express written permission of the author.

Printed by Amazon
Paperback edition © May 2019

ISBN-13: 9781094711072

Editor: Kelly Hartigan (XterraWeb) editing.xterraweb.com
Cover design by Robin Harper https://wickedbydesigncovers.wixsite.com
Photographer: Sara Eirew
Cover Models: Ripp Baker and Pamela Tremblay Mcallen
Formatting by The Deliberate Page www.deliberatepage.com

CHAPTER 1
Summer

"WE SHOULD'VE WORN bikinis," my bestie Hannah jokes, plucking at the lacy tank top clinging to her chest like a second skin, as we navigate our way through the throngs of people toward the bar. The popular Newark bar-slash-club is teeming with people, loud music pumping from speakers as the Indie band on stage works the crowd like pros.

"That would've been one guaranteed way of achieving my goal," I shout in her ear with a grin. "Why didn't I think of that?"

"You seriously think you'll have any issue finding a hookup in here?" Jordan—Hannah's boyfriend—inquires, quirking a brow as he glances around the room. "You could wear a sack and easily find someone to rid you of that pesky V-card."

Hannah thumps her boyfriend in the upper arm. "Don't be so flippant. Summer has standards, and the guy needs to meet the criteria."

"What criteria?" he asks, shoving his way to the bar and propping his elbows on the grimy countertop.

I scoot up alongside him, with Hannah on my other side. "He needs to be older and know what he's doing. I haven't waited this long to give it up in a sweaty encounter with some drunken frat boy who needs a compass to locate my clit."

Jordan smothers a laugh as the bartender approaches. He casts a skeptical glance over us, but the magical bands around our wrists, and the line of thirsty customers, are enough to convince the overworked bartender to let his suspicions over our age go, and he accepts Jordan's order of three beers without question.

That hundred bucks I spent on a fake ID is already paying dividends.

With beers in hand, we navigate our way around the other side of the bar where it's not so packed.

"Damn, why does it have to be so hot," Hannah moans, fanning her face with her hands.

"We won't stay long," I promise, patting her arm. "Once I find my prey, I won't be hanging around." My eyes flash with intent as I take a sip of my beer, scanning the talent in the room.

Jordan rolls his eyes. "You're something else, Summer."

I shrug, smiling back at him. "You know what I'm like when I set my mind to something."

"Pigheaded," Hannah quips, smirking as she brings the bottle to her mouth.

"Determined," I correct her.

"You know I can call Justin, and he'd come to the city in a heartbeat for you," Jordan says. "He'd help you out for sure."

"I love Justin. You know I do, but only as a friend, and it'd be weird having sex with him. I value his friendship too much to risk it."

Justin is Jordan's best friend from Bridgeville, our hometown, and when Hannah and Jordan started going out in freshman year of high school, Justin and I kissed a few times. I know Hannah and Jordan would have loved for us to become a couple too, but I realized, almost immediately, that Justin and I would be much better off as friends. Still, that hasn't stopped my bestie and her boyfriend from trying to play matchmaker over the years. But you can't force chemistry. It's either there or it isn't.

"Are you sure you'd rather do it with a random?" Hannah asks, for like the millionth time.

"We can't all be as lucky as you." I clink my bottle against hers, smiling warmly at Jordan, while I continue to check out the guys in our vicinity. "And you didn't have three overprotective big brothers cock-blocking you at every turn."

"True dat." Jordan scrubs a hand over his stubbly chin. "Charlie had every fucking guy terrified to even ask you out."

"Hence why I'm still a virgin starting college."

"It's not that unusual, Sum," Hannah says, "and I'm just worried you're going into this without thinking it through."

"I don't need to think it through," I confirm, my eyes homing in on the heaving dance floor with interest. "I'm ready. I want to have sex, and I want it to be a night to remember. That wouldn't have happened with any of the guys back home. I want to find some hot, older guy to rock my world and ensure I'll never forget the night I lost my virginity. And I want to walk away in the morning with no regrets and zero plans to see him again."

I extend my hands into the air, swaying my hips in time to the music. "I'm finally free, Han. Free to do anything I want. Be anyone I want. And the last thing I want to do is hold off for a boyfriend and tie myself down freshman year of college. No offense to you two, but I want to spread my wings before settling down."

"None taken," Hannah says with affection. "And if you're sure, then you should go for it."

"I'm glad you approve," I say, putting my beer down and handing hers to Jordan. "Because you're dancing with me."

I tug the hem of my short black minidress down, smoothing a hand over the front to remove the wrinkles. It's a simple dress, but it's well made, and it hugs my delicate curves in all the right places. I've always been a believer that less is more which is why I'm not wearing too much makeup and I've got my pink Converse on my feet instead of the red stilettos Hannah favored.

"C'mon." Hannah gives Jordan a quick kiss before looping her arm through mine. "Let's get this show on the road."

We push our way into the middle of the dance floor and move in time to the music. I toss my long, dark, wavy hair over my shoulder, shimmying my hips back and forth and losing myself to the rhythmic beats. I've no clue who the band is, but they're awesome, and it's not long before I've forgotten all about guys and I'm letting the music carry me away. My eyes are closed, and I'm swaying my hips with my hands roaming my body, absorbing the melody and lyrics, feeling the music all the way through to my bones, when Hannah nudges me in the side.

"Hottie alert dead ahead," she shouts in my ear. "And he hasn't taken his eyes off you in the last five minutes."

I jerk my eyes open, looking straight in front of me, and my gaze instantly locks on the guy in question. He's standing at the front area of the bar in a small circle of guys and girls. But he's not paying any attention to the surrounding conversation. He's blatantly staring at me, not even attempting to disguise his interest.

He's smoking hot, and the way he's devouring me on sight has my body tingling all over.

"I think my ovaries just exploded," Hannah hollers over the loud music, flattening a hand over her chest as her eyes drink him in.

"Mine too," I murmur, readily agreeing as I confidently return his inquiring gaze. His biceps flex as he brings a bottle of beer to his mouth, and I watch in fascination as his throat works while he drinks. Watching him swallow is one of the sexiest things I've ever witnessed, and my panties are already wet, my core aching in a way I haven't felt in forever.

He doesn't take his eyes off me as he drinks, and his intense stare sends a shiver coursing through me. His long, slim fingers grip the bottle with ease, and now I'm imagining his big hands exploring every inch of my body. Setting his beer down on the bar, he runs a hand through his dirty blond hair, muscles rolling in his arm with the motion.

Hannah and I are captivated, watching him as if we've never seen a hot guy before. And I know it's obvious as fuck. Because we're standing in the middle of the dance floor, motionless, with our jaws trailing the ground, bits of drool clinging to the corners of our mouths. The guy's voluptuous lips twitch at the corner, and I curl my fingers at him in a "come hither" gesture. His smile expands as he walks toward us, and a shot of liquid lust pools in my core.

"Holy fucking hotness," Hannah exclaims, and I couldn't agree more.

I hold his gaze as he walks this way, unashamedly ogling him, making sure he knows I return his interest. With the way his shirt clings to his broad shoulders and toned chest, it's clear this guy works out, and I'm betting he has a body made for sin.

Check box number one.

While I'm not the greatest judge of age, he's definitely no frat boy, and he exudes confidence and maturity that confirms he's older.

Check box number two.

He's weaving his way through the masses, and I swear I hear a collective swoon from the largely female crowd. A few girls make grabs for him, but his focus is singular, and locked on me. He's already making me feel hugely desired, and I'm seriously turned on, and we haven't even spoken yet.

Check box number three.

His cocky swagger is like an aphrodisiac as he stalks toward me, quickly eating up the distance with his long strides. I can't tell the color of his eyes yet, but he's sexy and good-looking, and he sure looks like he knows how to use his equipment.

Check. Check. Check.

I throw out my mental checklist, already knowing this guy fits the bill.

I keep a heated smile on my face as he approaches, my heart beating excitedly behind my rib cage.

He stands directly in front of me, towering over my five-foot-six-inch frame, like some Greek Adonis. "I'm Ryan," he says, in a rich deep voice that does funny things to my insides. "And you're beautiful."

His gorgeous, big blue eyes suck me in, and a shiver runs through me.

It's hard not to gawk.

This guy is seriously gorgeous.

Dark cobalt eyes framed by a thick layer of long lashes. Chiseled jawline with just the right amount of stubble peppering his chin and cheeks. Strong nose. Kissable lips. And that hair. My hands curl into fists as I fight the craving to drag my fingers through the dark blond strands to see if they feel as silky as they look.

Snapping out of my daze, I extend my hand. "I'm smitten, and you're sexy as hell."

His chest rumbles as he chuckles, taking my offered hand and bringing it to his lips. My knees buckle when he presses a kiss to my knuckles, delicious tremors ricocheting all over my body. "Dance with me?" he asks, moving behind me before I've even replied. His arm wraps around my waist, and he pulls me flush against his lean, hard body. I place my hands over his, loving the feel of his skin against mine.

My body's on fire as we move in sync to the music, and it's not from the dense heat in the room.

Remembering Hannah, I look around, but she's disappeared. I glance over my shoulder, at the place where we left Jordan, breathing a sigh of relief when I notice her draped around her boyfriend.

Ryan pushes my hair aside, nuzzling into my neck, and a little moan escapes my lips. "You feel so good pressed up against me," he whispers, grazing his lips along the column of my neck, his body moving fluidly against mine as we dance a provocative dance.

I arch my head back, granting him more access. "Don't stop," I plead. "I want more."

His body shakes with silent laughter as his mouth turns more urgent. He presses hot, wet kisses up and down my neck, nibbling on my earlobe, as his hands begin to softly explore. His fingers brush against my sides, moving up and down my body. My movements become harder, and I push my ass back into his groin, gasping as I feel the hard length of his erection pressing into me.

We're grinding against one another in a way that's hugely obvious, and my body is humming and purring, my arousal elevated to "don't give a fuck if I'm in public dirty dancing with some hot, random stranger" mode. My heart is soaring in my chest, my pulse throbbing in my neck. I've done nothing like this before, and the exhilaration is addictive. Sure, I've made out with guys, blown guys, and let a few go down on me, but it was all closeted, in quick, drunken fumbles at parties.

My brothers would freak the hell out if they could see me now, but that acknowledgment only pours more fuel on the flames.

I have spent my entire life in the quiet little town of Bridgeville.

A place I'm proud to call home.

A place I love wholeheartedly.

But it's insular and suffocating at the best of times. I couldn't sneeze around town without someone finding out about it. I'm unbelievably excited to be starting UD in a few weeks, for a variety of reasons but especially because of the freedom it offers. I love my parents and my brothers to the moon and back, and I'm so damn lucky I have them watching out for me, but their smothering protectiveness has clipped my wings, and now it's time to let them soar.

I've so many ambitions. So many plans. And I can't wait to begin this new phase of my life.

Ryan's hand subtly grazes the side of my breast, and my core throbs painfully. We're pressed tight against one another, with no gap between us, his enticing body melded against my spine, and I want more.

I want all of him.

I don't care that I don't know him.

That we've barely exchanged any words.

This is exactly how I want it to be.

One hot illicit night with a stranger.

A memory to cling to when I'm old and gray.

It's clear this isn't his first rodeo, and I'm under no illusion. His moves are practiced and assured.

He does this a lot, but I honestly don't care.

Reaching my arm back, I cup the nape of his neck, angling my head around as I pull his face down to mine. Our lips collide in a searing-hot kiss I feel all the way to the tips of my toes. He takes over, his mouth gliding with skill against mine. Keeping his lips locked on mine, he repositions me with a gentle touch until my front is pressed against his. He leans down, and I stretch up, my arms circling his neck as his arms wrap around my waist. His tongue licks the seam of my mouth, requesting entry, and I open freely for him. Stars explode behind my closed eyelids as his tongue plunders my mouth, licking me all over, and I whimper against his lips, pulling him tighter.

He grabs hold of my ass, prodding his erection into my pelvis, and then my hands are exploring, roaming the ripped planes of his muscular back down to his delectable ass. We're panting and groaning, and I'm ready to combust when he pulls back, peering down at me with lust in his eyes. "Want to get out of here?"

I nod, barely able to string a coherent sentence together.

He presses his lips to mine in a tender kiss that's completely at odds with the way we were just ravishing one another. "Fuck, you're so sexy. I can't remember the last time I was this horny."

His words shouldn't thrill me, but they do. "Try forever, in my case," I honestly admit.

His mouth twists into a devilish smile as he leans in closer. "You've gorgeous legs," he whispers into my ear, sweeping his fingers up the side of my thigh, and my legs almost go out from under me. "And now I'm imagining them wrapped around my neck."

My core throbs in a way it's never throbbed before, and butterflies scatter in my chest at the thought I might get what I'd hoped for. Ryan is all man, and the thoughts of him moving over and in me has me in a nervous-excited space. "That can be arranged," I tell him in a breathy voice, hoping he doesn't see through my façade. I doubt he'd be as keen if he knew how inexperienced I am.

"Your place or mine?" he inquires, taking my hand in his much larger one.

"Mine." I had already agreed to this with Jordan and Hannah in advance. They want me to be safe, and close by, in case anything happens. "I'm staying at the Regency for the weekend."

"You're an out of towner?" he asks, looking happy at that news.

"Yes," I semi-lie. While I'm technically an outsider now, I won't be come August when classes start. But he doesn't need to know that. The less we know about one another, the better. "Is that a problem?" I inquire, already guessing it's not.

"Nope." He plants a hard kiss on my mouth. "Quite the opposite." He waggles his brows.

"You want no attachments. Got it."

His eyes drill into mine. "If that's a problem for you—"

"It's not," I rush to reassure him. "Not at all. I'm only interested in one night. I'm not interested in forming any attachment either."

"Cool." He tugs me forward, assertively forging a path through the crowd.

Curious by nature, I ask, "Do you do this a lot?" as we exit the dance floor.

"Define a lot." I can hear the smirk in his tone.

Maybe I should be offended or disgusted, but I'm not. All I can think is this guy will have mad skills, and he couldn't be any more perfect. He's not interested in making small talk for hours to charm me into his bed. He's direct about what he wants, and that speaks to me on a base level. We're both on the same page, and I want to lose my virginity to him. We're attracted to one another, and I can tell this will be a purely physical encounter.

It's exactly what I'm looking for—mind-blowing sex with a random stranger.

One night.

No expectations.

No strings.

No ties.

"There's no such thing," I cheekily retort. "And I couldn't care less."

He spins me around as we reach the edge of the dance floor. "You genuinely mean that." I nod. "That's really fucking refreshing," he adds, caressing my cheek. "I'll give you a night to remember." His voice drips with promise, and my core pulses in response. "I'll worship you like a queen." And, as he lowers his mouth to mine, kissing me deeply and unhurriedly, I don't doubt him for a second.

CHAPTER 2
Ryan

"YOU SURE YOU want to do this?" the guy—Jordan, I think she said his name was—asks her for the umpteenth time as we pile into the elevator. He's getting on my very last nerve.

And it's not like I don't get it.

He's protective of his friend in the same way I'm protective of my sister Gabby, and I have huge respect for him for it. But *I* know where to draw a line. This guy hasn't stopped the whole ride back to the hotel. Now, we're finally on the home stretch, and he has to go there again.

"Han. Please. Take him into your room, and fuck his brains out so his mind stops churning," the hot little thing at my side says. She darts in, kissing his cheek. "Stop, Jordan. You're not my brother. And I've got this."

"Like I said in the Uber, you can trust me to look after her. She's safe with me," I reiterate.

And you have a photo of my driver's license, I mentally add, rolling my eyes as I recall his aggressive request and the way he scowled at my ID. I'm guessing it's to do with the obvious age gap, but who the fuck cares. We're both consenting adults, and that's all that matters.

Hannah hauls Jordan away, finally leaving us in peace.

My hookup takes her key card out of her purse, unlocking the door. "I'm sorry about that," she says as we walk into her hotel room. "He's a little overprotective."

"A little?" I quirk a brow. "I'm protective over my sister, and he makes me look like a pussy in comparison."

"Enough about Jordy." She slides her palms up my chest. "I want to get tonight back on track."

"Sounds good." I grab her waist, reeling her into my body as my lips descend on hers. There's nothing tender about this kiss or the way she's arching her tight, hot little body into me. The peaks of her nipples are taut through the material of her dress, turning the hard-on in my pants into a solid wall of muscle that begs to drive inside her. I lift her up, and she automatically wraps her gorgeous legs around my waist. My palm slips under the hem of the ridiculously short dress she's wearing, meeting smooth, bare flesh and my cock jerks in anticipation. I wasn't lying when I told her I haven't been this horny in ages. This girl has seriously turned me on, and I can't wait to get her writhing underneath me.

I place her down flat on the bed, hovering over her on my knees. "You sure this is what you want?" I ask her again, because a guy can never ask too many times.

"Hundo P," she confirms in a breathy tone, betraying evidence of her age.

Back at the bar, I had given no consideration to her age until I got up closer. Despite the band around her wrist suggesting she was twenty-one or older, I guessed she was younger. Before we left, I asked her outright, almost changing my mind when she confirmed she was only eighteen.

At twenty-six, I'm a good bit older, and I rarely go for women who are that young. But there's just something about her. And she's obviously as into this as I am into her, so where's the harm? It'll be one night of fun, and then we'll never see each other again. I don't see it as an issue.

She sits up, stroking my cock through my jeans, and any last-minute reservations fly out the window. I rip my shirt up over my head, fighting a knowing grin as her jaw slackens at the sight of my naked chest. "Fuck. Me," she blurts, her eyes mentally caressing me.

"I fully intend to, sweetheart." I stretch around to unzip her dress. "Take it off," I command as I stand, quickly getting rid of my jeans and shoes. She stands up on the bed, shimmying the dress down her hips and kicking it away. My cock throbs, precum leaking out of the tip, as I drink her in. She's so sexy standing in front of me in a black lace thong and matching bra, with her hands on her slim hips, shooting me dark, seductive looks. But there's also an innocence about her that's endearing.

As soon as the thought pops into my head, another unwelcome one does. I want to ignore it, but I can't. I crawl onto the bed in just my boxers and pull her down onto my lap. "You have done this before, right?"

"Of course," she squeaks, and I instantly know it's a lie.

"Fuck." I lift her off me, rubbing my hands down my face. "I know that's a lie, and I can't do this. I'm sorry." I lean over the end of the bed, reaching for my jeans.

"Because you don't fuck virgins, or some other reason?" she asks, hurt lacing her tone.

I cup her face. "Because your first time shouldn't be like this." I peer into her beautiful blue eyes, wishing I could be selfish enough to forego doing the right thing. "You won't ever get your first time back, and it should be with someone you love."

She straddles my lap before I can stop her, resting her hands on my shoulder. "Was yours?"

"Fuck, no," I admit before I think to lie. "And I've regretted it ever since."

"Why?" Genuine curiosity is etched across her face. "Because you didn't love her, or it wasn't any good?"

"Both, although I'm just as much to blame as she was. I didn't have a fucking clue how to pleasure a woman back then."

A triumphant glimmer appears in her eyes. "And that's exactly why I want to do this with you. Why I set out to lose my V-card tonight to an older guy."

My eyes almost bug out of my head. "You had this planned?"

She nods before frowning. "Well, not with you, because you were the one who approached me. But, yes, I wanted to do the deed tonight. I'm only in the city for the weekend, and I don't want to waste the perfect opportunity."

She runs her fingers along the fine hairs at the nape of my neck, and fuck, if I don't feel it in every part of me. This girl's touch affects me in a way I haven't felt in years.

That's another good reason to get the fuck out of here, but I'm stalling, because she intrigues me.

And my cock's still stiff as a brick, and he's a greedy motherfucker who doesn't understand what it means to have a moral code.

I shouldn't be contemplating this, but I know, deep down, that I haven't completely ruled it out. "Why now? And why a stranger?" I inquire, smoothing a hand up and down her spine. Her skin is like silk under my callused fingers which isn't helping my cause.

"Because I'm ready. I want to have sex. I want to explore that side of myself that's undiscovered. If I'd found someone back home I'd wanted to have sex with, then I wouldn't be a virgin, but there's been no one, and I…" She trails off, her brow furrowing as she tries to find the right words. Her brow smooths out, and she smiles at me, digging her fingers into my hair as she speaks.

"I want it to be memorable. Most all my friends said it was a non-event, and I don't want that. I want to remember tonight for years to come. I know I could find someone to hook up with once I start college, but I don't want to give it away to some guy with fumbling hands and a lack of regard for my needs."

Her confidence is super sexy, and I work hard to swallow my lustful growl.

"I want it to be with someone who knows what he's doing," she continues. "Someone who will make it enjoyable for me. Someone who will ensure it's a pleasant memory." She kisses me sweetly. "Someone like you."

She sits back on her heels, examining my face carefully. "But I won't beg for it either." She straightens her spine, drilling me with a determined look. "I'm eighteen, and I know what I want. There's nothing wrong with you and me being together like this, but if you can't get past the fact I'm young and inexperienced, then it's best we end this right now."

"I get why your friend was so protective now," I murmur, resting my hand gently on her hip.

"Jordy and Hannah are the best, and I love them for worrying about me, but this is my decision, and they ultimately respect that." Her eyes penetrate mine. "I have given this a lot of consideration, and I know what I want. I want to have sex with you." She leans in and kisses me deeply before pulling back, her face flushed, her lips slightly swollen. "So, what's it to be? Will you fuck me?"

Her eyes glimmer with challenge and determination, but I detect the vulnerability she's working hard to disguise. Rejecting her would hurt her, and I don't want to dent her confidence or cause her any pain.

She wants this.

I want this.

And I *will* make it good for her.

I can give her what she wants, and we'll both walk out of here happy and sated.

Gripping her hips, I pull her body in tight against mine. "No. I will not fuck you." She opens her mouth to respond, but I place my fingers over her lips, silencing her. "I will make love to you, because that's the way it should be when it's your first time." Taking her wrist, I plant a tender kiss to her skin, loving how she shivers at my touch. "I'll ask you one final time. And whatever way you answer is fine." I kiss her wrist again, never taking my eyes off her. "Are you sure you want to do this with me?"

She nods her head enthusiastically. "Yes. I want you to make love to me. I'm even more sure now." Reaching around, she unclasps her bra, quickly tossing it aside, baring her naked chest.

My eyes lock on her tits, and my cock throbs behind my boxers. They're small, but a decent handful, and perfectly formed with neat rose-colored nipples. I'm already salivating, my body craning to be inside her. "You're so beautiful." I kiss her lips before lowering my head to her left nipple, gently sucking it into my mouth. Her skin is so soft and pliable, her small bud tightening the minute my tongue suctions on it. I tenderly knead her other breast, enjoying the little moans she emits as her hips rock against me. I trail my nose along the delicate skin of her exposed neck before I devour her mouth with all the pent-up need mushrooming inside me.

Flipping us around, I place her flat on the bed, resting her head on top of the pillows. I kiss her for a few minutes until she's moaning and writhing underneath me, and then I work my way down her body, kissing, sucking, licking, and caressing every inch of her beautiful skin before lowering my mouth to her pussy, inhaling her intoxicating scent.

"Please," she whimpers, bucking her hips up as I rub my nose along her slit through the thin lacy material.

Hooking my thumbs in the side of her thong, I slide it down her legs and off her body. I stand, my eyes drinking in her gorgeous nakedness as I kick off my boxers and grab a couple condoms. My dick pulses as she feasts on it with her eyes, licking her lips as her eyelids darken with lust. I crawl up over her body, tossing the condoms on the bedside table. "You are fucking gorgeous, and I'm feeling very honored," I admit over her lips as I keep my body propped up by my elbows.

"Well, thanks, but could you stop talking now and get in me already?" She quirks a brow as she grabs hold of my ass, pulling me down on top of her.

I chuckle before brushing my lips against hers. "So impatient." I shake my head, grinning. "I need to make sure you're ready. Trust me to do this the right way."

She wraps her legs around my waist, angling her hips up into me, and I groan as my cock presses against her silky, warm flesh. "Trust me, I'm ready. If I was any wetter, we'd both be drowning."

A laugh bursts free of me. "Are you always this direct?"

"Always." She smiles as her hands absentmindedly caress the cheeks of my ass, causing precum to leak from the tip of my cock. "In my family, we have a rule we always speak our minds." She shrugs. "And no one lets an argument or emotions fester. I've grown up with straight talking, and I don't know any other way to be."

In a lot of ways, I could say the same of my family. Except for the festering part, but I shove those thoughts aside before they distract me. "I like that." I slide down her body, watching her eyes roll back in her head as I kiss my way along her hot flesh. "I like you."

"I like you too," she pants. "But I'd like you a lot more if you got to it."

I chuckle against her stomach as I move lower. Pushing her legs aside, I sink to the apex of her thighs, licking my lips in anticipation. "Has anyone ever gone down on you before?" I ask as I line my mouth up with her glistening pussy.

"Yes. I'm a virgin, but I'm not completely inexperienced."

I scowl at her response, not liking the thought of anyone touching any part of her, before I realize how hypocritical my thoughts are. "Well, buckle down, honey, because no one has eaten you like this." Before she can reply, I plant my mouth against her inviting pussy and ravish her with my tongue and my lips.

She is absolutely drenched, yet when I push a finger inside her she's so tight I almost change my mind. But my dick won't let me. And I don't want to disappoint the gorgeous girl moaning and squirming on the bed.

Slowly, I work my finger in and out until I feel her loosen up, and then I add another one. When her moans ratchet up, and she's arching her back off the bed, I suction my mouth over her clit and suck hard as my fingers continue to pump in and out of her, going faster and faster until she detonates, shattering under my touch in a way that sends my heart soaring. I watch her as my fingers and mouth continue to milk her climax, and the look of sheer bliss on her face almost has me coming on the spot.

When her body relaxes, I move up to kiss her before grabbing a condom.

"Let me." She takes it from my hands, rolling it down over my aching cock. "You're huge," she exclaims, a look of concern washing over her face for the first time. "Are you sure that thing'll fit in me?"

I work hard to smother a smile. "It'll fit and I'll take it slow. I promise." Gently, I push her down, lowering my body carefully against hers. I kiss her long and hard, peppering her face and neck with kisses while skimming my hands over her body, caressing her lush curves.

Her body is toned yet supple, and I could touch her all day long and never tire. I dip my finger inside her once more to check she's ready. Then I line up my cock and slowly inch inside her, keeping my face locked on hers the whole time. "If you want me to stop, you only have to ask." I stall as a glimmer of pain flashes in her eyes. "It will hurt a little at first," I confirm so she knows what to expect.

"I'm good," she rasps. "Don't stop. Just go slow."

It takes colossal willpower to hold myself back, but I do, because I don't want to hurt her. When I feel myself pushing through the tight ridge, I stop, watching her expression carefully. "You okay?"

"Keep going," she says through gritted teeth, and I push on until I'm fully seated inside her.

The feeling is indescribable.

Her walls hug my cock, and I know I won't last long. I move really slowly as I kiss her, my hands caressing her breasts while I carefully plunge in and out of her. Gradually, I feel her softening, and she moves instinctively against me.

"Faster," she pants, digging her fingers into the cheeks of my ass and tightening her legs around my waist.

I rock into her faster, still holding back, all the time kissing and worshiping her body. When I feel her gripping me tighter and her body tenses up with impending climax, I lose my restraint, pumping into her more rapidly, allowing myself to let go. She orgasms a split second before I do, and our joint mutual groaning and heavy breathing fills the air. My skin is slick with sweat as I pump my hips two final times before collapsing on the bed, pulling her with me, keeping our bodies fused together.

Pushing damp tendrils of hair back off her glowing face, I peer deep into her eyes. "You all right?" I examine every inch of her face to gauge her mood. "Was that okay?"

"I'm just perfect." Her smile is radiant as she beams at me. "And it was more than okay. That was amazing. Now I understand what all the fuss is about."

I cup her face and press a tender kiss to her lips. "That was incredible. Thank you."

Her arms encircle my neck, and she pushes her delectable tits into my chest. Her eyes sparkle with mischief as she grins at me. "How soon can you be ready to go again?"

My cock instantly hardens at her words, and I push my hips into hers, ensuring she feels what she's doing to me. "How soon is too soon?"

In a flash, she's straddling me, her long hair cascading down her back as she rocks on top of me in a seductive pose that cranks my lust to a new all-time high. "No such thing as too soon," she purrs, grinding down on my cock, and I can't contain my grin as I grab a fresh condom from the bedside table.

CHAPTER 3
Summer

"TWO-BED PLACES WILL be scarce at this late stage," my brother Charlie says on Sunday evening as we tuck into the sumptuous pot roast dinner Mom made.

"I'm confident we'll find something," I reply, in between mouthfuls of gorgeous beef, not overly worried, even if our apartment-hunting expedition this weekend was unsuccessful.

Jordan's last-minute decision to join Hannah and me at the University of Delaware has messed up our plans. Before, us girls were happy to share a dorm room, but now, we're apartment hunting off campus so we can all live together.

"I'm sure Austin will let you stay with him if you can't find a place," Mom says, adding another dollop of creamy mashed potatoes to my plate.

I almost choke on the lump of beef in my mouth. "I'm sure Austin does not want me cramping his style," I splutter.

"Or cramping yours," Charlie teases with a wink, and I discharge a "shut the fuck up" look in his direction.

"Besides, he doesn't have room for all three of us."

"I don't know why you think it's a good idea to move in with a couple anyway," Charlie says, pushing his empty plate away and rubbing his flat stomach. "That was awesome, Mom. Thanks."

Mom removes his empty plate, messing up his dark hair, before leaning in to kiss his cheek.

"They're my best friends. And I don't want to share with a stranger."

A knowing smile slips over my mouth at the mention of the word *stranger* as my mind instantly conjures up images of Friday night and my tangle between the sheets with a hot, sexy stranger. My body tingles all over, and my core aches, reminding me I'm still sore after our marathon sex session. I never knew I could contort my body into so many positions or that I could orgasm so many times, especially as a complete novice, but Ryan worked my body like a pro, and I was putty in his skillful hands. We didn't catch a wink of sleep all night, and we couldn't get enough of one another. He was so gentle and considerate, and I really couldn't have chosen a better guy to do the deed with.

It was, hands down, the most amazing night of my life.

"Why are you grinning like a crazy person?" Charlie asks, his blue eyes narrowing suspiciously. My youngest brother graduated from UD recently with a degree in agriculture and natural resources, so he's well attuned to college life, and I'm guessing he understands this past weekend was about more than just apartment hunting.

"I'm just happy. Is there a law against that?" I retort, offering him my sweetest smile.

"Uh-huh." He eyeballs me with intensity. "Maybe you *should* stay with Austin."

"Don't start." I roll my eyes. "You need to quit the protective big brother shit. That might've worked when I was still in high school, but I'm eighteen and starting college soon. You, Austin, and Marc don't get to pull that crap on me anymore."

"That's what I'm afraid of." He scrubs his hand across the thin layer of stubble on his chin. "College guys are horny fucking bastards, Sum. You need to watch yourself. Especially with those frat boys. They are total fucking manwhores."

"Charles Benjamin Petersen." Mom admonishes Charlie with a slap to the back of the head. "I will not tolerate that foul language at the dinner table."

"Aw, come on, Ma." He rubs the back of his head. "I'm only looking out for my baby sister." He accepts a cup of steaming hot coffee from her with an innocent smile plastered upon his face.

"You can look out for your sister without resorting to cussing," Dad says, finally lifting his head from his newspaper. "No disrespecting your momma."

"Sorry, Mom." Charlie looks sheepish, and I grin, pleased it focuses the conversation on my brother and not his statement.

But the reprieve doesn't last long.

"Your brother has a point though," Mom adds, pinning me with her serious face as she takes my half-eaten plate away and hands me a coffee. I groan, mentally preparing myself for it. "I know you're on the pill, but make sure you always use a condom. *Always.* Trust none of those boys, no matter what loving endearments they whisper in your ear."

Charlie spits coffee all over the table, and Dad turns pale. "Jeez, Mom. You shouldn't be encouraging that sh—stuff."

"Give it a rest." I roll my eyes again as I mop up the mess he made with a paper towel. "It's not like I'm going to sleep my way through campus or anything close to it."

Although I plan on indulging my newly discovered sexual appetite whenever I feel like it, it doesn't mean I won't be safe. I'm not completely reckless. But now I've gotten a taste for sex, there's no holding me back.

"What about young Justin?" Dad muses, putting his paper down and giving me his full, undivided attention. "I always thought he was sweet on you. You should date him."

My eyes almost bug out of my head remembering all the times Dad sent less than friendly vibes in Justin's direction any time he dropped by our farmhouse. "Justin's a friend, Dad. Besides, he has a full ride to Oregon State, and he'll be thousands of miles away from me."

"Exactly my point." He wiggles his eyebrows, and his tan, weather-beaten brow creases with the motion.

"Benny." Mom shakes her head, strands of reddish-brown hair tumbling around her face with the motion. "Summer can date who ever she pleases, and you'll just have to get used to it." Her tone brokers no argument, and I'm glad to have at least one member of my family on my side. "She's not your little princess anymore."

"I'll always be your princess, Daddy," I refute, getting up and pressing a kiss atop his head, noticing more gray hairs among the dark strands. "Having sex with boys won't change that."

This time, it's Dad's turn to choke on his coffee.

"I'm calling Austin," Charlie cuts in, removing his cell from the pocket of his jeans to phone my eldest brother. "If you room with him, he can at least vet the guys first."

I snatch the cell from his hand before he can make the call. "If you're trying to deliberately piss me off, you're doing a stand-up job." I faux glare at my brother. "For the last time, I am *not* staying with Austin. And, I'm well able to vet guys myself, but thanks a bunch for the vote of confidence."

"I literally cannot wait to get out of here," I grumble to Hannah an hour later, flopping down on her bed. "You should've heard the crap coming out of Dad's and Charlie's mouths. Their attitudes are like something from the Dark Ages."

"Charlie's just spent four years fucking his way around UD, so he's probably right to worry," she unhelpfully adds.

"I don't know if that's true, but if it is, then he's a total hypocrite. Of all my brothers, he's usually the one I can count on to have my back, but he put Austin and Marc to shame today. And it's not as if I'm planning on riding the entire male campus. It's ridiculous."

She nudges me in the side, grinning. "Imagine the hissy fit he'd throw if he knew about Friday night."

Rolling onto my stomach beside her, I laugh. "Oh, my God. He'd blow a gasket. They all would." I prop my head up with my hand, facing her. "It's just as well I won't ever see Ryan again. It's safer for him that way," I quip.

"I don't know how you can do that."

"Do what?"

"Have an incredible night of amazing sex with an awesome guy and just walk away knowing you'll never set eyes on him again. Aren't you even the tiniest bit tempted to hook up with him again?"

"Nope," I instantly reply, popping the P. "It was a onetime deal, and we're both happy with that even if I have been replaying every second of my time with him on a continual loop in my head." I roll onto my back, smiling up at the ceiling like the cat that got the cream. "He was truly something else."

"You know Jordy still has a copy of his driver's license on his cell. If you want to contact him, I can get his name and address for you."

I shake my head. "Tell him to delete it. I won't be contacting Ryan again. As hot as he is, and as incredible as the sex was, I don't want to be tied down, and I very much doubt he's interested in dating a college freshman. In fact, I got the distinct impression he doesn't date, but he clearly hooks up. *A lot*. Because he had all the right moves."

There's a dreamy quality to my voice, like every time I think of him. And I want to retain that feel-good factor. Attempting something more could ruin all the good memories I have of him, that night, and handing over my V-card.

Hannah copies my move, and we lie side by side on her bed, both staring up at the ceiling. "I'm so glad your first time was a good experience. You were right to wait and do it like you did."

"I've no regrets," I honestly admit, turning my head to look at her. "My only fear is that he's set an impossibly high standard now. That no college guy will ever measure up."

"You could have fun testing that theory out," Hannah suggests, smiling wickedly.

"That I can," I agree, with a matching smile.

August can't come quick enough.

"So, I hear someone's no longer in possession of her V-card," Justin says with a cheeky grin on Friday night as we sit on the bed of Jordy's truck at the side of the field.

"If your bestie wasn't so busy groping my bestie, I'd punch him in the nuts for telling you that." Not that I specifically asked Jordan to keep it private, but it was an unspoken rule.

"I won't tell another soul. I was just teasing."

I dangle my legs off the edge of the truck as I take another sip of my warm beer. Out on the field below us, the party is in full swing. "It's cool. I'll be out of here in a few weeks, and I give zero fucks once I'm gone."

"You say that like you plan on never coming back home."

I shrug. "I'll be back. The rents would never let me get away without regular visits, but I don't plan on settling back here after I graduate. I want to go traveling for a year or two, and then I'll probably move permanently to the city if I can get a teaching job somewhere close by."

"You have it all worked out."

I snort. "Hardly." I nudge his shoulder. "I have a rough plan for my life, but I'm deliberately keeping it loose so I can take advantage of any amazing opportunities that come my way. This feels like the start of something epic, and I never want to lose that feeling."

"I admire you so much, Sum. You haven't changed since you were a kid, and you're still the same sweet, adventurous girl I remember."

Thinking back to last weekend, I'm wondering how sweet he'd think I was if he knew the things I let Ryan do to me. "Knock it off, dude." I elbow him in the ribs. "If anyone has his head screwed on right, it's you. You've always wanted to play ball in college and join the NFL, and you're on track to achieve your goals." I smile up at him. "I. Admire. You."

"Promise me you'll keep in touch. I'll really miss you." His voice softens, and I lift my eyes to meet his piercing green ones.

"Aw, are you getting all sentimental on me, Juju?" I joke, using the pet name I gave him when we started high school.

"I am, Sunshine." He raises my pet name with one of his own making. We exchange identical grins. "I've spent years dreaming of playing college football, and I'm fucking ecstatic about playing for the Beavers. But I'm feeling a little nostalgic these last few weeks, and one part of me hates that everything's changing."

He shrugs, and, for a split second, he looks so sad, and I just want to take that look off his face, so I scoot over right beside him, wrap my arm around his back, and snuggle into his side. "That's only natural," I say to appease him, because I'm feeling zero nostalgia at the prospect of moving away for college. But I'm only moving to Newark, which is under two hours away. I can come home anytime I feel homesick. Maybe I'd feel differently if I was moving clear across the country like Justin is. "And I'm sure you'll be fine once you adjust. You'll be too busy with classes, football, and hooking up with hot college chicks to feel homesick or lonely," I add in a jokey tone, trying to lighten the moment.

"Yeah, probably," he agrees, wrapping both arms around me, and holding me close. We're not usually this touchy-feely, but I'm sensing Justin needs this now, and there's nothing wrong with two old friends hugging one another. We're both quiet, silently watching the party rage on in the distance while trying to ignore the moans and groans coming from the front of the truck.

"Sum," Justin says after a few beats, tilting my chin up with his finger. I look into his eyes, confused when I see his expression. "Do you ever wonder what would've happened if we'd kept dating?"

Calling the few kisses we shared back in the early days dating is a stretch, but I'm not about to split hairs with him. "Not really," I truthfully admit.

"Why didn't we?" he whispers as his eyes drift to my mouth.

I gulp over the sudden lump of nervousness wedged in my throat. "Because we weren't feeling it," I remind him.

"Maybe the timing wasn't right," he whispers, his eyes searching mine for permission as he lowers his head toward me.

I should pull back, because starting something with one of my best friends just before we separate for college is not a good idea, but there's a part of me that's curious to see if Justin's kiss will ignite my blood the way Ryan's kiss did.

The curious part wins, and, as Justin moves in for the kill, I offer no resistance, letting him kiss me.

CHAPTER 4
Ryan

"ARE YOU SURE you're okay with this, man?" Austin asks me for the umpteenth time, as we carry the new mattress into the spare guest bedroom.

"It's cool. She's your sister. We can hardly leave her stranded with no place to stay." We drop the mattress down onto the bedframe, walking back out to our living area.

We only moved into this apartment five months ago, just as we celebrated one year in business.

Although it's early days, the state-of-the-art gym we own and run together is doing better than expected, and our membership is growing exponentially as word of mouth increases.

Being ahead of our five-year plan so early in the game is encouraging, and we're both excited for the future. It's a shit-ton of hard work, and neither of us has much downtime which is one reason why I don't mind that Austin's baby sister Summer is moving in with us for a while. This place is empty often, and it's not like I'll see that much of her, anyway.

"Hopefully, a place will free up in one of the freshman dorms and this is only a short-term thing," Austin adds, grabbing a couple bottles of water from the refrigerator and tossing one to me.

"I'm back!" Miley calls out as the front door slams. Her face lights up as she rounds the corner and sees her boyfriend. "I got the cutest bed set for your sister," she says, placing her shopping bags on the kitchen counter before waltzing into Austin's open arms.

It's actually kinda funny to see him like this. I met Austin freshman year of UD, and we instantly clicked. We moved into a house off campus with my best buddy Slater and another mutual friend, Michael, during our sophomore year, and we all lived together until we graduated.

It's fair to say all of us enjoyed the college life until Michael had to move back home to care for his sick dad, Slate fell for my sister Gabby, and I ended up dating her best friend Myndi. Austin was the only single one in the house for a couple years, and he made the most of it. It was around that time we resorted to calling him Powers in a nod to Austin Powers, the legendary manwhore extraordinaire.

When I want to piss Austin off, I call him Powers in front of Miley, and it never fails to rile him up.

In all the time I've known him, he's never had a steady girlfriend. Until now. The instant we hired Miley to work the front desk at the gym, I knew my buddy was smitten. It didn't take him long to convince her to go out with him, and they've been together four months now, and it's getting more serious by the day. I'm happy for him although I've lost my wingman, and sometimes it's difficult being around them because it reminds me of what I had with Myndi.

As usually happens, my mood dips to the floor as soon as thoughts of my ex enter my mind, and I work hard to consciously evict her from my head. Thinking of that shit doesn't do me any good.

"I'll dress her bed and finish the room," Miley says, pecking Austin on the lips one final time. "I hope she likes it."

"She'll love it, babe." Austin can't resist kissing his girl again. "Summer's very laid-back, and she'll be delighted you went to so much trouble for her."

"I'm so excited to meet her," Miley adds, bouncing on her feet, her loose blonde curls swaying with the motion. "And having another girl around here regularly will be nice." Planting her hands on her shapely hips, she drills me with a pointed look, her warm brown eyes chastising me. "Instead of dealing with the rotating line of females out of your bedroom."

I shrug, casting a grin her way. "Can't help it if the ladies want to sample my goods. Who am I to deprive the lovely ladies of Newark of the opportunity of a lifetime?"

She rolls her eyes. "I swear, your ego gets bigger every time we talk."

"Just stating the facts."

"Yeah, about that." Austin rubs the back of his neck, looking a little sheepish as his blue eyes follow his girlfriend out of the room. "Could you dial things back while Summer's here? She's only eighteen and way too impressionable. Those assholes on campus will be all over her, and I've my work cut out trying to protect her as it is. Last thing I need is her seeing your revolving door of hookups and getting ideas."

Mention of her being eighteen brings me back to my hookup from last month. I don't even know her name, but she left a lasting impression. For reasons unknown, I haven't been able to shake her from my mind. And I've had zero interest in screwing any woman since which is most unlike me.

When I close my eyes in bed, I replay every second of that incredible night we spent together, and I can almost feel her pliant, warm body underneath me.

Almost smell the sweet scent of her perfume.

Almost hear the exquisite sounds she made as she came apart in my arms.

The fact she trusted me enough to give me her virginity blows my mind. And while I know I rocked her world, there's no denying she rocked mine too. There was nothing about the experience that was in any way uncomfortable. It felt as natural as breathing, and that unnerves me. No sexual encounter has ever affected me as much, and my preoccupation with it, with *her*, has raised alarm bells I haven't heard in years.

I'm glad we parted ways without exchanging contact details, because I have a feeling that girl would've been dangerous for my heart.

Austin flicks his fingers in my face, dragging me out of my mind. "Earth to James. Where'd you go, man?"

"What were you saying?"

"Can you go easy on the hookup while Sum's here?"

"In case you hadn't noticed, I haven't been hooking up that much lately anyway, so it's cool." I clamp my hand on his shoulder. "I'd do anything for Gabby, so I get it."

"And that's another thing," he adds, looking awkward. "You can't hit on her. She's off-limits to you."

I'm surprised he's gone there. He should know he doesn't need to articulate it. But now he has, I'm going there too. "Pity *you* didn't get that memo when my sister was living with us." I pin him with a knowing look.

"I only kissed Gabby one time. It was nothing. And she's happily married now, so no harm done." He shoots me a wolfish look, and I decide to mess with him.

"So, I can kiss Summer, and you'd be fine with that?"

"Hell to the no!" He glares at me. "If you put your mouth, or any part of your anatomy, anywhere near my sister, I will throw you off the roof of this building." He crosses his arms over his chest, narrowing his eyes in warning. "And don't think I'm joking. I mean it, James. She's too innocent, too fucking young, for you. Keep your hands to yourself."

I chuckle. "You're too easy to wind up, Powers. Relax. I won't touch your little sister. Scout's honor." I salute him, and he flips me the bird, just as my cell vibrates in my pocket. I grin as I spot the caller. "Speak of the devil," I tell my sister as I answer her call. "Powers and I were just talking about you."

"So that's why my ears are burning," Gabby quips down the line.

"Powers was just reminiscing about what a fantastic kisser you are."

Austin flips me the bird again, shouting into my cell. "Your brother is an asshole."

Gabby laughs. "Tell him I agree, and why has it taken him so long to work that one out?"

"I'll tell him no such thing." I prop my butt on the back of the couch and cross my feet at the ankles. "So, what's up?"

"We're having dinner here on Sunday, and we want you, Austin, and Miley to come."

"I don't know if we can get away, Tornado. The gym is getting busier by the day."

"I'm glad to hear it's going well, but I'd never have invested in your new business if I knew it meant I'd hardly get to see you. We miss you. Especially Billy and Daisy. We haven't seen you in ages. Can you not get someone to cover for a few hours?"

Her pleading tone works as an effective guilt trip. It *has* been ages since I've caught up with Slate and my sister, and I miss my nephew and little niece.

"The whole fam will be here, and everyone's dying to see you," she continues, adding more guilt on the pile. "*Please*, Ryan. Just come for a couple hours." Gabby and I have always been super close, and, while I have a great relationship with my two older brothers too, I've always had a special bond with my only sister. And I struggle to say no to her. "Okay, I'll work something out." Her contented sigh trickles down the line. "Hang on a sec. Let me talk to Austin."

I put my cell down to address my buddy. "Gabby and Slate have invited us to their place for dinner on Sunday. We can get Derrick to cover, right?"

While Austin and I manage the business on a rotational basis between us, Derrick is one of the personal trainers we employed from the start and the only other guy we trust to look after stuff in our absence. He's filled in a few times when we've both had outside plans, and he knows the ropes.

"Sure. I'll message him now. Tell Gabby we'll be there."

I lift my cell to my ear. "You hear that?"

"Yep. I'm so happy you guys are coming, and tell Miley not to bring anything but herself this time."

"Austin's sister Summer might come too. She's moving in with us for a while."

"The more, the merrier, and I look forward to meeting her." We shoot the shit for another few minutes, and I end the call when the doorbell chimes.

Miley comes racing out of the guest bedroom. "I'll get it!" she squeals, rushing past Austin toward the front door like she's on skates.

"Wow. Enthusiastic much?" I say to Austin, re-pocketing my cell.

He grins, running a hand through his short brown hair. "If you think Miley's excitable, wait until you meet Summer. I have a feeling those two will hit it off."

"You're really selling it, dude," I deadpan, wondering exactly what I've agreed to. Excited chatter drifts toward us, and Austin grins wider. I know he's happy she will be staying with us, and I can't fault him for that. His family is close knit, like mine, and from the way he's spoken about his only sister over the years, I know he loves her in the same way I love Gabby.

Pushing off the couch, I straighten up, plastering a welcoming smile on my mouth as the girls round the corner and come into view.

All the blood drains from my face when I lock eyes with Austin's beautiful sister.

Fuck my life.

This cannot be happening.

Summer's familiar blue gaze widens in shock for a split second before she hurriedly composes herself. Austin sweeps her up into his arms, oblivious to the sudden tension in the air and the furious beating of my heart.

Out of all the girls in this city, I had to sleep with the one girl completely off-limits. Austin will literally kill me if he finds out I had sex with his baby sister. Worse, that I took her virginity.

Summer stares, bug-eyed, at me over his shoulder as he hugs her, clearly as shocked as I am.

"Don't say a word," I mouth to her. At least not until I've had time to talk to her alone and we can work out what the hell we're going to do.

"Well, duh," she mouths back, rolling her eyes, and my lips twitch at the corners.

"Let me look at you," Austin says, shucking out of her embrace and holding her at arm's length. "You look different," he adds. "But I can't put my finger on what it is."

My eyes subtly glance over her. She has her dark hair tied back in some kind of messy bun, which only serves to highlight her stunning face. Her skin is devoid of makeup, and it's flawless with a light dusting of freckles across her nose and upper cheeks. Her eyes are big and bright, and it's cheesy as fuck to say this, but she glows.

She exudes warmth and vitality, and the first impression I had of her wasn't wrong. She's so comfortable in her skin, betraying maturity that belies her age. I can't imagine anything fazing this girl, and what you see is what you get. There is no pretense or falseness about her, and it's refreshingly different.

No wonder I've struggled to forget her.

She's wearing a tank top under an open blue-and-pink checkered button-down shirt and minuscule jeans shorts. My eyes are glued to her long, lean, bare legs, and my cock twitches as visions of our hookup resurrect in my mind's eye. I'm picturing how her legs were wrapped around my neck as I plunged deep inside her, and I still remember how silky smooth her skin felt under my hands as I traced my fingers up and down her legs while I fucked her.

My cock is now straining against the front of my jeans, and I'm terrified Powers will notice. *Down, boy*, I caution, forcing the image of a naked Summer from my mind. I think of the most mundane things while willing my hard-on to deflate.

"What's different?" Austin asks her again with a slight frown. "Did you do something with your hair?"

She shakes her head, fighting a grin. I think I understand why she appears different to her brother, and I rub a tense spot between my brows as I consider the clusterfuck my life has just become.

A massive smile graces Summer's lush mouth as she grins at her brother. "I'm all grown up now, Austin." She flicks a subtle glance in my direction. "In every sense of the word. Maybe you're finally noticing that."

CHAPTER 5
Summer

"YOU BETTER NOT be saying what I think you're saying," my overbearing big brother spews, his handsome face turning an unflattering shade of red.

"I am, and you'll get over it." I offer him a sweet smile, trying to ignore the fact my heart is trying to beat a path out of my chest.

I cannot believe the guy I gave my virginity to is standing right over there.

And I've no clue who he is to my brother.

He looks scared shitless at the direction our conversation has taken, but he shouldn't worry. There's no way in hell I'm telling my brother what went down between us. I won't have Ryan's murder on my conscience.

Austin splutters, for once lost for words. Miley loops her arm through mine, winking conspiratorially at me. I've known her for all of five seconds, and I already know I'll love her. Although, I suspected I would. The girl who tamed my big brother is clearly someone special.

"Aren't you going to introduce me?" I ask Austin, quirking a brow as I motion toward the spot where a mute Ryan is standing.

"Uh, yeah." Austin scrubs the back of his neck, and I stifle a laugh. My veiled confession has really thrown him for a loop. I swear he still looks at me like I'm five sometimes.

In some ways, I'm not as close to Austin as I am to Marc and Charlie purely because of the eight-year age gap. Austin left for college when I was ten, and though he visited regularly, he missed out on most of my childhood. In other ways, my relationship with him feels closer, more natural, and more akin to friends than siblings.

Unless it comes to the subject of boys.

Then he's every bit as smothering as my other two brothers.

"This is my buddy James. Say hi to your new roomie."

New roomie? Oh, hell to the no. Someone please pinch me. This cannot be real. *He's* Austin's roommate, friend, and business partner? I don't understand. The world spins for a split second, and I'm confused. Did Ryan lie about his name that night in the club?

"Nice to meet you, Summer," Ryan, James, whatever the hell his name is, says, stepping toward me and extending his hand.

"Likewise." I drill him with a penetrating look as I grip his large palm firmly. Fuck, he's even more gorgeous in the light of day, and my memory has not done him justice at all.

His dark denims hug his muscular thighs like a second skin, and his tight T-shirt highlights his ripped arms and chest to perfection. He returns my intense gaze with one of his own as we shake hands, and desire coils low in my belly. Delicious tingles whip up my arm once we make skin-to-skin contact, almost like I've been electrocuted.

His eyes darken momentarily, letting me know he felt it too.

Interesting. I'd supposed my reaction to him that night was one-sided because it was all so new. Now, I'm wondering if there isn't more to our chemistry. Not that I want to explore that. The fact he's my new roomie is an added complication I don't need.

"Where's your stuff?" Austin asks, his brow creasing as he looks to where my hand is still joined with Ryan's.

I let go and dig my car keys out of my pocket. "In the trunk of my car. Have at it, big bro." I waggle my brows at him, dropping the keys in his palm, and Miley giggles.

"I'll help," Ryan offers, and the guys leave as I allow Miley to escort me to my new bedroom.

"I hope you like it," she says, nervously opening the door. "I painted it, and the guys assembled all the furniture." She waves her arms around the room. "But if you don't like anything, we can return it to the store, and you can pick replacements. We can even repaint it."

The room is much larger than I was expecting with muted gray walls and a big window, which lets in lots of light. The focal point is a king-size bed covered in a pristine white comforter. A pale pink velvet quilt and an abundance of gray and pink fluffy cushions elevate it from something simple to something elegant. Two framed prints in complementary colors hang on the wall behind the bed, and two white bedside tables rest on either side. One has a small pink lamp atop it, and the other has a potted plant. A desk and overhead shelving unit on the right-hand side of the room will come in handy once classes start. The only other furniture in the room is a three-door fitted closet off on the left.

"This is amazing." I spin around to Miley, flinging my arms around her. "I love it, and I wouldn't change a single thing. Thank you so much." She hugs me back with the same enthusiasm, and I'm thinking maybe living with my brother won't be as bad as I expected, provided Miley's around.

"Told ya," Austin says, smirking at Ryan as they enter the room, depositing my bags and boxes on the floor.

"Told him what?" I inquire.

"That you two would hit it off." Austin pulls Miley into his arms, kissing the top of her blonde head, and my heart swoons.

"If you love her, it stands to reason I'd love her too." I smile at my brother, so happy to see him happy.

And he doesn't even flinch at the mention of the 'L' word.

Wow.

My brother really is head over heels for this girl.

"And how could I not after Miley did all this for me?" I cast a glance around the room. "And I believe you both helped too. You didn't have to go to so much trouble, but thanks so much. I really appreciate it."

"I think I might have to ditch you in favor of your sister," Miley jokes, squeezing Austin at the waist.

"I wouldn't blame you if you did," Austin instantly replies, pulling me into his other side. "She's pretty fucking awesome."

I laugh, and my eyes meet Ryan's as he hangs back in the doorway with a strange smile on his face. He notices me watching him and he snaps out of it. "You guys want to go out for lunch or eat in?"

"I've got to unpack," I explain. "But you guys should go out. I'll grab something later." I could use the time to clear the fog from my brain and try to wrap my head around the fact the guy I gave my virginity to is my new roommate for the next few months.

"Why don't we grab lunch from the deli place around the corner, and then we can all eat here?" Miley suggests, earning herself a kiss from my brother.

"Sounds like a plan," he agrees, taking her hand. "We'll go, and doofus here can put the coffee on." He nudges Ryan in the ribs as he passes by. Ryan stares at me for a minute before following the loving couple out of my bedroom.

Blowing air out of my mouth, I shake my head in disbelief, tossing a bag on my bed. Removing items of clothing, I hang them up in the closet or fold them neatly into the accompanying drawers, while I contemplate the curveball thrown at me.

"Can we talk?" Ryan asks in his deep voice, startling me.

I jump about ten feet in the air, dropping the sweater in my hand. "Don't sneak up on me like that!"

"Your door was open. I was hardly being covert." He ambles into the room with his hands buried in the pockets of his jeans as I quickly shove the sweater into my closet.

"You can't tell him. Like ever," I blurt, plopping onto the bed and patting the space beside me.

"Well, I'm glad we're on the same page. I value breathing," he teases, sitting down beside me.

"As do I," I agree, and he chuckles. "But, seriously, Austin can never know. You've no idea how overprotective he is of me or perhaps you do. Maybe now you realize why I was still a virgin."

"Trust me, I've no desire to ever tell him. He would never forgive me." He looks down at the floor, clenching and unclenching his fists, and I frown. When he looks up at me, remorse is written all over his face. "If I'd known who you were, I'd never have gone through with it."

"Don't do that," I groan, shaking my head. "Don't say you regret it and stomp all over my happy memory."

"I'm not saying I regret it." His features soften, and it would be so easy to get lost in his baby blues. "I don't regret it. Not at all." He cups my face, and my heart races around my chest. I feel his touch all the way through to the tips of my toes. "I could never regret such an amazing night, but I've broken the bro code, and Austin would be furious if he found out. He made me promise to keep my hands off you, but I didn't realize I'd already messed everything up." He worries his lower lip between his teeth, and I have a sudden, almost uncontrollable urge to nip at his lip. I sit on my hands to quell the craving. "Why didn't you mention you were going to college here?"

I arch a brow. "We didn't exactly share personal details other than intimate body parts." My core pulses in remembrance, and I squeeze my thighs together, hoping he doesn't notice.

"True." He grins, and his eyes sparkle, and I get lost in their hypnotic depths. He peers into my eyes, and electricity crackles in the space between us. All the tiny hairs lift on my arms and my mouth is suddenly dry. A muscle clenches in his jaw as he continues to stare at me, and my chest is heaving the longer he looks at me. He's so unbelievably gorgeous, and I don't know how I'm expected to live here with him and keep my hands to myself. He blinks in fast succession, looking up at the ceiling, and it breaks whatever spell we were under. "Austin will never speak to me again if he finds out, and I wouldn't blame him. You're his little sister. If—"

"You didn't know. We didn't know," I rush to reassure him, fighting the urge to reach out and touch him. "Why'd you say your name was Ryan, anyway?"

He looks perplexed. "Because that's my name."

"I thought your name was James?"

His lips kick up at the corner. "My name is Ryan James, but your brother always calls me James."

I nod a couple times. "Ah, now it makes sense. I've heard Austin talk about you for years, but he has always called you James. Not that it really matters. Even if I knew you were Ryan, I would still never have made the connection in a million years. What are the chances, huh?"

"I know, and it's not like it matters. We can't change what happened." He drags a hand through his dirty blond hair before pinning me with earnest eyes. "But nothing else can happen between us. It was a strictly onetime thing, and you're way too young for me even if you seem older."

"Agreed," I say, ignoring the little stabby pain in my heart. "I never expected to see you again, and I was cool with that. I don't want things to be awkward while I'm living here, so I can forget about it if you can."

He stands, nodding. "Perfect. I'm glad we had this talk." He opens and closes his mouth in quick succession, and I wonder what he's holding back. After a couple beats, he slants me a friendly smile as he backs out of the room. "I'll let you continue your unpacking."

"So, Summer," Miley says, placing her elbows on top of the table. "Do you have a boyfriend?"

"Nope. I want to enjoy the full college experience, and a boyfriend would only get in the way."

"Oh, wow, okay." She emits a tinkling laugh.

"Do I even want to know what the full college experience entails?" Austin asks, ramming the last piece of his sandwich into his mouth.

"Shouldn't you know? Or has it been that long since you graduated you've forgotten?" I push a loose strand of hair back off my face while I perform a mental countdown in my head.

"Don't fucking push me, Sum," Austin warns, and I hadn't even counted to two before he reacted predictably.

I lean back in my chair. "Oh, relax. I doubt I'll be even half as wild as you were."

"Even half would be disastrous," Ryan adds, fighting a smile. "Let's just say your brother made the most of his college experience and leave it at that." He shifts in his chair, and his thigh brushes against mine, heating my body upon contact. Our eyes meet for an infinitesimal moment, a spark igniting in the tiny space between us, until he pulls his leg back and turns his head around.

"Yes, please," Miley cuts in. "It's not like I'm keen to hear old war stories either."

"Babe." Austin slings his arm around her shoulders. "That was the past. You know I only have eyes for you now."

Ryan makes a gagging sound while I sort of melt into a puddle. I would never have thought Austin had it in him to be so romantic, but it's lovely to see.

"Shut your face, dude," Austin says, elbowing his buddy in the ribs. "I still remember how gaga you were for Myndi, and you spouted worse shit, believe me."

The smile instantly wipes off Ryan's face, and his chair screeches in protest as he shoves it back, standing abruptly. Without saying a word, he stacks our empty plates before taking them to the sink.

"Shit, man. I'm sorry," Austin says. "I know better than to mention the she-devil."

I'm dying of curiosity here, but I bite my tongue to stop my probing questions because I can see how tense Ryan is at the mere mention of this girl, whoever she is.

"It's fine," Ryan says through gritted teeth as he rinses the plates before placing them in the dishwasher.

"So, does anyone know of any drama groups in the area?" I ask, deliberately changing the subject in the hope it'll defuse the tension in the air.

"Not by name," Miley says, "but there are a bunch around Newark, and I believe there's a theater company started by students in the college."

"I remember hearing something about that," I say. "I'll check it out next week."

"You act?" Miley asks.

I nod. "I've been a member of the local drama group back home since I was twelve, but it's only a hobby, really. I thought it might be fun to get involved in something new while I'm in college."

"Won't that interfere with your weekend plans?" Austin asks.

"What weekend plans?" I frown. "Is there something you know that I don't?"

"Won't you be flying out to watch the Beavers' games? There's a lot of talk about Justin online. He's definitely on the NFL watch list."

"Who's Justin?" Ryan asks, scowling a little as he retakes his seat alongside me.

"Summer's new boyfriend," Austin unhelpfully supplies, deliberately winding me up.

"He's not my boyfriend. He's just a good friend."

"Charlie said you were dating him."

I roll my eyes. "Charlie's got a big mouth, and he loves to stir shit. He was just trying to wind you up in the hope you'd tighten the leash on me."

"So, Charlie didn't catch you giving Justin head in his truck last weekend?"

"Austin!" Miley pinches his muscly arm, a look of abject horror on her face. "Oh, my God. You can't say stuff like that to your sister!"

I reach over and pat her hand. "In our house, no topic is off-limits. Trust me, before you pay the fam a visit, you'll want to leave your morals and your embarrassment at the front door. You never know what'll pop out of their mouths, so don't say I didn't warn you."

"Nice attempt at deflection." Austin smirks, and I flip him the bird.

"Oh, whatever." I sigh. No point in denying it. Although I'd rather yank my toenails off with tweezers than have this conversation in front of Ryan, Austin will just keep badgering me if I don't fess up. "That was me, but it doesn't mean I'm dating Justin. I'm not. We messed around the last few weeks, but it wasn't anything serious. He's in Oregon, and I'm here, and I've zero interest in doing the long-distance thing."

"So why even bother?"

I don't want to explain to my brother how we sort of fell into it. I didn't stop to question it. When he kissed me that night at the field, I wanted to see if being with another guy would feel different after experiencing sex for the first time. And while Justin didn't set my body on fire the way Ryan did, he definitely set my heart rate pulsing, and I enjoyed spending time with him these last few weeks. If we hadn't been moving away for college, who knows what might've happened, but we are, and I won't waste any time thinking about what could've been. I didn't have sex with him, although it tempted me, but I knew if we'd taken it that far it might alter our friendship, and I value it too much to risk it.

"Why exactly do you care?" I ask.

"I'm just looking out for you."

"Trust me, you've nothing to worry about with Justin, and if you're done grilling me, I'd like to get back to my unpacking." I give Miley and my brother a kiss on the cheek each. "Thanks for lunch." Turning to face Ryan, I say. "And thanks for cleaning up."

"No problem." His jaw is taut as he forces a smile, and as I walk back to my room, I can't help wondering if he's pissed over Justin or if it was mention of that Myndi girl that soured his mood.

CHAPTER 6
Ryan

"DUDE, ARE YOU listening?" Derrick asks from the doorway to my office, snapping me out of my head. Since Summer moved in with us yesterday, I've been hugely distracted, and not in a good way. "What hours do you want me to cover on Sunday?" he repeats.

"From one until closing."

"Cool, and thanks. The extra money will come in handy with the wedding. Clara will bankrupt me before we've even made it down the aisle," he semi-jokes. Having briefly met his fiancée, I'd say he's not too far off the mark. She gives new meaning to Bridezilla. Rather him than me. I shudder at the thought.

"No problem, and if you want additional shifts, just let me know. It might be nice for Austin and me to take a bit of a breather from time to time."

"Awesome, thanks, boss."

"Derrick, your four p.m. is here," Miley says, appearing at his back.

"I'm outta here. Later." He jogs off down the corridor, while Miley lingers in the room.

"Austin called. He's stuck in traffic on his way back from the meeting at the PR firm. He asked if you'd look after Summer and her friends."

Fucking great. Just what I need. *How the hell am I going to evict this girl from my mind if I can't get away from her?*

I had a hard time sleeping last night knowing she was in the room next door.

Hard being the operative word.

Even jerking off twice in the shower this morning has done nothing to dampen the semi I seem to be permanently sporting around her. "Of course," I tell Miley. "Let me know when they arrive."

"Oh, they're here already. I showed them to the locker room and told them you'd meet them in the reception area."

"Okay. Thanks, Miley."

She smiles before closing the door on her way out. I rest my head on my arms on top of the desk, groaning. *What the fuck have I gotten myself into?*

When I feel sufficiently calm, I walk to the lobby to greet Summer and her friends.

I'm not surprised to see the same couple from the night we met waiting with her. Austin mentioned they were her best friends, and they're essentially the reason Summer's rooming with us. They couldn't locate any available two-bedroom apartments within their budget, and the one-bed place they found wasn't big enough for all three. So, according to Powers, Summer insisted Hannah and Jordan take the place while she'd wait for a spot in the dorms to open, living with us in the meantime.

"Hello again," I mumble as I reach them, keeping an eye on Miley as she chats to a client from behind the front desk.

"Hey, Ryan." Hannah smirks, waggling her fingers at me. "It's great to see you again."

"Thanks for stepping in for Austin," Summer adds, smiling up at me. "But if you're too busy, we can wait for my brother."

I work hard to keep my gaze focused on her face, but it's challenging. She's wearing a sports bra top and yoga pants that leave little to the imagination. Her tits silently beckon me, and my fingers itch with a craving to touch her. With her firm, tan midriff on full display and those long, slender legs encased in a clingy black fabric, she's like my every wet dream. My cock hardens under my training shorts, and I discreetly adjust myself before anyone notices.

"I second that suggestion," Jordan says, eyeing me warily, and I wonder what the hell his problem is.

"I can spare time." I deliberately ignore his sullen tone and expression, jerking my head to one side. "C'mon. I'll give you the grand tour."

"This doesn't look like any gym I've seen before," Summer says when I show them into the main CrossFit training area.

"That's because it isn't." I smile with pride. "This is our CrossFit area, which is only one part of the overall facility. CrossFit is a training program that builds strength and conditioning through varied and challenging workouts with a heavy emphasis on nutrition and diet. As you can see, we use minimal equipment," I say, pointing at the frames which several clients are using.

"You don't have weights?" Jordan grumbles, pouting like a pussy.

"We do, just not in this section of the gym. Follow me." I walk toward the door at the far end of the room, explaining as we go.

"The vision Austin and I had for this gym was a state-of-the-art facility which offers a wide variety of programs to suit different needs at a reasonable price point."

I hold open the door, allowing the girls to pass through to the corridor. "Keep walking to the end, and go into the door on your left," I instruct, taking up the rear. It takes colossal willpower to avoid ogling Summer's shapely ass, but I feel Jordan's eyes like laser beams searing into my back. Dude really doesn't like me.

We enter the main gymnasium. "As you can see, we offer a traditional workout area too with all the usual weights and ellipticals." I point over our heads. "If you look up there, you'll see one of our trained consultants conducting a spin class. That section is reserved for our classes. We have a full daily schedule including Zumba, yoga, cardio, tai chi, and we also offer personal one-to-one training sessions."

"Wow." Summer spins around, her head whipping from side to side, taking it all in. "This place is very impressive. You should be proud of what you've both achieved."

"Thank you. We are, and we've worked hard for it."

"You play hard too, I bet," Jordan says, butting into the conversation.

"You have a problem with me, buddy?" I fold my arms over my chest and stare neutrally at him. This is my domain, and if he gives me shit, he'll find his ass out on the sidewalk, pronto.

"Jordy," Hannah hisses under her breath.

"Let him say what's on his mind."

"Guys like you make me sick," he spits out, his hands clenching at his sides. "You'd think at your age you'd be past the manwhore stage, but I guess some people just never grow up."

"Jordan, you are way out of line here," Summer calmly says. "Ryan has done nothing wrong, and if anyone needs to grow up, it's you. We were two consenting adults, and it was a onetime thing. The only one making a big deal out of this is you."

"You didn't see him ogling your ass on the way over here. It's fucking disrespectful." He glares at me, and I really don't get this guy. *What the fuck concern is it of his if I stare at Summer's ass? What am I missing here?*

"You were ogling my ass?" Summer asks, fixing her gaze on me. Her mouth pulls into a lopsided grin, and she doesn't look in any way pissed.

"It was right there in my face." I shrug, smirking. "Can't blame a guy for looking." Especially when I know what said ass looks like without clothes on.

"I think Austin might have something to say about that," the douche barks.

All good humor disappears as I step up to him. I'm at least a good three inches taller, and a heck of a lot wider, than him. He's a stupid fucker if he thinks he can challenge me, especially in my place of business. "Are you threatening me?"

"Just stay away from her. You shouldn't have touched her. Aren't there any women your own age you can hit on?"

"What happened between Summer and me is nobody's business but our own. I get that you don't like me, and I couldn't give a flying fuck, but I thought Summer was your friend, and she deserves a lot more respect from *you*."

"Ryan is right," Summer says, stepping in between us and forcing me to take a step back. "And you've got to let this go. I don't interfere in your love life, and I expect the same in return. If you value my friendship, you'll tell none of my brothers. It has nothing to do with them or you."

"And what about Justin? Doesn't he have a right to know?"

Ah, now I'm getting it. He's acting the big man on behalf of his friend.

"No." Summer shakes her head and stands her ground. "I'm not dating Justin, and I've made no promise or commitment to him, nor has he. I'm a free agent, and I can do what or *who* I want. I really don't want to fall out with you over this, but you've got to drop it."

"Summer. Come on. You've got to know how Justin feels about you. He's my best friend, and you expect me to say nothing when this douche is trying to get in your pants again?"

What the actual fuck? I admit I stared at her ass for longer than I should have, but I haven't given him, or her, any sign I'm planning on hitting on her again. Summer is as off-limits as girls go.

"You obviously don't understand the concept of a one-night stand," I say, working hard to keep my tone professional. "Or the fact she's my best friend and business partner's little sister. What happened between us is in the past, and I'm really struggling to see how this is any of your concern. And I stared at her ass for all of ten seconds which doesn't equate to hitting on her."

"I have a pretty spectacular ass," Summer says, wiggling her butt and winking. "I'd stare at my butt too, if it was possible."

I don't understand how she's keeping such a cool head. If he was one of my supposed friends, I'd be tearing strips off him, but she's laughing and cracking jokes to ease the tension.

"You don't have any boxing classes scheduled now, do you?" Hannah asks, shooting daggers at her boyfriend.

"Not something we offer."

"Well, do you have anything to hit because my fist is dying to punch the alien being who has invaded my boyfriend's body, and I'd rather not mess up his pretty face."

I like this girl, and I'm glad Summer has at least one decent friend. "We have pads and you could do bag work if you like?"

"Babe." Jordan moves to his girlfriend's side, but she holds up her hand, keeping him at bay.

"Don't babe me. I'm crazy mad at you right now. And have you forgotten Sum is only in this position because she selflessly stepped aside so we could live together? Something I'm sorely regretting right now."

He scrubs his hands up and down his cheeks before exhaling loudly. "I'm sorry, babe."

"I'm not the one you should apologize to." Hannah plants her hands on her hips, challenging her boyfriend with a heated stare.

Jordan looks like he swallowed something nasty as he turns to face Summer. "Sorry, Sum. You know it's only because I care."

"I know, Jordy, but you've got to let this go."

"I will." He kisses her on the cheek, narrowing his eyes at me while neither of the girls are looking.

What a tool.

"You owe Ryan an apology too," Summer says as he moves to return to his girlfriend.

A muscle clenches in his jaw as he swings his gaze around. "Sorry, man," he clips out, sounding utterly unapologetic.

I could call him on it, but I'm sick of this juvenile bullshit, so I let it go. "No problem. Forget about it."

⬤

"Where's Summer?" Austin asks, stalking into my office a half hour later and flopping down into a chair.

"She's working out on the main floor with Hannah and that asshole Jordan."

Austin chuckles. "What did the little punk do?"

"Try breathing," I mutter, not wanting to elaborate.

"He's always been a mouthpiece, but he's harmless."

"I'll take your word for it. How did the meeting go?"

"Great, although you should've been there. We'll have to appoint a manager. We can't keep splitting stuff up and working all the hours we have been."

"I know, but we can't afford to appoint someone permanently yet. Business is doing well but not that well." I lean back in my chair, locking my hands behind my head.

"Maybe we should look for some venture capital. The figures look good, and with our expansion plans, it's a good prospect for an investor."

"I'm not keen to bring in someone else. Not unless we really have to. We're lucky with Gabby as an investor because she has zero interest in getting involved in the business, but if we go external, we'll be answerable to someone else, and I like the way things are now." Gabby's ex was a tech genius, and he left her a bunch of money after he passed. She has more than she needs, especially considering the great job Slater has, so she was happy to invest in our fledgling business.

"I'm grateful to your sister, and we both know we wouldn't be here today without her support but—" He leans forward, wetting his lips.

"But what?"

"I want to have a life outside these four walls. I want to have time to take my girlfriend to dinner or go away with her for a weekend."

I sit up straighter. "We both knew what we were getting into when we started this business. You can't turn around after barely eighteen months and say you've changed your mind."

"I haven't changed my mind. I just want more work-life balance."

"And you think I don't?" I get up and come around the front of the desk, resting my butt on the edge. "I know the hours are a killer, but it won't be forever. Every startup business is like this, and we're already ahead of the curve. We can't take our foot off the pedal now. This is the time to work even harder." I eyeball him, because I need to know if he's still with me on this. "It won't be forever, and we'll get to reap the benefits in a few years."

Air whooshes out of his mouth as he nods. "I know, man. And I don't want to give you the impression I'm having doubts because I'm not. This has already exceeded my wildest dreams, and working with you has been great. It's just—"

"You're in love, and you want to spend more time with your woman," I supply.

"Yeah, I do."

"I'm happy for you, bro. And, look, if you want to take Miley away for a dirty weekend, I'll work something out. Just tell me when, and I'll come up with a plan."

"I can't up and leave you to manage by yourself."

"Quit with the martyrdom. Make your plans and I'll work around it. And I'll see if I can come up with some options that will allow us to take a step back more regularly."

CHAPTER 7
Summer

"I'M PAYING AS soon as I get a job," I tell my brother as I complete the last of the paperwork confirming my gym membership. Austin insists on waiving the membership fee, and while I love that he wants to do that for me—and it's nice of him to offer Jordan and Hannah a twenty percent discount too—his business is still new, and I doubt they can afford to just give memberships out for free or at discounted rates. Jordan and Hannah have passed anyway, as they can use the sports facilities on campus for free, but they appreciated the gesture.

"Don't sweat it, Sum. You can make it up to us by helping keep the apartment clean and cooking the odd dinner."

"Deal." I stretch up and kiss my brother's cheek. "Love you, and I'm grateful for all you're doing to help me out." I didn't want to move in with my brother. Didn't want to rely on him when I'm reveling in my newfound freedom. But now I'm here, I'm finding I'm not all that unhappy about it. I refuse to believe my hot, sex God roomie has anything to do with my change in attitude, and I'm happy to languish in denial.

Austin wraps his strong arms around me, squeezing me tight. "I love having you around. I feel like I was never really there for you growing up, and I like we'll get to spend time together now."

"Me too," I say, but the words are muffled against his warm chest.

"Aw, you two are so sweet," Miley says, coming around the desk with a wide smile on her face. "It makes me wish I had a big brother."

"Big brothers are the best," I agree. "Do you have any siblings?" I ask, easing out of Austin's arms.

"Only one older sister. She lives in London, so I don't see that much of her." Her smile fades, and I feel for her. I don't know how I'd cope if I didn't have my family close by. They mean everything even if they drive me to distraction often.

"I'm going to head home for a few hours," Ryan says, coming up behind us, and speaking directly to my brother. "I'll be back at nine to relieve you," he adds, dangling his car keys between his fingers.

"Can you take Summer with you?" Austin asks before turning to face me. "Unless you have other plans?"

Jordan and Hannah have already left, and I made no other plans. "Nope. A ride would be great."

A cheeky grin appears on Ryan's gorgeous mouth, and I think I know where his mind has gone. "Perv," I mouth at him over Austin's shoulder as we hug goodbye. I give Miley a hug too, and then I wave at my brother and his girlfriend as I join Ryan and we exit the building.

It's still bright out, and glorious sunshine beats down on us, prompting me to lift my face up to the sky. I adore the sensation of the warm sun on my skin, and it reminds me of copious summers spent outside on the farm, attending to chores and messing around in the woods and by the small stream at the back of our property.

I follow Ryan out into the parking lot, trying not to notice how the muscles in his back and arms ripple invitingly as he moves. And I'm definitely not checking out his toned ass or remembering what his butt cheeks felt like in my hands as I urged him to bury himself deeper inside me. Desire coils low in my belly, and my mouth suddenly feels as dry as the Sahara Desert.

"Liking what you see?" he asks over his shoulder, smirking at my blatant drooling. I open my mouth to reply truthfully when he groans, holding up one large palm. "Forget I said that, and definitely don't answer." He holds the door open for me, his face pulled into a tight grimace.

"Okay?" My brow puckers as I pull myself up into the car. My arm brushes against his as I slide into the passenger seat, sending a rake of shivers all over my body. I've never had any guy affect me so potently, and the feeling is off-putting. Ryan shuts my door and jogs over to his side, jumping into the car and starting the engine. "Nice wheels," I remark as he fiddles with the air conditioning.

"She's a beauty all right. Technically, it belongs to the business, so your brother and I share it." He backs out of the parking garage and into the busy rush hour traffic.

"Do you mind if I put music on?"

"Knock yourself out." He pushes a few buttons on his iPhone which is hooked up to the sound system in the car. "There you go."

I scroll through songs until I find one that reminds me of senior year of high school. I fight a smirk as I press the play button, instantly knowing Ryan will hate this choice.

Predictably, his brows climb to his hairline as the song starts. "'California Gurls'? Seriously?"

I'm jumping around on the seat, making robotic movements with my arms, as I bop my head to the catchy beat. "I fucking love this song. We did a spoof version of *Pitch Perfect* for our senior year play, and I was Katy Perry in our rendition of this song." I put my hands up in the air, dancing around like a crazy person as I belt out the lyrics. Ryan watches me with clear amusement, and it's just as well the traffic has come to a virtual standstill because he's paying scant attention to the road.

When the song ends, he shakes his head, chuckling with the biggest grin on his face. "I would've paid good money to see that show."

"I got a standing ovation I'll have you know," I mock pout, poking him in the ribs.

"I'm sure you did. You're a fantastic singer although the jury's out on your dancing," he teases, moving the car forward as the traffic eases.

"I've got moves," I protest.

"I know you do," he blurts before cussing under his breath.

"Let me guess," I say, arching a brow, "forget you said that too?"

"So, are you studying drama?" he asks after a couple beats of awkward silence, purposely ignoring my question.

"Nah, drama's only a hobby. I want to be a teacher, so I'm majoring in early childhood education."

"Is that something you've always wanted to do?"

"Pretty much." I pull my legs up into my chest, resting my face sideways on my knees. "I was one of those freaky kids who loved school, and I adore children, so it seems natural to want to work in that environment. I feel like I can relate to them, and the thought of playing a nurturing role, helping kids develop and grow and learn, makes me feel all warm and fuzzy inside."

"That's great, Summer. I wish I'd had that focus at your age. I didn't have a clue what I wanted to do when I started UD, and it's only the last couple years I found something I was passionate about. You're ahead of the curve, in so many ways."

I almost blush at his compliment, and a heady warmth invades my chest. "Were you a business major like Austin?"

He nods as he maneuvers the SUV around the corner in the apartment's direction. "Yeah. Not that I had any burning ambition to work in business, but it seemed like a good idea at the time and it's served me well now."

"How come you didn't study something sports related?" I ask, because it's clear that's where his passion lies, along with Austin's.

"I wasn't as into sports back then. I liked to run, but I didn't see it as something I'd want to pursue as a career," he admits, "but I can't really complain. I'm where I am now thanks to my passion for sports and the business degree I earned. Sometimes, although you might feel lost and aimless, you're on the right path even when you don't realize it." He enters the parking lot of the building, swinging into the designated space.

"That's profound."

He kills the engine, staring blankly at the windshield, and his voice is strangely numb-sounding when he speaks. "So many times, I've thought my life was going in a certain direction only for something to derail it, but I finally feel like I'm in the right place and that all the shit I went through happened for a reason. To lead me to this point."

"What shit?" I blurt before I can question the wisdom.

He visibly shakes himself out of whatever place his mind had wandered to, forcing a fake smile on his face as he opens his door. "It's nothing. It's in the past, exactly where I want it to be."

I'm still pondering his words as I slowly unbuckle my seat belt. My door swings open, and Ryan gently holds me at the waist, helping me down. My heart rate speeds up at his touch, and my body tingles all over. Little goose bumps sprout on my arms, and I'm acutely aware of his proximity. He looms over me and heat rolls off his body in hypnotic waves, almost knocking me off my feet.

He has so much *presence*.

And he's so masculine in a way that both thrills and scares me.

All the other guys I've been with—Justin included—seem so boyish when compared with this man. Visions of his large hands roaming my body, as he explored every inch of my bare skin, surges, unhelpfully, to the forefront of my mind, and I'm hot all over.

"Hey, you okay?" He holds onto my elbow, attempting to steady me, but his touch knocks me even further off-kilter, doing little to ease my temporary lack of balance. "You're not dizzy after your workout, are you?"

I snort. "Hardly. Calling it a workout is a huge stretch of the imagination." I wasn't even exerting myself, yet I still found myself breathless. I shuck out of his hold, feeling like a stranger in my body, and not liking it one bit.

"You obviously exercise regularly," he says, his eyes quickly scanning my body before a familiar scowl paints his lips.

"Not in a gym." I lift my arm, flexing my biceps. "These muscles are thanks to farm work, but it's clearly no match for working out with weights and machines because I was virtually dead after fifteen minutes on that stepper."

He chuckles, ushering me across the parking lot toward the elevator. "I can schedule a session with one of our personal trainers, if you like. They can devise a training plan that will help you build muscle strength and stamina."

"That would be cool," I agree, stepping into the elevator alongside him.

"I'll grab a quick shower," I say when we enter the apartment, conscious I smell like moldy ten-day-old socks. "And then I'll fix dinner."

Ryan tosses his keys on the counter, shrugging off his hoodie and flinging it on the back of a stool. "You don't have to make dinner. I can fix something myself."

I roll my eyes. "Don't be ridiculous. It hardly makes sense for both of us to cook separately, and I want to earn my keep."

"I won't argue if you insist," he complies with a wink, sauntering toward his bedroom.

I'm walking toward the bathroom a couple minutes later, wrapped in my fluffy bathrobe, when I hear the shower start up in his bedroom. I'm surprised Ryan wangled the master suite out from under Austin, but I'm grateful because it means I'm only sharing the main bathroom with my brother, and I won't risk bumping into the guy I gave my V-card to in a minuscule towel.

As I stand under the stream of warm water, I can't help thinking of Ryan standing naked in his shower only a few meters away, and my body grows hot and needy as my mind's eye conjures up his image. I try to dismiss the visual, as I do every time it surfaces in my mind, but I'm a lost cause.

Before I know it, my hand is gliding down over my stomach, and my fingers are caressing my swollen clit as I close my eyes and revisit the night I lost my virginity.

I come seconds later, leaning against the tiled wall as wave after wave of powerful bliss rockets through me. My chest is heaving, and my legs are shaking, as I turn off the water and step out. Wrapping a towel around my body, and another one around my head, I swipe my hand across the steam coating the bathroom mirror, staring at my flushed reflection.

Before I met Ryan, my plans had been to come to UD with no ties or expectations other than to enjoy my freshman year of college and to enjoy my single status once I was no longer under my brothers' watchful eyes. But, already, I feel my resolve wavering, and I don't like it.

I don't want this guy to get under my skin.

I don't want to feel a growing attachment toward him.

I don't want his touch to ignite the lustful fuel flowing through my veins.

I don't want to picture him fucking me when I'm getting myself off.

Hannah and Jordan's lumpy couch is looking more and more appealing by the minute. I sigh, wondering why it's proving so hard to shake this guy from my thoughts.

It was only sex, I remind myself. A hot hookup. An amazing one-night stand and a clear onetime thing. Perhaps, because it's so new, and he's the only one I've had sex with, it's natural I feel some kind of connection with him. It doesn't mean I have feelings for him other than an ongoing desire to jump his bones again.

I'm drawn to him because of the sex, I conclude, nodding at my reflection in the mirror as I lie to myself, buoyed up by the fresh thoughts skating through my mind.

There's an easy cure for this ailment.

A surefire way to get Ryan out from under my skin.

I need to have sex with someone else.

CHAPTER 8
Ryan

SUMMER ISN'T AROUND when I step into the kitchen, so I set about making dinner for both of us. I have the chicken and veg cooking in the skillet and the noodles bubbling in the pan when she finally emerges from her bedroom, dressed in tight yoga pants and a loose shirt.

"I would do that." She leans in and sniffs the steam rising from the stove. Her delicate floral scent wafts through the air, and her perfume, combined with the curve of her ass in those pants, stirs my lust, reminding my libido that it's still in full working order. "That smells yummy, and I'm starving." Her tummy rumbles at that exact moment as if to prove a point.

"It'll be about ten minutes." I flip the ingredients in the skillet with a practiced twist of my wrist. "Help yourself to a drink. Miley has wine coolers you can steal or there's beer too," I say before remembering she's underage, and I'm not sure if Austin would approve of me offering her alcohol. "Forget I said that. Grab two bottles of water."

She rolls her eyes, smirking as she opens the refrigerator. I try my best not to ogle her gorgeous ass in her form-fitting yoga pants as she bends over. "I'm going to suggest they use that statement as your epitaph," she teases. "And I'm eighteen, not eight. I've been drinking since I was fifteen, and I know how to handle myself, so I'll have a beer. Thanks."

She tosses a bottle of water at me so fast I almost don't catch it. I watch as she closes the refrigerator with her hip before popping the top on a beer, arching her head back as she takes a sip. Her throat works elegantly as she slowly drinks, and it shouldn't be such a turn-on, but I'm fucked if it isn't. My cock thickens in my shorts, and I discreetly adjust myself before she notices.

This is becoming a regular occurrence in her presence, which is hugely disconcerting.

I can't be lusting after her.

It's wrong on a million different levels.

But try telling that to my greedy hormones.

She's only been here a little over twenty-four hours, and I'm almost permanently hard. I seriously need to get laid. Maybe then I'll be able to evict her from my thoughts.

"I'll be back," she says, striding out of the kitchen like a woman on a mission. I hear her messing around with the TV, but I keep my focus on making dinner while silently cautioning my dick to get with the program.

"Can you lower the heat on that and come with me," she asks, a couple minutes later. I glance at her, my curiosity instantly piqued when I spot the mischievous expression on her face and the long blue wig she's sporting on her head. "I have something to show you."

Intrigued, I turn off the heat on the stove before trailing her into the living room. "What the hell is that?" I point at the image frozen on the TV screen.

"You said you would've paid good money to see me, so let's see if that's true." A giddy smile transforms her entire face as she presses play on her phone and the recording streams on the screen.

Summer is wearing the same long blue wig in the video, along with the most indecent outfit I've ever seen. My jaw drops to the floor as my libido fully reawakens at the sight of her in those tiny sparkly blue shorts and outrageous bra top. The fake cupcakes jutting out from her bra jiggle around as she sings and dances to "California Gurls" on the screen. My cock is saluting her at full mast now, and damn, does she look good up on that stage. She exudes confidence and sexiness, and she's having the time of her life.

I'm so distracted by the screen I haven't realized she's performing the routine alongside the TV until she's halfway through.

It draws my eyes to her, and I lose all interest in the video as she expertly performs the dance moves right there in front of me. She sways her hips from side to side, rolling her stomach back and forth as she flings her arms up and out. When she dips down and wiggles her chest, I almost come in my boxers. My throat is dry, and my heart is racing around my rib cage like it's barreling around a competitive track.

I remember watching Katy Perry in the video for this song, and Summer has nailed all of her cheeky facial expressions and her sultry moves. When it gets to the part where Katy sprayed stuff from these tubes glued to her tits, Summer fakes the movement with a comical look on her face, and a hysterical laugh bubbles up my throat. I let it loose, because pretending I'm amused is better than admitting how fucking aroused I am right now.

Rapturous applause breaks out on the screen accompanied by catcalls and a few shouted, obscene proposals.

"Well?" Summer is slightly breathless, her cheeks stained red, as she faces me with her hands on her hips. On the screen, she's blowing kisses to the audience, and then she turns and wiggles her butt at the crowd.

My knees almost go out from under me as I crack up laughing, and once I start, I can't stop. I'm doubled over, clutching my stomach, in almost physical pain, as tears peel out of my eyes.

At first, she fake pouts, pretending to stomp her foot in anger before she joins me in my laughter. Both of us are roaring laughing, with tears streaming from our eyes, and it helps release some of the sexual tension I've been holding onto since that night.

I'm wiping tears from my eyes as she shuts down the feed and disconnects her cell from the TV. "Fuck, Summer. You're one crazy chick. I can't believe you got up there on stage like that." I shake my head, still chuckling.

"I was pretty nervous that night," she admits. "And I knew my dad and brothers would flip, but once I got up there, I lost myself to the music, and it was fun." Her face glows as she reminisces.

"You were amazing, but if you were my sister, I'd have totally fucking lost the plot when those assholes spouted that shit."

"Please don't mention the war. Austin and Charlie almost came to blows with these two guys in the row behind them. My dad and my uncle had to separate them." She giggles. "Fun times."

"Something tells me you enjoy getting a rise out of your brothers," I tease as I head back into the kitchen to rescue dinner with her trailing hot on my heels.

"They deserve it," she says, removing plates and silverware from the cupboards. "I could barely pee without them breathing down my neck. Their overprotectiveness is legendary."

"You're their baby sister. What do you expect?" I heap food onto both our plates, carrying them over to the dining table. We usually sit at the counter to eat but the table is more comfortable.

"Not to be suffocated unfairly," she retorts, sliding into the chair across from me.

"You sound just like my sister Gabby. She used to say the same about me and my brothers."

"I can't wait to meet her," she says, rolling noodles around her fork. "Austin said she's married to your other friend Slater and they have a little boy and girl?"

I nod, chewing my food quickly before replying. "Yeah. Billy is four and Daisy is just five months old. I feel bad because I've had little time to visit lately."

"I'm sure your sister understands. Running your own business is a twenty-four-seven commitment. I've seen it with the farm. You're always on the go."

"I think it's getting to your brother," I admit, recalling our earlier conversation. "He wants to take Miley away for the weekend, but finding cover for both of them is an issue."

She chews her food slowly, looking lost in thought. Then her eyes come to life, and she leans across the table. "He should take her to London to see her sister! I could cover the front desk, so that only leaves you to find one additional pair of hands to help."

"You'd do that?"

She looks at me like I've grown ten heads. "Sure. He's my brother, and if he's stressed, I want to help. It's not rocket science, right? I pick things up quick, and I could spend a few evenings after classes with Miley so she could train me."

I shouldn't agree to any plan which involves spending more time with her, but I'm eagerly nodding before my brain has had time to catch up, and I can't find it within myself to be unhappy about it either.

"Just a tiny bite, please?" Austin pleads with his sister from the passenger seat of our SUV as we make the road trip to Lewes on Sunday afternoon.

"You'd swear I never feed you," Miley grumbles from the back seat.

"You are not getting a *crumb* of this apple pie," Summer chastises her brother from her position alongside his girlfriend. "It's a present for Gabby."

"She won't mind if there's a slice or two missing, and you have the apple jelly too."

"Not happening, asshole," Summer confirms with finality. "And you shouldn't ruin your appetite before dinner."

"Are you eighteen or eighty?" Austin teases, sticking his tongue out at his sister.

"Says the guy who's acting like he's five." I can feel Summer rolling her eyes at him, and I snicker.

"Glad to see you're in a better mood," he says. "She must've been some lay."

"Shut the fuck up." I take my eye off the road for a split second to glare at him. I do *not* want to have this conversation around his sister.

"So, you're back to your manwhore ways?" Miley inquires, lifting a brow.

"I hate that word," Summer pipes up, and I swallow the sudden lump in my throat. Our eyes meet in the mirror, and my heart rate accelerates at the mischievous smile on her face. "If Ryan meets a random stranger in a club, there's an obvious attraction, and they're both into it, then why shouldn't he go back to her hotel for sex? And how does that make him a manwhore?"

Holy fucking shit.

Bile travels up my throat as I risk a glance at Austin before drilling Summer with a subtle "what the fuck" look through the mirror. *What the hell is she playing at?* I know Austin thinks she's just referring to the girl I met last night, but it's too close to the truth for comfort. Distracted, I fudge the gear stick, and the car lurches forward, jostling our bodies with the motion. "Sorry," I mumble, trying to get a grip.

Austin opens his mouth to say something, but Summer hasn't finished. "If I told you I got laid last night too, would that mean you'd call me out on my slutty ways?" she adds, and I almost crash the car at her statement.

"Who was he?" Austin growls, shooting me a slightly worried look before swiveling in his seat and narrowing his eyes at his sister.

"Oh, don't get your panties in a bunch, Powers. It was hypothetical. I hate the way society labels men and women in touch with their sexuality. If people are single, the sex is consensual, and they want to explore different partners, why does that automatically mean they're a manwhore or a player or a slut?"

Steam is practically billowing out of Austin's ears. I don't know if it's her casual use of his nickname or her liberal views that has him on edge, but he's a grenade waiting to explode.

"Summer," he grits out, rubbing a spot between his brows. "I don't know what you've been doing or who you've been talking to, but that is not an acceptable attitude for an eighteen-year-old freshman to have."

"She's an adult, Austin," Miley says, leaning forward in her seat. "And Summer was just expressing an opinion. You need to lighten up."

"Maybe *you* need to get laid more often, and you might not be so tense," Summer bravely says.

"Summer."

Austin's tone carries considerable warning, and I don't want us arriving at Gabby and Slate's place with tension lingering in the air, so I intervene. "For the record, I didn't get laid last night." It had been my intention, and the gorgeous brunette glued to my side at the club had made it clear she was up for it, but I wasn't feeling it, and I rushed out of her apartment, spewing apologies as I left her semi-naked and wanting. "I'm in a good mood because I'm spending time with my family, so can we just focus on having a nice dinner instead of goading one another over sex?"

The conversation turns casual after that, thank fuck, and in next to no time, I'm pulling into the driveway of Gabby and Slater's house.

"Wow, nice place," Summer says, sliding out of the back seat before reaching in to remove her purse, the pie, and the homemade jelly.

"Here. Let me take that." I hold out my hand for the pie, but she places her purse in my palm instead.

"Thanks!" She waggles her brows, grinning, before making a beeline for the front door.

I'm mumbling under my breath as I use the key fob to lock the car, trailing behind the girls as we walk toward the house. Austin chuckles at my dilemma, and I'd flip him the bird if my hands weren't otherwise occupied holding Summer's purse. "Shut it, ass face."

"She has you wrapped around her little finger already, and she's not even living with us a week."

"She's kind of hard to say no to." And that's a fucking understatement.

"She's a little minx, but she has a heart of pure gold." He scratches the back of his neck in an obvious tell. "You don't think she was serious back in the car, do you?"

We're veering into dangerous territory, and I want to get the fuck out of Dodge as fast as I can. "She's not a little girl anymore, Austin. She's beautiful and spirited, and she'll get attention. You'll just have to deal with it." I sigh as I watch the front door swing open. "I'm sure you haven't forgotten the shit we got up to our freshman year. You can't expect her to act like an angel when you were the devil incarnate," I joke.

"The thought of any fucker putting his hands on her makes my blood boil." His hands clench into fists at his sides, and an icy shiver tiptoes up my spine. "And I know it's hypocritical as fuck, but I pray she doesn't run into any guys like us. I think I could adjust to a boyfriend, but a string of random fucks?" He shakes his head, a deep frown creasing his brow. "Not a chance in hell."

I wet my dry lips, hoping he doesn't notice the beads of sweat forming on my brow. I'm glad we had this chat because it helps remind me she's off-limits. Austin would lose the plot if he found out I took her virginity or that I can't get her out of my fucking head ever since. This is a timely reminder and one I need to heed because I've too much invested in our friendship to risk it.

"You have a stunning home," Summer is saying to Gabby in the hallway when I step foot inside the house.

"Bro." Slate welcomes me with a slap to the back. "Good to see you. You too, man," he adds, nodding at Austin.

"We must arrange a few beers soon," Austin suggests. "After Miley and I get back from London," he adds in a low tone.

Slate raises a brow. "What's in London?"

"Miley's sister, and I'm planning a surprise trip so keep that to yourself."

"Uncle Ryan!" Billy's high-pitched screech cuts through Slater's response and I bend down as my adorable nephew comes charging down the hallway.

"Billy!" My mom calls to him from the end of the hallway. "Walk, don't run!" She flaps her hands in the air in consternation.

Paying her no heed, Billy flings himself into my arms, and I bundle the little dude up, cherishing the feel of his small body against me. "I missed you," he says, tightening his arms around my neck, and my heart swells with love.

"I missed you too, buddy." I stand, keeping him in my arms. "So, so much." I kiss the top of his head before messing up his dark hair.

He twists around in my arms, coming face to face with Summer, and his eyes pop wide. "You're pretty," he tells her, his cheeks reddening a little.

I can't disagree with him.

Summer is wearing a simple white sundress, flat gold sandals and minimal makeup, with her hair hanging in loose curls down her back, and I've never seen a woman look more gorgeous. Every time she looks in my direction, she steals my breath away.

"Thank you. And you're so handsome I think I'll run away with you." When she smiles at him, her entire face lights up, and I swear the little guy swoons, right along with me.

"I'd run away with you," the little charmer supplies, nodding eagerly as he opens his arms to go to her.

Summer scoops him up, and he clings to her like he's afraid she'll vanish if he doesn't hold her tight enough. "You smell pretty too," he adds, nuzzling his nose into her hair.

Gabby laughs, and Slater slides his arm around her waist as they smile at their son.

"What have they been putting in the water around here?" I joke, leaning in to kiss my sister on the cheek. "Or have you been sending the little dude to Casanova classes on the sly?"

"I think he's just inherited some of your traits," Gabby quips, yanking me into a bone-crushing hug. "I missed you, little big bro." She squeezes me so hard it's a wonder I can still breathe.

"Missed you too, Tornado." I kiss the top of her blonde head before holding her at arm's length. "You look fantastic." She truly does. There's no evidence she only gave birth a few months ago, and she's practically glowing. I may have had concerns when she and Slater first dated, but I can't deny how amazing they are together and how great it is to see her happy after all the heartache she experienced.

"Thanks. I'd like to say the same, but you look like shit." She brushes her hand over the five days' worth of growth on my chin, rubbing her thumb along the bruising shadows under my eyes. "Are you getting any sleep?"

"I'm sleeping and eating and shitting." She swats my arm, scowling at my crude language, and I pull her into a gentle headlock, like old times. "Stop fussing. I'm fine," I say, messing up her hair.

She punches me in the gut, and I'm momentarily winded as she escapes my clutches, straightening up and brushing tangled strands of long blonde hair from her face.

"No hitting, Mommy," Billy chastises, wagging his finger at Gabby, and we all crack up laughing. He's still wrapped around Summer like a koala, showing no signs of giving her up.

"You want to give Summer a break there, dude?" I suggest, opening my arms for him.

"She's mine." He circles his arms tighter around her neck, glaring at me, and another round of laughter breaks out.

"Wow. I'd hate to see what he's like when he's older if he's this possessive already," Austin jokes.

"I'm betting he'd still have nothing on you, Marc, and Charlie," Summer is quick to reply.

"Girl, I think we have lots to talk about," Gabby says, prying Billy out of Summer's arms and putting his feet on the ground. "Why don't you rejoin your cousins outside?" she suggests, kissing his cheek. "I'm sure Uncle Ryan will play basketball with you."

His little hand wraps around mine, and he looks up at me eagerly. "C'mon." He leads the way. "I'll let you be on my team."

"Duty calls." I wink at Summer as we pass, and she waves us both off.

"It's okay, Uncle Ryan," Billy says when we're out of earshot.

"What's okay, buddy?"

"If you want the pretty girl to be yours."

My mouth drops to the floor as I stare at my nephew, slack jawed.

"You can look after her until I'm old enough to marry her," he adds with a level of supreme confidence that only comes with youth. "But promise you'll treat her like a princess because my daddy says every boy should treat every girl like that." And with those parting words of wisdom, he drags me outside with my jaw trailing the ground behind me.

CHAPTER 9
Summer

"THAT WAS DELICIOUS," I proclaim, beaming at Gabby with a full stomach. "Thank you so much."

"I'm glad you enjoyed it, and we're thrilled you could join us today. You're welcome to visit anytime." Her happy smile is genuine, and she looks so like Ryan when she smiles. They share the same blue eyes, blonde hair, quick wit, and charming personality.

"I appreciate that," I say, raising my voice. The kids are racing around the table having grown bored with sitting down a long time ago. I smile as I watch them giggle and shriek.

Ryan's eldest brother Dean is here with his fiancée, Alice, and his two twin daughters from a previous marriage. Mia and Tia are seven and most definitely the leaders of the pack. Ryan's other brother Caleb is here with his wife Terri. They have Ryder, who's basically the same age as Billy, and their seventeen-month-old son, Roman. Ryan's mom and dad, Lucy and Paul, complete the guest list, and they've all been friendly and welcoming.

"Okay." Gabby stands, talking in a commanding voice. "Who wants ice cream?" The kids all squeal in delight, skipping and jumping after Gabby as she walks into the kitchen. I gather up plates and follow her in. After depositing the dirty dinnerware in the dishwasher, I help her with the ice cream, and then we bring the kids outside, settling them on the picnic bench. Billy takes hold of my hand, refusing to let me go until Gabby bribes him into releasing me. I kiss his cheek, promising I'll come out and play after we've eaten dessert.

"He's really taken a shine to you," she says as we work side by side serving up apple pie and cheesecake for the adults.

"He's adorable. I wasn't joking when I said I'd run away with him. You must be so proud."

"I am. He's a great kid." Her eyes glisten proudly. "They both are."

"I hope Daisy wakes soon. I'm dying to meet her."

Gabby glances at the clock. "She's having a power nap today, but she had a turbulent night, so I'm not surprised."

"You must be exhausted."

"It comes with the territory." She shrugs. "We live in a perpetual state of sleep deprivation, but I wouldn't swap my life for the world." A sad, nostalgic look sweeps across her features momentarily.

Miley and Lucy appear in the kitchen then, and together, we return to the dining room, handing out dessert before reclaiming our seats.

"This apple pie is to die for," Paul, Ryan's dad, says a few minutes later. "Ryan said you made it yourself from apples grown on your family farm?"

I nod. "Yes, and the apple jelly too."

"You know, we've had Austin over to dinner plenty of times, and I don't think I've ever asked him much about the farm," Lucy says. "I thought it was a cattle farm?"

"It used to be," Austin responds before I can. "But Dad had to diversify over the years."

"We grow a variety of vegetables, fruits, and flowers," I continue. "And we sell the produce locally online and via the farmer's market in Milton. Although the focus is on beef and duck, the farm wouldn't be profitable without the other side of the business."

"You seem very knowledgeable," Lucy adds. "Do you plan on working on the farm after college?"

I shake my head. "Definitely not. That's my brother Charlie's forte. He recently returned home to work on the farm after getting his agricultural degree."

"Summer wants to be a teacher," Ryan confirms. "When she's not performing Katy Perry songs on stage, that is." We share a conspiratorial grin.

"How the hell do you know about that?" Austin asks, quirking a brow.

"Summer put on an impromptu show the other day." Ryan smirks at the memory.

"She what?" Austin splutters, almost choking on his pie. "You better not have been prancing around the apartment in that excuse for a costume."

"Oh, for the love of all things holy, keep your hair on. I wasn't wearing the costume." His shoulders visibly relax, and I can't stop myself from pushing his buttons. "Although I would have if I'd thought to bring it with me. Ryan deserved the authentic experience." I shouldn't wind Austin up but he's making it too easy.

My brother is lost for words, and I'm struggling to contain a grin when Ryan sticks the knife in. "She played me the video from the show though, and damn, that was some costume."

"Why the hell would you show him that?" Austin asks, getting worked up and now he's just pissing me off. However, we're guests in Gabby's home, and I don't want to bring tension to the table, so I work hard to offset my annoyance.

"We were talking about it in the car on our way back from the gym, and I thought it'd be funny to show him."

"Do I look like I'm laughing?" Austin growls, and I notice Miley clamping her hand down on his thigh under the table in warning.

"This is priceless," Slater says, showcasing a mad grin. "I never thought I'd see the day where Austin would be all loved up or act like he has the biggest stick up his ass, and now I've witnessed both. Today's a good day." He rubs his hands together, as Gabby swats the back of his head.

"Don't tease our guests. It's not hospitable."

Slater snorts. "We're talking about Powers."

Austin flips him the bird just as the baby monitor emits a loud wail. Slater stands, but Gabby tugs on his arm. "I'll go. Summer wants to meet Daisy."

I hop up out of my seat with no further encouragement, practically skipping out of the room after Gabby.

"Hello, my little princess," Gabby murmurs as we pad carefully into the baby's room.

A nightlight rotates a smattering of tiny stars across the ceiling in the dimly lit space. Daisy cries, kicking her legs out and reaching her arms up to her momma. Gabby holds her close to her chest, gently rocking her. "Would you mind switching on that lamp?" she whispers, gesturing at the dresser off to the side of the crib.

I switch it on, and the room comes into clearer view. "Wow. This is a beautiful room." It's painted in a pale shade of green with matching white wooden furniture. One wall has large daisies floating across it as if they were blowing in the breeze, and the wall at the back of the crib spells out Daisy's name in large white foam lettering. Fitted shelves hold tons of cuddly toys and family photos, including a cute one of Billy holding his baby sister in his arms.

Gabby watches me looking at it as she changes her baby's diaper. "That was minutes after Daisy was born," she explains. "Billy was so excited to meet his sister, but it completely overwhelmed him when the time came to see her."

"I can tell from his expression." I run my finger along the frame, my heart full as I take in the wide-eyed shell-shocked stare on her son's face.

"He loves her so much," Gabby admits, tickling her daughter as she dresses her.

I return to her side, smiling at the gorgeous little blonde princess. She's gurgling and kicking out her legs, and I want to bundle her up into my arms. "It'd be hard not to. She's beautiful, Gabby." I place my finger in the baby's hand, and her tiny fingers latch on. "She looks so much like you with her blonde hair where Billy is dark-haired like Slater."

Gabby smiles quietly at me as she lifts her daughter up. "Would you like to feed her?"

"Oh, yes, please." My grin is wide. "I didn't want to be rude, but I'm dying to hold her."

"C'mon then. Let's go down to the living room, and I'll get you set up."

I'm seated on the brown leather couch, while Gabby has gone to the kitchen to fetch a bottle, cradling her gorgeous daughter in my arms. Sounds of conversation and laughter trickle in from the kitchen as the rest of the adults enjoy an after-dinner coffee. Daisy gurgles, and I can't stop peppering her face with little kisses. I'm rewarded with the biggest smile, and my heart seriously melts.

I can't wait until my brothers settle down and pop out little Petersens. I know Mom's dying for some grandkids too, and I'm betting they will subject Austin and Miley to lots of teasing about weddings and babies when my brother finally plucks up the courage to bring her home.

Even though she's hungry, little Daisy is impeccably well-behaved, giggling as I blow raspberries on her chest.

"You have mesmerized both my children," Gabby says with a smile as she steps into the room. "Are you sure you aren't Mary Poppins in disguise?"

I laugh as I prop the baby up higher on my shoulder, accepting the warm bottle from Gabby and bringing the nipple to Daisy's mouth. All the years of babysitting the neighbor's kids means I'm well accustomed to babies. Daisy latches on instantly, sucking greedily on the bottle, and I run my finger along her soft cheek as I smile at her. "I wish. How cool would it be to fly over the city via umbrella?"

"It might be a bit cold and wet," she jokes with me.

"It'd be worth it though." I coo at Daisy as I gently snuggle into her while she feeds. "I'm happy to babysit if you ever need a sitter."

"You might be sorry you offered," she quips.

"Not at all. Honestly, if I can help, I'd be happy to."

"That's sweet of you. Thanks." She sits back farther in the couch, casting a glance at the large family photo, of her with Slater and the kids, hanging over the mantelpiece, an automatic smile cresting upon her face. "Date nights are rare these days, but if we have something to go to, usually my parents babysit, or sometimes Dean and Alice if they don't have the twins with them." She folds her hands in her lap. "Ryan used to babysit Billy a lot when he was a baby, but he's way too busy now with the gym, and I'd only feel like I was imposing."

"I'm sure he wouldn't mind once he could arrange cover."

"I know he wouldn't," she agrees, her eyes drifting to the photo on the side wall. Her expression turns nostalgic, and I stare at the man locked in an intimate pose with Gabby, trying to keep the curiosity out of my eyes, but I'm a naturally nosy person so it's difficult.

"That's Dylan," Gabby volunteers. "Billy's father."

"I didn't want to pry, but I was wondering. I'm sorry," I add, realizing my faux pas upstairs. "I shouldn't have presumed anything about Billy and Slater."

"It's okay. Slater gets that a lot when he takes Billy out, and it's a natural assumption."

"Does Billy see Dylan often?"

"Dylan passed shortly after Billy was born," Gabby quietly admits, and I feel awful for opening this topic of conversation.

"Oh, my God. I'm so sorry. I'm too nosy for my own good."

Gabby pats my arm, smiling. "It's fine. We don't shy away from talking about Dylan. Billy knows all about him, and he loves bragging he has two daddies, one of whom is an angel looking after him from heaven."

Her smile is radiant and full of love and pride for her son. She looks up at the picture again, and my eyes follow suit. It's a beautiful photo but tinged with sadness now I know the history behind it. They are both sitting on the floor, and Dylan has his arms wrapped around Gabby's baby bump from behind. She's leaning back into his chest, staring up at him, and he's meeting her eyes, the look of love and adoration transparent in his gaze.

"He was my first love," Gabby continues explaining, "and I thought we'd be together forever, but fate had other plans." She wipes a lone tear aside. "I will always love Dylan, and I love that I have a piece of him in Billy, but Slater is the love of my life, and he has made me so incredibly happy. He adopted Billy, and he treats him as if he's his own flesh and blood, and don't even get me started on how he is with this little one." She squeezes her daughter's toes. "I'm lucky to have him, and I love the life we share."

Slater appears at that exact moment, as if he's in perfect tune with his wife. From the expression on his handsome face, I'm guessing he heard the tail end of our conversation. "I love you," he tells her, not fazed at the fact I'm right here. Sitting down, he slides his wife onto his lap, wrapping his bulky arms around her. I've been watching the way they are together, and it's obvious they are very much in love.

Someday, I hope to have what they have. When I've lived my life to the fullest and I'm ready to settle down and start a family.

"We're so very lucky," Slater says, kissing his wife on the cheek, as he talks. "And after the things we've experienced, we never take a single day for granted."

"I love that," I truthfully admit, draping Daisy over my shoulder after she's finished her bottle. I gently rub her back, and she emits a loud burp almost instantaneously. "And it's how I want to live my life. With no regrets. Grasping every opportunity to live life to the fullest because you never know what's lying in wait around the corner. It's part of the reason I want to go traveling after college before I settle into my career. There is such a vast world out there, and I want to explore."

I carry Daisy over my shoulder, continuing to rub her back as I wander back into the kitchen, letting Gabby and Slater have some precious alone time. Miley and Lucy have been busy cleaning up the kitchen, and some of the others have meandered outside to watch over the kids, while Ryan, Austin, and Paul are still sitting around the kitchen table drinking coffee.

"You look right at home there, Summer," Paul says when he spies me.

"I adore babies, and this one is precious." I sit down, turning her around in my arms, still holding her close.

"Stop hogging the precious one," Ryan jokes, holding out his arms. "Hand the cutie over." I carefully deposit his niece into his arms and our fingers brush. As usual, delicious tremors ricochet up and down my arms from the contact, and from the way Ryan jerks a little, I can tell he's definitely feeling it too.

The back door swings open rather forcefully, and a little ball of energy barrels through. "Pretty girl," Billy says, raising a smile to my lips. "Can you play basketball with me?"

"Her name is Summer," Ryan reminds him.

"I know." Billy pouts, comically folding his arms across his small chest. "But Daddy Slater calls Mommy beautiful, so why can't I call Summer pretty?"

I extend my hand toward him and he links his small fingers in mine. "I don't mind if you call me pretty girl once I'm allowed to play ball."

"You can play anything of mine. Anything." He looks so sincere, and my heart melts again. Seriously, these kids are making me feel broody in a way I've never felt before. Which is crazy because I'd never consider having a child at my age. I definitely want kids, a whole host of them, but when I'm much older and I'm at a place in my life where I can devote my full attention to them.

"Wow, Sum." Austin says. "You're hooking them young these days."

"Age is only a number," I toss out. "And I'm sorely tempted to kidnap your sister's kids and never give them back," I admit, eyeballing Ryan.

"I can't say I blame you because they're gorgeous kids, but you're wearing rose-tinted glasses. Kids are a shit-ton of work. Come babysit them overnight sometime, and I bet you'll be eating your words," he says, nuzzling his nose into Daisy's neck. She giggles nonstop, and he's fascinated by her. There's something magical about watching a big, burly guy cradling a cute baby in his arms, and my ovaries swoon as Ryan continues to lavish affection on his niece.

Billy tugs me outside, and I spend twenty minutes running around the backyard with all the kids playing ball. I haven't had this much fun in ages. They really are a great bunch of kids and such a lovely family. My parents would get on famously with Ryan's.

I stop to take a breather, heading back inside to grab a bottle of water. The sound of angry voices greets me as I step into the kitchen.

Ryan is standing in the middle of the kitchen with a face like thunder. Gabby has a worried expression on her face as she stares up at Slater, pleading with her eyes for him to do something. The only other people in the kitchen are a strange man and woman who weren't there before.

The man is standing protectively behind the woman, his arm resting on her shoulder as he whispers in her ear. She's stunning with shoulder-length wavy reddish-brown hair and expressive green eyes. "I'm sorry, Ryan," she whispers. "I didn't know you'd be here."

His gaze lowers to her swollen belly, and a flash of pain glimmers in his eyes before he conceals it. "Whatever, Myndi. It's not like I care." But as he looks up at her, challenging her to disagree, it's blatantly obvious he cares, and a sharp pain spreads across my chest at the realization.

CHAPTER 10
Ryan

I CAN'T FUCKING believe this. This is like my every worst nightmare rolled into one. It's been over two years since Myndi and I broke up, and I'm still pissed over the way she treated me. Seeing her again brings a host of repressed emotions to the surface, and I'm not in the mood to revisit my past.

She moved to Australia shortly after all that shit went down, and except for Gabby and Slate's wedding last year, I haven't had to face her since then.

I knew she was in a new relationship, and I couldn't give two fucks about the stuck-up jerk in the blazer and button-down shirt glowering at me. She's welcome to her nerdy doctor boyfriend, but seeing her like this is akin to a slap in the face and I'm ill-equipped to deal with the host of conflicting emotions running through me.

She looks up at her boyfriend, and they communicate silently with their eyes.

I remember a time when we used to do that.

A time when I thought maybe, just maybe, I was wrong about love and marriage.

But I wasn't wrong.

I'd gotten it right all along.

He nods, and she turns back around to face me. Remorse and pity emanate from her in spades, and I fucking hate that. I want nothing from her.

Especially not her pity.

And her remorse is too fucking late.

"Can we talk in private?" she asks, beseeching me with her eyes.

"We've nothing to talk about." I cross my arms over my chest, trying my best to avoid looking at her swollen belly.

"We both know that's not true."

"You had plenty of time to talk before you emigrated to Australia, and I seem to recall the only words you had for me were harsh ones. I'm not in the mood for a repeat."

"I was in the wrong," she admits, reaching her hand out.

I flinch, stepping back from her touch, almost tripping over Summer. I didn't realize she'd come back inside, and I hate she's a witness to this. I grab onto her elbow to stop her from falling. "Sorry. I didn't see you there."

"It's fine." Her soft smile is laced with concern, and fuck, if that doesn't thaw the new layer of ice around my heart.

"Is this your girlfriend?" Myndi asks, her tone hopeful as she pins Summer with an eager smile.

"She's mine," Billy cuts in, strolling into the room like he owns it. "But I told Uncle Ryan she could be his until I'm old enough to marry her. He promised to treat her like a princess," he tacks on the end, like that totally justifies it.

"Oh, jeez." Gabby bites down on her lower lip to stop from laughing. "I think you need to have a word with our son," she murmurs to Slate, and Slate promptly brings Billy out of the room for a man-to-man chat.

Myndi's gaze bounces from me to Summer, and she looks awkward as hell. I really don't give a shit if she's embarrassed, but I won't disrespect Summer. "Not that I owe you any explanation, but Summer is Austin's sister. She's living with us at the moment."

"Oh. I'm sorry for jumping to conclusions." She offers Summer her hand. "It's nice to meet you. Ryan and I used to date in college, and I lived in the house with him and your brother for a while. I see the resemblance now."

I harrumph, and Myndi's baby daddy looks like he wants to rip my head from my shoulders.

I'd like to see him try.

"Please don't remind me," Summer says. "Most of the time I try to forget we're related."

Myndi laughs, and it rubs me the wrong way. I can't stomach being in her presence any longer. The ghosts of the past are choking the life out of me every second I'm around her. "I'm going outside. It'd be nice if you left by the time I return," I spit out, as Gabby gasps.

"I'm so sorry. He's—" I don't hear the rest of Gabby's apology as I storm outside.

"Hey, man. You okay?" My brother Caleb approaches me with caution, because they all know how crazy that woman makes me.

"I'll be fine once I don't have to look at her face." Caleb shares a loaded look with my other brother Dean. "And no, before you ask me for the thousandth time, I don't want to talk about it. Why the fuck is she here, anyway?"

"Gabby didn't know they were coming," Dean coolly states. "You know she'd never ambush you like that. I'm not even sure if Gabby knew Myndi was pregnant."

"They're best friends. Of course, she knew," I bark, venting my frustration in the wrong direction.

"Don't fucking take it out on Gabby, Ryan," Caleb snaps back. "She lost her best friend in all this, and she's never once blamed you for that."

"Because it wasn't my fucking fault!" I yell.

"Keep your voice down," Dean cautions. "There are kids around."

I attempt to rein in my anger, but I'm too wound up. Air whooshes out of my mouth as I drag my hands through my hair. "Fuck." I chew on the inside of my mouth. "Seeing her again just brings so much shit to the surface, and it's not something I enjoy thinking about."

"I get it," Dean says, nodding as he squeezes my shoulder.

Dean is the only one who knows everything that went down with Myndi. I wanted to confide in Slate, but I couldn't ask him to keep it a secret from my sister, and if her best friend didn't tell her the truth, then I wasn't bringing them into it either.

"And I understand," he continues. "Every time I have a confrontation with Annie, I'm in a foul mood for days after."

Annie is Dean's ex-wife, my nieces' mother, and a Class-A bitch. It doesn't matter that she's apparently happily re-married; she still loves trying to wind my brother up any chance she gets.

The door opens behind me, and our parents join us. Great. Just what I need. "You okay, son?" Dad asks, looking me directly in the eye.

"I'm fine," I lie, tension tightening my jaw and twisting in my gut.

"Maybe you should talk to her," Mom softly suggests. "It might help if you unburdened whatev—"

"Seriously, Mom? You're in no position to lecture me on this," I snap. Shaking my head, I harrumph at the audacity of that woman to interfere, given her track record and when she hasn't a clue about the situation with my ex.

"What exactly does that mean?" she asks with a frown, sharing a troubled glance with my Dad.

"Nothing." I push past her. "Forget it. I'm going for a walk to cool off. I'll catch you later."

I veer left, away from the yard where the kids are playing ball.

Slate and Gabby purchased this house primarily for the lavish gardens. It stretches over two acres, and they have all the outdoor space they could ever need. I walk for five minutes until I come to the small covered seating area nestled between leafy trees and flowering shrubs. Plonking my butt down on the love seat, I cradle my head in my hands, wondering why I keep letting that woman get to me.

Why I enabled those cruel words she spoke to dig so deep into my heart, damaging it beyond repair.

Why I ever believed I was destined for love and marriage and the kind of family life my best friend shares with my sister.

"Hey."

I pick my head up as Summer's sweet voice rings out.

She shoves a bottle of beer at me. "Thought you could use this. Miley says she's good to drive us back."

My fingers curl around the cold glass, tingling where my skin comes into contact with her hand. "Thanks." I whip the bottle away as if her touch is toxic.

It might as well be.

For the first time in over two years, I've met someone who threatens these steel walls I've built around my heart, and I don't fucking like it one bit.

I don't want to feel the things I'm feeling for this girl, and I'm terrified it goes beyond lust.

I made a promise to myself when things turned to shit with Myndi.

A promise I wouldn't let myself fall again, and I won't break it. Not even for someone as gorgeous and sweet as Summer.

"I'm not great company right now. You should head back." I don't even look at her as I attempt to dismiss her.

In true Summer fashion, she ignores me, dropping onto the seat beside me. "I like it out here, and we don't have to talk. I'm good with silence."

We sip our beers, rocking back and forth on the seat, in amicable silence, and the irony isn't lost on me.

After a while, she sets her empty bottle down on the ground and clears her throat. "You know, I believe people come in and out of our lives at different times to teach us something. Maybe it's something about ourselves. Maybe it's something about the world. But I think every experience helps shape us. Helps prepare us for the future. Even the bad stuff. Even the stuff that seems like it might break us."

I twist around to face her. "You want to know what I think?" She nods eagerly. "I think that's the biggest crock of shit I've ever heard," I spit out, still riled up. "That you're way too young and naïve to know what you're talking about. And I doubt you've faced any bad shit in your life." I'm being a jackass, but I'm too pissed to tone it down.

She purses her lips, staring calmly at me while she contemplates how to reply. "You're right. About it all, except the crock of shit. You might not share my beliefs, but that doesn't give you the right to be rude about my opinions. Yes, I haven't had to face many obstacles in my life. I know I'm luckier than most. But just because I have limited personal experience doesn't mean I'm wrong."

I pick at the label on my beer, mulling her words over, as she stands. Panic is instant. "I'm sorry. Don't go," I blurt before I've had time to rethink it. "I didn't mean to disrespect you or your beliefs. It's just hard for me to look objectively at it when my experiences have tainted my opinions."

"I understand, and you're forgiven," she says, running her hands over the bark of a large, old, oak tree.

"Just like that, huh?" I inquire, climbing to my feet.

She spins around, her dress swirling around her thighs with the motion, reminding me of the ballerina on the top of the music box Gabby had as a kid. She used to watch that little ballerina rotate for hours at a time, forcing the rest of us to suffer that sickly sweet melody repeatedly. "I don't bear grudges. Life's too short."

"I hope you never change, Summer," I truthfully say, shoving my hands in the pockets of my jeans to ignore the urge to touch her. "There aren't many like you in the world."

She beams at me, dropping a curtesy that's cute as hell. "Why, thank you, kind sir." She turns back around to the tree, straining her neck to look up. "I have an idea." There's a devilish glint in her eye as she looks over her shoulder at me. "Let's climb this tree."

I stare at her blankly for a few seconds, sure I must've heard that wrong. But she's already on the move, expertly placing her feet on the bark, and pulling her torso up as she climbs.

"Why?"

"Because it'll be fun." She says this like my question was preposterous.

"You've done this before," I remark, watching her scale the tree with skill. I place my hands on the bark, deciding I may as well join her in crazy town.

"Well, duh." She looks down at me, laughing. "I grew up on a farm with an orchard and a small forest. Climbing is practically my middle name." Her eyes shimmer with excitement and adventure, and I force my gaze away as she climbs higher, flashing her panties at me. I concentrate on climbing the tree and not looking up, but it takes mammoth self-control. I must be as crazy as she is to even contemplate this. It's been years since I did anything on the spur of the moment, and the feeling of exhilaration is just what I need to distract my troubled mind.

She's light on her feet, her body flexible, as she climbs higher and higher, while my heavier limbs struggle to keep pace with her. Eventually, I catch up, and I sit on the thick branch directly across from her. She has her hands planted on either side of her, her legs dangling over the edge, as she swings them back and forth with no fear.

"I tried to persuade my parents to let me live in the woods at the back of our property after I watched *The Hunger Games*," she tells me without invitation. "I wanted to be like Katniss. Minus the killing part, obviously." She grins at me. "I was convinced I could survive out there, blanketed in Mother Nature's arms, and that I could fend for myself."

"What happened?"

"My parents agreed to let me spend one night outside, and I barely lasted four hours." She giggles. "Although that was Marc and Charlie's fault because they snuck into the woods once it was dark and started throwing things and making noises, and I got so frightened I ran all the way back to the house leaving my tent and my bag behind." She rolls her eyes. "It's a wonder I still speak to any of my brothers given the stuff they pulled on me growing up."

"It's a rite of passage. Gabby can tell you about all the shit Slate, my brothers and I pulled on her over the years."

She smiles. "I wouldn't have it any other way, because then it'd mean they don't care."

Silence engulfs us, and I scan the land down below and in the distance. "It's peaceful up here."

"It is," she agrees. "I love it, and you can see so much."

I lean back against the trunk of the tree, swinging my legs up onto the branch. "Myndi accused me of cheating on her," I admit, suddenly wanting to talk to Summer about it although I'm not brave enough to tell her everything.

"And did you?" she asks in a curious tone devoid of malice or accusation.

"No. I would never do that. *Never*." Not after what I witnessed as a kid.

Cheating is a major deal breaker for me.

I rub a tense spot between my brows. "If I had ever felt like that, like I wanted to be with someone else, I would've ended things with her before betraying her trust. She knew how I felt about cheating, but she still wouldn't accept that I was innocent."

"Why did she believe you'd cheated on her?"

A pain slices across my chest as I revisit one of the most painful times in my life. "Because this bitch manipulated the situation one night when I was out at a club without Myndi. Catching me completely off guard, she pulled me into a kiss, and her friend recorded it in the seconds before I realized what was happening and pushed her off me. I was so fucking mad, especially when I discovered she posted it on social media within minutes, tagging my girlfriend, ensuring she'd see it and jump to the wrong conclusion."

I pull my knees up to my chest, staring out at the darkening sky. "Myndi had already decided before I even got home to explain. She knew that bitch had been chasing after me for months. Knew I'd been continuously turning her down, but she didn't want to hear my version of events, choosing to believe that photo instead."

I gulp over the lump in my throat. "And it's not like I didn't understand her initial reaction because the photo was pretty damning, and Myndi's ex had cheated on her, so she had understandable trust issues. But the difference between her and me is that if it'd happened in reverse, I would've given her the benefit of the doubt because *I* trusted *her*. I'd never given her any reason to doubt my loyalty, yet she immediately believed the worst. I thought she'd cool down the next day, but she didn't. She refused to believe me, some other shit went down she blamed me for too, and that was it for me."

"That sucks, and I'm sorry it happened to you."

"Well, I'm not," I honestly admit. "Because it proved that we never would've made it as a couple, and it was better to find that out before I'd invested any more of my time in a relationship that was going nowhere."

"Is that why you don't date anymore?"

"Who told you I don't date?"

"I kinda guessed that first night we met, and Miley confirmed it."

Fucking Miley and her big mouth. Not that it matters. It's good that Summer knows this in case she's harboring any silly notions of her and me.

"I didn't date before Myndi, and I haven't dated after her, and that's what I prefer. I enjoy casual hookups when I need to fuck, and I make sure the girl knows it's only a onetime thing. That it's only sex. A pure physical release and nothing more."

"And you haven't grown tired of it? You don't feel lonely?" Again, her questions are inquisitive, not critical in the slightest. It's so easy to talk to her. To be honest with her. Because she genuinely doesn't judge.

"Nope." It's not a lie if I'm deluding myself. "This way, there are no complications." I swing my legs back around, looking her straight in the eye. "No feelings involved. And that's exactly the way I like it."

CHAPTER 11
Summer

I CAN TELL he's convinced himself he believes it, but deep down, he knows it's not the truth, and that makes me sad for him, because he's so closed off, so guarded, so unwilling to open his heart again that he might miss out on the greatest love of his life. Of course, I don't voice those opinions, because he'd just chalk it up to my innocence and inexperience again, and I don't want him thinking I'm hitting on him either, so I keep those thoughts to myself.

But I feel for him. I truly do. I've no plans to tie myself to a guy, but my heart is wide-open, and if love finds me, I won't turn it away.

I'll embrace it.

Jump off the cliff with gusto, allowing myself to free fall, trusting that I'll land safely. Yes, I might be damaged or broken when I hit solid ground, but I know I'll survive.

Ryan would never leave the platform, missing out on the entire experience, and I hurt for all those lost opportunities he's most likely already foregone.

"We should get down," he says, dragging me out of my head. "It's getting dark and we need to head back to the city."

"Okay." I make a move, but he shakes his head.

"Let me go first."

I don't argue, letting him descend first and giving him a head start before I climb down. A gentle breeze blows around me as I descend, still lost in thought, and I'm a little distracted.

I'm about twenty feet off the ground when I lose my footing. It happens so fast, and it's so unexpected, that I do the one thing you should never do—panic. My hands grapple at the tree trunk, my fingers desperately trying to hold on even as I feel myself falling.

"Fuck! Summer!" Ryan shouts from somewhere below me.

I close my eyes, humming under my breath as I go into that Zen place in my head, preparing for the inevitable hard landing. It's not as if this is the first time I've fallen out of a tree. I've a history of broken bones to prove it, so I'm expecting the worst.

But it doesn't happen. Instead, I land in a pair of strong, warm arms, and relief washes over me. With my eyes still shut, I wrap my arms around Ryan's neck, resting my head on his broad chest, inhaling his potently masculine scent.

Might as well take advantage of the opportunity while I can.

Being held by him again is nice. His heart is beating frantically under my ear, mirroring the pounding organ in my chest.

"You scared the shit out of me," he exclaims, his voice gruff. "You're lucky I'd reached the ground, or you could've been seriously injured."

My eyes flicker open, and I lift my head, peering into his piercing blue eyes. "Thank you for saving me."

He makes no move to put my feet on the ground, and I raise no objection. My heart is thumping wildly, doing cartwheels and somersaults behind my rib cage as we stare at one another. Something indecipherable passes in the tiny space between us, and despite my previous protestations, I know I want him. I'm only fooling myself by pretending otherwise.

I want him so badly I could cry.

I need to feel his lips on mine again.

To savor the feel of his tongue as it sweeps inside my mouth.

To burn from the fiery tingles scorching a path across my skin in all the places where he touches me.

His chest rises, his pupils darken, and I imagine his mind has gone to the same blissful place mine has. My tongue darts out to moisten my dry lips, and his eyes follow the motion. "You shouldn't thank me," he half-whispers, his eyes still glued to my mouth.

"Why not?" I whisper back, circling my arms more firmly around his neck as he holds me closer to this chest.

"Because I'm about to do something I shouldn't." He lowers his head, lining our mouths up, and his warm breath fans over my face. "Now is the time to say no if you don't want this," he whispers across my lips.

Determination flows through me, and I bridge the tiny gap between us, pressing my lips to his.

Our mouths glide effortlessly together. Once, twice, three times. Just a barely there kiss each time. A fleeting meeting of lips.

But it's everything.

Everything.

I feel his touch everywhere as if he's kissing me all over my body. *How the hell can a few feather-soft kisses make me feel so damn much?*

He angles his head, moving his lips more precisely over mine as the kiss deepens, and I eagerly open my mouth, ready to welcome his tongue when my brother pours ice water over our moment.

"Summer! James!" Austin hollers, his voice way too close for comfort. We rip our mouths apart, and I wriggle out of his hold as he quickly puts me down. I move away from him, and one infinitesimal second later, my annoying, cock-blocking brother is right up in my face. "There you are."

"Yes. Here we are." I smother my frustration as adrenaline courses through my body and my core aches with need. My heart pounds against my chest as I consider how close we came to being discovered.

Holy shit.

If Austin had arrived and found me wrapped up in Ryan's arms, kissing him, there would've been hell to pay.

Talk about a close call.

"It's time to go," he says. "I don't want Miley driving back in the pitch-dark."

"We're ready." Ryan's voice sends shivers cascading up and down my spine, but I purposely don't look at him, and he's keeping his distance from me too. "Let's go."

"And he hasn't mentioned it all week?" Hannah asks, on Friday at lunchtime, as we share a table in the campus cafeteria. This is the only day of the week where our different schedules enable us to have lunch together.

My first week as a college freshman is just about over, and I lived to tell the tale. Truth be told, I'm loving all my classes, and I've made friends with a bunch of guys and girls who share some of the same electives, so things are good.

"Not a word. In fact, I've hardly seen him. If I didn't know how busy he was with the gym, I'd say he's avoiding me." And even though I spent two nights this week training with Miley, Ryan still evaded contact with me.

"How do you feel about the kiss now?" she inquires. I had called Hannah the minute I got back to my room Sunday night and told her everything.

Ryan was quiet and distant in the back seat of the car as we drove to Newark from his sister's house, pretending to sleep most of the journey, but I knew from his breathing he was awake.

I shrug. "Whatever. It's not that big of a deal. Austin interrupted before we were properly kissing. It won't happen again, and that's probably for the best."

"Probably?"

"I mean it *is* for the best." I stab a piece of chicken, popping it in my mouth. "Nothing can come of this attraction between us. I know it. He knows it," I add, once I've chewed my food.

"Well then, we're going to that frat party tonight. You need to find another pair of hot lips to distract you."

"You won't hear me complaining, sister."

"Who else is going to the frat party tonight?" Austin asks as we eat dinner alone at the apartment later that day.

"Hannah and Jordan and a bunch of people from class," I confirm, shoveling a forkful of pasta in my mouth.

"Be careful. Some of those frat boys are complete assholes with no agenda except fucking as many girls as they can. Don't leave your drink unattended, and don't go off with someone you don't know."

"I know how to take care of myself, Austin, and you've got to quit this shit. I know you mean well, and I appreciate that you care, but you've got to stop treating me like a little girl. I'm an adult now, and I can fend for myself."

"I want nothing to happen to you. And I want to protect you from assholes who might break your heart. Is that so wrong?" He places his silverware down to take a sip of his water.

I reach across the table, curling my hand around his. "I love how protective you are, but there are some things you can't and shouldn't protect me from."

I bite down on my lip, carefully considering my next words. "I need to make mistakes, Austin. Because it's all part of the learning process. Part of growing up and discovering who I am and who I want to be. I'm not planning on falling in love or getting my heart broken, but if it happens, I'll embrace it fully. And if anyone is doing the protecting after that, it'll be me. I'll be the one protecting my heart until I'm ready to give it away again."

My brother smiles at me. "You always had such a wise head on your shoulders, yet you're so innocent and excitable at the same time. I hope you know how special you are, Sum. You'll make some guy so fucking lucky someday."

He looks down at his plate, toying with his food, looking contemplative. "It goes against my nature to say this, but I'll stop. Or, at least, I'll try to. I respect your wishes once you promise you'll do your utmost to stay safe."

"I have no desire to be utterly reckless."

He scowls. "That's hardly a reassuring statement."

"Austin, you've just got to trust me, and know that if I need anything, you'll be the first one I come to. I promise."

He sighs, nodding. "Okay. And for the record, I do trust you. It's those dicks on campus I don't trust."

I'm finishing curling my hair when my cell pings with an incoming text from Hannah letting me know they are on the way up in the elevator. Unplugging the curling iron, I apply a light layer of lip gloss before casting one final glance over myself in the mirror.

It's my first frat party, and I've no clue what the usual dress code is, so I'm playing it relatively safe tonight, and my ripped jeans, stiletto heels, and black lace-trimmed tank top scream sexy without looking like I've tried too hard. Grabbing my gray leather jacket and a silk scarf from my bed, I pull them on and then tip my head upside down, loosening out the waves in my hair so they flow naturally down my back.

Satisfied with my appearance, I exit my bedroom just as the doorbell chimes, almost colliding with Ryan in the hallway.

"Shit, sorry. You okay?" He grips my elbow to keep me from falling, and his touch electrifies me.

Like always.

"I'm fine." I shuck out of his hold, offering him a brief smile.

His eyes rake up and down my body like a sultry caress, and butterflies scatter in my chest. He's only wearing plain sweats and a tee, and his feet are bare, but he looks totally hot. This guy could wear a sack, and I'd still want to bang him. The air is fraught with the usual tension, but neither of us makes a move to separate.

I'm acutely aware of how close we're standing to one another, and the chiming of the door for the second time, but I can't drag my gaze away from him, and it appears he's the same. His eyes drink me in, his gaze caressing me with intent, and he may as well be undressing me for the way it makes me feel.

When Ryan focuses his singular attention on me, it's intense and all-consuming, and it's difficult to remember how to even breathe.

"You look…" he says before backtracking. "You're going out?"

I nod, as the doorbell rings again, finally snapping me out of my trance. "Yep. Heading to my first frat party, and I need to answer the door before Hannah busts her way through it."

I walk as quick as my heels allow, swinging the door open as Hannah has her finger poised over the doorbell. "About damn time," she says, pushing past me. "I desperately need to pee." She runs off in the direction of the bathroom, and I step aside.

"Come on in," I say to Jordan and the two guys standing behind him.

I lead them into the living room when I hear Ryan tinkering about in the kitchen. I'd rather avoid another confrontation between him and Jordy. There's still no love lost between them. "Summer, this is Dalton and Sean," Jordan says, introducing his friends.

"Hey." I smile. "Good to meet you."

"Trust me, the pleasure is all mine," the taller, dark-haired guy says taking my hand and planting a kiss on the back. "I'm Dalton."

"I'm Sean," the second guy says, nudging his friend out of the way and stealing my hand. "And you're fucking hot."

A snort resonates from the doorway, and I glance over to where Ryan is propped against the doorjamb, eyeing the guys warily. Crappity crap. Things are about to go south.

"Who are you?" Sean asks, the same time Dalton says, "Got something to say, buddy?"

"He's the douche I was telling you about," Jordan pipes up, and I glare at him. I will beat his stupid ass if he told them the story of how I lost my virginity.

"Relax," he whispers in my ear. "I didn't tell them everything. I just warned them he might be here."

"You're really begging for an ass kicking," Ryan says, sauntering into the room with a nonchalant look on his face.

"Do I look like I care?" Jordan retorts, squaring up to him.

"What's going on?" Hannah asks, arriving into the room with impeccable timing.

"Nothing," I say, grabbing Jordan and shoving him toward his girlfriend. "Let's go."

"Lead the way, babe," Dalton says, draping his arm around my shoulder without invitation.

Tossing his arm off, I purposely ignore Ryan as I walk toward the door.

"Summer. Wait a sec," Ryan says just as I'm about to step foot out into the hallway.

"I'll meet you at the elevator bank," I tell the others, beseeching Han with my eyes. Taking the cue, she drags Jordan and the guys away as I turn around to face Ryan.

"If you're planning on lecturing me, save your breath," I say before he's opened his mouth. I fold my arms across my chest, daring him to challenge me.

His Adam's apple bobs in his throat as he fixes those gorgeous blue eyes on me. "You sure you want to go out with them? Those guys seem like dicks."

I shrug. "Maybe, but I don't see how it's any of your business." I'm not being rude, just stating a fact.

He's quiet for a few beats, and then he exhales loudly. "You're right, it isn't." A muscle pops in his jaw. "Have a good night." With a brief nod, he goes into the apartment, slamming the door, leaving me staring at the wooden frame, wondering what the hell is going on between us.

CHAPTER 12
Ryan

"WE'RE GOING TO head, man," Austin says, clapping me on the back. Miley is tucked under his left arm, smiling up at him like he hung the moon.

"I think I'll stay." I gesture with my eyes, capturing the bartender's attention. "I'll have another." I point at my almost empty beer.

"Thought as much." Austin grins, his eyes darting to the curvy brunette pressed into my side. "Later, bro."

Miley kisses my cheek, whispering in my ear. "You are so much better than this."

Her words piss me off, and I scowl at her, ignoring the warning look Austin shoots my way.

The brunette maneuvers herself into the space between me and the counter, pushing her ample tits into my chest. "How about we go back to my place?" she purrs, setting her hands on my shoulders and leaning in close.

"I'm not interested." I gently remove her hands from my body.

"What?" She plants her hands on her hips, narrowing her eyes at me. "But we've been flirting for the last hour."

"No. You've been flirting. I've just been sitting here listening to you blabber on."

Her cheeks inflame, and her nostrils flare. I'm being an asshole, and it's not her fault I'm in a fucking shitty mood and taking it out on her. "Look, Sasha."

"My name's Sandy, asshole."

"Sandy. I'm sorry. You're beautiful and great company, and at any other time, I would be up for going home with you, but I've had a crappy week, and I'm just not in the mood."

Her features soften. "Do you want to talk about it?" she asks, and now I feel even worse. Because I just want her to leave me the fuck alone. I don't want to talk to anyone. I want to drown my frustrations in my beer and anesthetize my brain so the images of Summer fucking that douche Dalton leave my mind. My head is a melting pot of confusion, thanks to Summer and Myndi fucking with my sanity. I certainly don't need to add another female to the mix, no matter how much a physical release might help.

"No, but I appreciate you asking. You should go. I'm lousy company tonight, and you deserve so much better."

She grabs her jacket and purse, surveying me with keen eyes. "Whoever the woman is, I hope she realizes how lucky she is." She kisses my cheek. "Take care, Ryan, and don't get too drunk."

Pity I didn't heed her warning. I'm in the taxi on the way back to the apartment, and I'm seeing double and triple of everything. But my head is too foggy to fixate on Summer, so it's mission accomplished.

I stumble into the apartment, heading straight to the kitchen where I down a couple bottles of water with a few pain pills as a precautionary measure.

Against my better judgment, I knock on Summer's bedroom door, telling myself I just want to check she got home safe. Austin is staying at Miley's again, and I promised him I'd look out for her when he's not here, so it's not like I'm doing anything wrong. Her room is dark, with no light seeping out from under the door, which indicates she's either asleep or not home yet. My vision is blurry as I check the time on my watch, but I decipher it's just past two a.m. Risking it, I gently open her door, cursing when I spot the empty room and her unmade bed.

My jaw locks tight as I head into my bedroom, stripping my clothes off and walking naked into my bathroom. I turn the shower on and step under the cold stream of water, needing the icy shock to help sober me up.

It's not unheard of for frat parties to go on until all hours. Hell, I remember coming home a couple times at eight and nine in the morning, but this is Summer we're talking about, and I don't like thinking of her out there somewhere, alone and drunk and vulnerable.

I'm considering options as the cold water batters my body like a thousand tiny knives penetrating my skin. But it works as an effective sobering agent, and my head is a lot clearer when I finally step out, shivering and shaking as I wrap a towel around my hips and another one around my shoulders.

I grab two more bottles of water and make a strong cup of coffee before retreating to my bedroom again. I turn on the TV, pulling a pair of sweats on as I prop myself up on the bed to wait for her. I'm giving her until three a.m., and if she isn't home by then, I'm calling her.

It's now three forty, and she's answered none of my calls or texts, and I'm going out of my mind with worry. I've just decided to head out in search of her when the front door crashes open, and the sound of footsteps in the living room confirms she's home.

I walk with urgency out of my room, my heart careening around my chest when I find her lying on her side on the couch, passed out, with Jordan and Sean looming over her.

"What the actual fuck?" I growl, storming toward them. "What the fuck did you do to her?"

"Sus drunkkkk," Hannah slurs, and I whip my head around, discovering her sprawled across the lounge chair.

"No one did anything to her," Jordan snaps, sounding coherent. "I'd never let anything happen to Hannah or Summer. I only had two beers, and she was by my side all night except for the times she was sucking face with my buddy here." Jordan smirks, elbowing Sean in the ribs as a muscle ticks in his jaw.

"I think I'm in love," Sean slurs, crouching down beside Summer. He reaches out to brush hair back off her face, and I'm done.

Yanking him up by the shirt, I pull him away from her, shoving him toward the door. "Get the fuck out of my apartment, and don't come back."

"Someone sounds jealous," Jordan taunts, and I'm this close to punching the annoying punk. I know he's doing it to wind me up, but I'm a ball of pent-up-frustration, and it won't take much to snap.

"Yeah, *Dad*," the other asshole says, shucking out of my hold and swaying on his feet. He's completely wasted. "It's obvious you've got a boner for her. Too bad you're too old."

Now I really want to punch something. Preferably his annoying, ugly head, but I doubt I'll win any brownie points with Summer if I go around beating up her friends.

"Get him out of here," I tell Jordan. "You and Hannah can stay if you want to wait for an Uber, but he leaves now."

"We're going." Jordan scoops Hannah up into his arms, before glowering at me. "Keep your hands off Summer," he warns.

"Mind your own fucking business," I snap. As if I'd take advantage of any girl in that situation.

"This *is* my business. She's Justin's girl, and I promised him I'd look after her."

"Who the fuck is Justin?" Sean asks, frowning.

"Not now." Jordan dismisses him, eyeballing me like I'm scum of the earth. "You had your fun with her. Now let her be. She doesn't belong to you, and it's pathetic how obvious you are around her."

"Get the fuck out," I demand, losing the last semblance of my patience. "And in case that isn't clear enough for you, you're not welcome here again."

"Fuck you, man."

Refusing to be dragged into any more of this juvenile bullshit, I ignore him, closing the door after them with relief. When I return to the living room, Summer is quietly moaning on the couch. "Summer?" I kneel beside her, sweeping hair back off her face as she slowly opens her eyes.

"Ryan," she mumbles, reaching out for me. "Don't feel so hot." She reeks of beer and cigarettes, and from the way her eyes are rolling around her head, I'd say she's drank more than her body weight tonight.

"Do you need the bathroom?" I ask as she gags.

She nods and I lift her into my arms, racing toward the bathroom.

I position her on her knees in front of the toilet, removing her jacket just before she retches. Grabbing a hair tie off the counter, I gently pull her hair into a messy ponytail, rubbing her shoulders as she pukes.

When she's expelled everything in her stomach, she slumps sideways, resting her back against the tub, moaning and clutching her head. "I've got the spinnies," she slurs. "Can't see straight."

A chuckle escapes my mouth as I bend down and wipe her mouth with a towel. "Stay put." I run into the kitchen and grab a bottle of water and some pills. When I return, she's lying on her side on the cold tile floor. "Shit." I gently shake her shoulders. "Summer. Wake up."

"Wha?" She groans, swatting her hands at me. "Go away. Sleeping." She's even fucking adorable when she's all messy and drunk. I prop her upright. "Open your eyes. I need you to take this."

She opens her eyes, staring unfocused at me. Lifting her hand, she traces her fingers across my cheek. "You're beautiful, you know that?"

"Isn't that supposed to be my line?" I tease, opening her mouth and bringing the bottle to her mouth. "Drink."

She downs it like a trooper, letting me open her mouth and place the pills inside. Her eyes never leave mine, and they're clearer and less tired looking now. "I can't stop thinking about you," she admits, keeping her eyes trained on mine. "I think that could be a problem."

"Tell me about it," I say, helping her stand up. She sways unsteadily, but I've got my arm wrapped firmly around her back and I won't let her fall. "You're too tempting for your own good, Summer."

"I like you," she murmurs, resting her head on my shoulder. "I like you more than I should."

She'll be so embarrassed tomorrow when she finds out she said all this. However, I doubt she'll remember. Which is why I give her the same honesty in return.

"I know, Summer. Believe me, I feel the same way."

"You do?" She tries to circle her arms around my neck, but they flop back to her side, and I chuckle again.

"I think this is a conversation for another day. You need to get to bed and sleep this off." Glancing down, I notice the puke on her shirt and the end strands of her hair. "But you need to shower first." There's no way she can stand up by herself, so I place her back on the ground while I start the shower and gather a towel and toiletries. I test the water, ensuring it's lukewarm before I kneel beside her, gently removing her clothes.

I try not to look as I strip her even though I know every square inch of her body intimately. I leave her in her panties and kick my sweats off so I'm only in my boxers. Then I lift her into the shower, placing her directly under the spray of water with her back pressed up against my chest. She shrieks as the stream of water beats down on her, but I keep my arm wrapped around her waist, telling her she's okay and I've got this.

I take my time washing her. Gently rubbing the cloth up and down her arms, over her tummy, across her breasts, and down over her shoulders and back. I'm painfully hard, even though I'm trying my best to be good here, but Summer only has to look at me to turn me on.

The little whimpers and moans of pleasure leaving her mouth aren't helping either. When my fingers massage the shampoo into her hair, I almost come on the spot as she gasps and writhes against me, rubbing her ass against my erection, confirming she's as horny as me. Thoughts of pinning her to the wall, and fucking her from behind, invade my mind, torturing me with visions of something I want but can never have. And even if I could, I would never do that now. Not when she's so drunk and incapable of thinking clearly.

"Oh, God, Ryan." She moans, slinging her arm back and around my neck. "I'm so horny. Fuck me. Please."

Kill. Me. Now.

It takes enormous willpower to turn her down especially when she slides her hand between our bodies, palming my hard dick. I want nothing more than to let her drop to her knees and suck me off, but I won't disrespect her like that. Not when she's not in her right mind to make such a call.

I remove her hand, keeping a hold of her as I reach over and turn the shower off. "You're drunk, Summer, and you need to sleep this off."

"No," she pouts, twisting around, so she's facing me. Her nipples are hard peaks jutting into my chest, fueling the arousal coursing through my body. "I need to sleep with you." She stretches up to kiss me, and I twist my head to the side so her lips press against my cheek.

"It's not happening, babe." I lift her out and swaddle her in a towel before slipping one around my hips. I tug my wet boxers off underneath the towel before urging her to do the same.

"You take them off me," she challenges with a glint in her eye.

"I can't touch you there."

"Why not? You did before?"

"Summer. Please. Just remove your panties. You can't get in bed with them on."

Her eyes flare. "Fine." She deliberately drops the towel, hooking her thumbs into the side of her panties and pulling them down her legs. She sways, and I hold her elbows to steady her as she removes the last item of clothing. I keep my eyes fixated on her face despite the almost overwhelming urge to lower my gaze to her gorgeous tits.

When she kicks the panties away, I swaddle her in the towel and carry her into her room. I place her down carefully on the bed, gently patting her skin dry. Her eyes roll back and forth, and she's close to passing out again.

Removing her sleep shorts and tank from under her pillow, I help put them on her before grabbing the hairdryer from her bedside table and sitting up behind her on the bed. I dry her hair as she leans back against my chest, and it's one of the most intimate moments of my life. Her eyes flutter open and closed, and she holds onto my arm, her soft touch and unspoken trust reaching places deep inside me.

When her hair is dry, I help her into the bed, tugging the covers up under her chin. "Sleep well," I whisper, as she clings to the last vestiges of consciousness.

I straighten up and her arm darts out, brushing my leg. "Don't go," she whispers in a sleep-drenched voice. "Stay with me."

"I wish I could," I whisper, brushing strands of silky hair back off her face as she finally succumbs to slumber. "I want to so very much, but I can't." I wait another couple minutes, making sure she's fast asleep before I slip out of her room. I snatch another bottle of water and a couple pills and leave them by her bed before returning to my room where I toss and turn in a restless sleep for the remainder of the night.

I drag my weary ass out of bed at eleven a.m. the following morning, yawning as I walk into the kitchen.

Summer's bedroom door is still closed, and there's no sign of life out here, so I figure she's still sleeping. We don't have to be at the gym until three, so we have a few hours to relax before our shifts start. She's covering the front desk alone today as a kind of dummy run before next weekend when Miley and Austin are in London. They're away from Thursday night until Tuesday afternoon, and Summer, Derrick, and I are filling in for them.

I make a pot of coffee, deciding to call my sister before I make breakfast. "I'm so glad you called," Gabby says when she answers. "I've wanted to call you all week, but Slate said to give you time. I'm sorry about Sunday, Ryan. I swear I didn't know she was dropping by."

The anguish and guilt in my sister's tone are like a punch in the gut. I never wanted her to get caught in the crossfire, let alone ruin her friendship with her best friend, but that's exactly what happened when Myndi and I broke up and I feel awful about that. "It's okay, Tornado. I know you didn't know, and I don't blame you. I'm the one who should apologize to you for ruining your dinner party."

"You ruined nothing, Ryan. We had a nice time. At least until that point."

"Why is she here?"

There's a pregnant pause before Gabby replies. "Her and Will are engaged, and they wanted to come back home before the baby is born," she quietly confirms, and I hate the little stab of pain that accompanies her words. "They have both secured jobs at the hospital."

I say nothing for a while. "All I ask is that you don't invite her over when I'm there."

"I'll keep my distance from her, Ryan. You're my brother. You come first."

Her loyalty warms my frozen bones. "I love you, Gabby. So fucking much, but you've sacrificed enough for me. She was your best friend. You don't have to cut her out of your life anymore. Not because of me. Just keep us apart. Never tell me anything about her, and things will be fine."

Silence engulfs us again. "What happened, Ryan? Where did it go wrong for you two because I don't understand?"

This isn't the first time she's asked me, but I couldn't tell her back then, and I can't tell her now. "It's water under the bridge now, Tornado. She's moved on."

"But you haven't," she supplies. "I know whatever happened hurt you, and I hate seeing you like this. I want you to find your person and be happy."

"I am happy," I lie. "I don't need a woman to make me feel complete."

"Oh, Ryan." Her voice cracks, and I hate to upset my sister.

"Stop worrying, Gabby. I like my life exactly the way it is. Not all of us are destined for marriage and a family."

I once harbored those dreams. Came close to turning them into reality. Until they came crashing down around me. Now I know I'll never have that, because I'm not cut out to be a husband or a father.

CHAPTER 13
Summer

MY TONGUE IS glued to the top of my mouth when I finally emerge from my alcohol-induced sleep coma. Beams of buttery sunshine stream into my room through the gap in the blinds, confirming it's time to get my lazy butt up out of the bed. I'm yawning as I sluggishly climb out from under my warm comforter, stretching my arms out over my head. My tummy rumbles as hunger claws at my insides.

Memories of last night resurrect in my mind while I toe on my slippers and wrap a robe around my body. I sit on the edge of the bed, brushing my hair as I piece back the events of last night. I remember how crazy the frat party was. I also remember consuming copious red cups. And dancing on top of a table with Hannah. Making out with Sean. Feeling sick in the Uber on the ride here.

Hell.

I drop the brush, cradling my head in my hands as I remember Jordan referring to me as *Justin's girl* and Ryan angrily kicking Sean and him out.

I puked.

A lot.

And Ryan took care of me.

Vague recollections of him showering with me awaken my libido, and my pussy pulses with renewed desire. I remember what I said to him and asking him to stay with me.

I suppose it could've been a lot worse.

I could've puked *on him*.

Or thrown myself at him.

Or said way worse.

Considering how smashed I was, I think I got away lightly.

As I glance at the water and pills by my bed, my heart does a funny little twist. Ryan could easily have taken advantage of me last night, but he was a perfect gentleman, and he took such good care of me.

The more I get to know him, the harder it is to deny that I crave his touch as much as I crave his company.

I pad out of my bedroom, taking a pee and brushing my teeth before wandering in the direction of the delicious aromas wafting from the kitchen. Ryan is standing at the stove, singing along to the song playing on his iPhone as he cooks something in the skillet.

"Morning." I round the island unit, making a beeline for the coffeepot.

"Fuck." He slams the skillet down on the stove. "Don't sneak up on me like that."

"Not my fault you were too busy singing to notice my arrival," I tease, pouring myself a giant mug of coffee.

He steps behind me, reaching over my head to extract two plates from the cupboard. Heat rolls off him, crashing into me, and every tiny hair on my body stands alert. My lips stall around the rim of my mug as he leans into me, setting the plates down and bracing one hand on the edge of the counter. With his other hand, he gently touches my arm. "How are you feeling today?" There's a slightly rough edge to his deep voice.

"Ugh. Okay," I splutter, as his finger brushes up and down my arm.

He's barely touching me.

It's the lightest of caresses, but it's wholly intimate, and I long to turn around and latch my mouth onto his. To wrap my legs around his waist and grind my hips against his hard-on. To yank his sweats down, push my panties aside, and direct his cock inside me. To feel him moving as one with me so I forget I exist on this planet without him.

"Good." He steps back, and I feel bereft. "I hope you're hungry and that you like omelets."

"I love them," I reply, my voice coming out a little more high-pitched than usual. I hop up onto a stool, quietly sipping my coffee as he silently works at the stove.

A few minutes later, he slides a plate with a delicious-looking tomato and ham omelet across. "Dig in." He takes the stool beside me, wasting no time devouring his brunch.

"This is so good," I say in between mouthfuls of the fluffy, cheesy goodness. "Thank you."

"You're welcome." He smiles at me, and my heart starts cartwheels.

It's futile ignoring what's happening between us.

I'm attracted to him.

I like his company.

And I want to get to know him better.

More intimately.

There. I've finally said it. I've finally admitted it to myself, and the world is still standing.

"And thank you for looking after me last night. I really appreciate how much of a gentleman you were." I eye him directly as we speak so he can tell I'm genuine.

"It's no problem. You were pretty wasted."

"I was." He chuckles, and I frown. "What?"

"You never react how I expect you to. It would embarrass most girls, but you own that shit."

I grin, shrugging. "No point deluding myself or you. And I'm not embarrassed for speaking my mind. I meant every word."

He stalls with his fork halfway to his mouth. Now it's his turn to ask, "What?"

I flash him my most seductive smile. "I meant it when I said you were beautiful and I really liked you."

"I could say the same, but it doesn't change a thing."

"Why not?" I set my silverware down, swiveling on my stool to face him. Our legs brush, and a jolt of electricity zips through me. His leg jerks, and I know he felt it too. "You can't deny we have chemistry. I know you're attracted to me as much as I'm attracted to you."

"I'm too old for you, Summer."

I scoff. "Seriously? *That's* your objection?"

"And your brother is my best friend. He most definitely wouldn't approve."

"I'm not suggesting we run off and elope." I roll my eyes.

"What *are* you suggesting?"

I haven't really given it much thought, but I don't want to waste the opportunity either. "A friends with benefits arrangement," I blurt. His eyes pop wide, and I blabber on before he can shut me down. "Having sex has awakened a side of me I've never explored. I want to discover my likes and dislikes. To explore my sexuality with someone I trust. We're attracted to one another, and neither of us is interested in dating or a relationship, so it seems like a perfect solution."

I pat myself on the back for coming up with such an ingenious plan on the spur of the moment. Especially when I'm so hungover.

"Let me make sure I've got this straight," he says, leaning back and staring at me with an incredulous expression. "You want me to educate you about sex, behind your brother's back, but you're not interested in any relationship outside of a sexual one?"

"That's about it in a nutshell." I nervously tuck my hair behind my ears, afraid he'll turn me down because it sounds so…clinical, so impersonal, when it's put like that. "But we'd be friends. Obviously. I mean, we are friends, right?"

"I'm not sure I could just be friends with you," he says with a hint of sadness in his tone. He cups my face in his large hands, examining my face. "And deciding to have sex behind your brother's back is a recipe for disaster. If he found out, he'd quite likely kill me."

"We'll be careful. He won't find out." I'm grasping at straws because it feels like I've already lost this battle.

His thumb presses into my lower lip, and he stares at my mouth, looking conflicted. I wait with bated breath for him to decide. When he lifts his chin to look at me, my euphoria dies when I spot the decision on his face.

"I think you're breathtaking, Summer. Truly. Inside and out. And making love to you was incredible, but I'm not the kind of man you should be mixed up with. You need to find a guy your own age. One who will respect you and treat you right." He stands, clearing away our plates. "Whatever this attraction is between us, it's got to end. Nothing else will happen. I'm sorry if that hurts you, but in time, you'll see it's for the best."

❤

"I'm such an idiot," I tell Hannah over lunch in this dinky little café the following day. "And I'm embarrassed. And now I'm stuck working with him, and it's awkward. We didn't speak at all in the car on the way to and from work, and at the gym, all our interactions were about professional matters, but it was weird and uncomfortable, and now, I'm terrified Austin will pick up on something and read into it, which would be comical, considering nothing's going on and it never will because he only sees me as this inexperienced little kid with nothing to offer him." "Wow. Breathe, girlfriend," Hannah says, slanting me a sympathetic look. "And it's his loss. Not yours. The world is your oyster, babe, remember?"

"It's hard to hold on to grandiose notions when I'm feeling deflated."

"You'll bounce back, and Jordan says Sean is crazy about you. He keeps asking for your number. You should go out with him."

"I thought Jordy is opposed to me dating other guys, or it's just Ryan he has issue with?"

She cringes a little. "It's Ryan, but that doesn't mean he won't vet any potential dates or hookups. He promised Justin he'd look out for you."

"Why? And what exactly does that mean?"

She squirms in her seat. "I don't really know. Jordy's loyal, and he won't say. I get the impression Justin has plans for you once you are both finished college, and I could be wrong, but I think he's relying on Jordy to ensure you find no one permanent in the meantime."

"Meanwhile, he's free to fuck around with whoever he wants with no interference?" I snap, grabbing my cell out of my bag.

"It's only a guess, Sum. And would it be so bad if he cared that much?"

"He doesn't have the right, Han! I know we were kind of dating before we left, but it was casual. Hell, we haven't even had sex, and who the hell knows where we'll be and who we'll be with in four years' time? If Justin is holding onto some romantic notion about us, then it's time I set him straight."

She nods. "I'll grab us more coffee while you make the call."

Justin answers just before I'm about to hang up, sounding groggy. "Hey, babe," he croaks. "It's good to hear from you."

We made a deal when we went our separate ways for college not to smother one another, so we've only shared a few texts in the last few weeks, and hearing his voice again is good. Still, I'm mad at him.

"What did you make Jordan promise you about me?" I spit out.

"What?" He sounds a lot less fuzzy now, and I detect the wariness in his tone.

"Jordan's acting weird. Well, weirder than usual, and I know you said something to him, and I want to know what it is."

"Look, can we talk about this later? Now isn't a good time." His voice spikes with a tinge of fear.

"No. I want to talk about it now. You—"

"Come back to bed, Justin," a feminine voice says in the background halting my words.

"You are fucking unbelievable," I say before hanging up. "Ugh!!" I cradle my head in my hands.

"What'd he say?" Hannah asks, sliding back into her seat. She hands me a fresh coffee.

"Nothing. He was too distracted by the girl he was in bed with."

"Shit."

"It doesn't matter. It just proves my point."

"Are you sure? You look upset."

"Of course, I'm upset. Everyone thinks they can tell me how to run my love life, and I'm fucking sick of it. Maybe I'll become a nun and forget about sex and boys because all they do is mess with your head. This is exactly why I want no entanglements. And it seems like even casual sex is more trouble than it's worth. Honestly, I give up."

"Are you all packed?" I ask Miley as I'm preparing to leave the apartment on Wednesday night. They are heading on their mini vacay tomorrow, and Austin finally let the cat out of the bag regarding their destination. Watching Miley squeal and then climb all over my brother was kind of disturbing, but at least someone's happy.

Ryan and I have been cohabiting in this awkward space all week, and I'm phoning the housing assignments coordinator daily, inquiring into whether a free dorm room has become available yet. Even Hannah and Jordan's floor sounds appealing at this stage.

"Yes," Miley squeaks, jumping in her seat. "I'm so excited, and I can't believe Austin arranged for me to visit my sister." Tears prick her eyes. "He's so thoughtful, and I'm so in love with him."

"Aw, that's super sweet." I grab her into a hug. "You help bring out the best in him, Miley, and I've never seen my brother so happy."

"I think he's the one," she whispers, glancing over her shoulder to ensure he's not in earshot. "Or is that weird for me to admit to his sister?"

"Not weird at all." I shake my head. "And I hope it's true because I'd love to call you my sister-in-law someday."

"What are you two whispering about over there?" Austin asks with suspicion in his voice.

"Just girl stuff," I say, with a shrug. "Nothing you need to worry your pretty little head about."

"Aw, you think I'm pretty, sis?" Austin kisses the top of my head before reeling Miley into his arms.

"The prettiest," I sweetly reply. "And that's my cue to leave."

"I'll drive you," Miley says, grabbing her keys and pecking Austin on the lips.

"I can walk. It's not that far, and it's a nice evening."

"I want to drive you so I can come inside and watch. Unless that'd make you nervous?" she adds, her brow puckering.

"It wouldn't but you don't have to."

"I want to. I want to support you. And I've never been to auditions. It'll be fun."

"Well, okay then. Thanks." I really hope Austin and Miley make the distance because I can't imagine anyone better than her for my brother. She has such a pure heart, and she already feels like my sister.

The look my brother gives his girlfriend in that moment melts me into a puddle of goo on the floor. "I love you," he tells her, nuzzling his head into her neck, and happy tears pool in my eyes.

"We shouldn't be too long," I say, hugging my brother once he's finally torn himself away from his girl.

"Break a leg," Miley says, slipping into a seat in the auditorium at the theater arts company where auditions for *Romeo and Juliet* are being held. Mom always says go big or go home, so I'm auditioning for the part of Juliet, even though I probably don't have a snowball's chance in hell of winning it.

"Thanks!" I give her a quick hug before meandering backstage. The girl in charge gets me to complete some paperwork and then advises me where to stand in line.

"Hey, beautiful," a husky voice says in my ear, and I look around, startled to see Sean standing behind me. I haven't seen him since last Friday night although I know he's still pestering Jordy for my number.

"Hey yourself." My tentative smile is rimmed with suspicion. "What are you doing here?"

He shrugs. "Auditioning. Same as you."

I narrow my eyes at him. "If this is some kind of attempt to ingratiate yourself, it won't work."

He chuckles, and a mop of light-brown hair falls into his warm chocolate-colored eyes. "I don't play games, and my reasons for being here are the same as yours. I love to act. Had a part in every play in high school, and I was a member of the amateur dramatics group in my local town. I didn't even know you'd be here."

Sincerity radiates from his expression and his tone and I give him the benefit of the doubt. "Sorry for jumping to conclusions."

"It's cool." His wide smile is disarming. "But now, I really hope I get the part if it means I'll get to spend more time with you."

"Provided I get the part, and I might be pushing expectations auditioning for Juliet."

His grin expands, and my eyes pop wide. "Hang on!" I glance down at the sheet in my hand. "You're auditioning for Romeo, and they've partnered us up?"

His eyes twinkle with mirth as he waggles his brows. Leaning down, he presses his mouth to my ear. "Just as well we've already kissed. There won't be any awkwardness when we get out on that stage, and it'll give us an edge over the other audtionees"

"Always playing an angle, huh?" I tease.

He shrugs again, still smiling. "I like to win, and I'll take every advantage I can."

"A man after my own heart," I joke.

"Truer words have never been spoken." Reaching out, he tucks a few stray strands of hair behind my ear as he smiles confidently at me. "And I won't be leaving here without your number either." He leans in close to my ear, and his warm breath fans over my skin. "I like you, Summer," he whispers, placing one hand on my hip. "And I'm not giving up until you agree to go out on a date with me."

CHAPTER 14
Ryan

SUMMER IS QUIET as I drive us to the gym on Thursday evening after dropping Miley and Austin off at the airport. I'm not surprised. It's been the pattern since our difficult conversation on Saturday. I remind myself I'm doing the right thing. *But why do I feel so lousy then?* And I miss talking with her. I miss her energy and her enthusiasm, and I hate that there's so much tension between us. It's my fault it exists, and I owe it to both of us to get things back on an even keel. Clearing my throat, I glance at her briefly before speaking. "How did your audition go last night?"

Her face showcases her surprise as she turns around. She's so beautiful. So natural and unaware of how she turns heads wherever she goes, and it only adds to the appeal. *Focus, Ryan.* I silently chastise myself as I so often need to do in her presence.

If only we'd met under different circumstances.

At a different point where she's older and the age gap doesn't matter so much.

At a point where her brother is more mellow and I can talk him around.

But dreaming won't get me anywhere. And I need to repeat that she's not meant for me. And that I don't do relationships. Even if they're offered with no strings attached.

Try telling that to my greedy dick though.

"I think it went well, but competition is fierce." She shrugs casually, offering me a small smile. "Now it's in the hands of the gods."

"When will you find out?"

"Next week. There may be a round two, or they'll announce the main cast straightaway. I'll just have to wait and see."

"I hope you get it."

"Me too." Her knee bounces off the floor of the SUV. "But I won't stress about it. If it's meant to be, it'll happen."

We're silent the rest of the journey, but it's not an uncomfortable silence, and for that, I'm grateful.

I see little of her the rest of the day as the gym is busy, and we're both kept occupied. After the last few clients have left, she helps me lock up, and then we leave for home. Summer lets out a massive yawn as she climbs into the passenger seat.

"Tired?" I inquire, slowly backing out of the parking spot.

"A little. That was a long shift, and I had a full schedule of classes today too."

"If it's too much—"

"It's not," she rushes to reassure me, cutting me off. "I'm just getting used to my new schedule is all."

She kicks off her sneakers, lifting her legs to the dash. The car swerves as I take my eye off the road for a split second, the lure of her long, slim legs too much to deny. Her lips kick up at the corners, and I silently curse myself for giving the game away. It's just so hard to be in her company and not stare at her. My body hasn't gotten the memo that she's forbidden fruit, and every second in her presence is a battle with my self-control.

"Any word yet on a dorm room?" I blurt.

"Keen to get rid of me?" Her eyes flash knowingly as she levels a smirk my way.

"No, I…" Air expels from my mouth in a loud rush. "It's nothing personal, Summer. I just think it'd make things easier for both of us."

She sighs, and I hate that the smile slips off her face. "I know, and I'm trying, but no space has opened yet, and there's a couple of girls ahead of me on the list." She rubs a tense spot between her brows. "I can always sleep on Jordy and Han's couch for a few weeks." She pulls out her cell. "I'll message her now to make arrangements."

"Don't." I drag a hand through my hair. "I don't want you sleeping on anyone's couch." Especially not that douchebag's. I don't trust him around her. His behavior is off, and I'm wondering if there isn't more to it. "And I don't want you thinking you're not welcome at our place. Because you are. This is my issue, and I'll handle it. Forget I said anything."

A big smile graces her luscious mouth, and I almost crash the car. Fuck.

Her whole face lights up when she smiles like that, and it's like getting sucker-punched in the nuts.

My vision blurs.

The world pales.

And I'm completely caught up in the moment.

"There you go again." She's fighting a laugh. "We really need to expand your vocabulary, Ryan."

The way she says my name is such a turn-on, and I realize exactly how fucking screwed up I am over this girl. I shouldn't want her. But I do. I want her so badly. And I don't know how long I can hold out before taking what I want.

"The problem isn't my vocab," I admit, pulling up to the curb outside my favorite takeout place. "It's that I continuously say shit around you I shouldn't."

"That only happens because you're trying to censure yourself. You need to just speak your mind."

"Trust me," I say, killing the engine and twisting around to face her. "If I spoke the things on my mind, I'd be in a whole new world of trouble." Before she can reply with some flirty response, I open the car door, sliding out. "I'm buying dinner. What do you want?"

Friday is a long-ass day at the gym, thanks to an arduous double shift. I desperately need to unwind, so when the staff asks if I want to join them for drinks after we're closed, I tag along. Summer is there too. Looking effortlessly pretty in a light, flowery summer dress and pink Converse. She's chatting and laughing loudly, drawing people to her without even trying. She's surrounded by a group of guys and girls, and every male member of my staff is entranced by her, none of them doing a thing to disguise it.

Not that I can blame them.

She's bewitched me too.

"She's a big hit with the clients as well," Derrick informs me, noticing the direction of my gaze, sliding a fresh beer into my hand. "You should hire her on a permanent part-time basis to cover for Miley."

"I already plan to talk to Austin about it when he returns," I truthfully admit. Even though I'm trying to create distance between us, there's no harm in hiring her because the gym is busy, and we don't get to interact that much. Summer needs a job, and we need someone flexible to cover for Miley, so it's a no-brainer.

"I think you might have to issue a memo to male members of staff though," Derrick adds with a grin. "Or else Austin will fire their asses left and right for hitting on his baby sister."

I snort. "You're not wrong. I'll definitely be having a word in a few ears."

I lose count of how many beers I drink the longer I stay rooted to my stool, growing more and more forlorn, and more envious, as I watch Summer flirting up a storm. If this was any other girl, I'd suspect she's doing it on purpose to piss me off. But I know that's not Summer's M.O. That she's just being herself.

When Matthias slides his hand down her back, coming to rest dangerously low on the curve of her ass, I've reached my limit. Jumping up, I drain the rest of my beer and stalk toward them. I glare at him, pointedly fixing my gaze on his wayward hand until he gets the message, yanking it back as if electrocuted. "Let's call it a night," I tell Summer, sliding my arm protectively around her shoulders and steering her away from the fawning crowd.

"Okay," she readily agrees, waving at the rest of our staff. "See you guys tomorrow!"

I call an Uber, and we jump in, both quiet on the trip back to the apartment.

The instant I step foot in the door, I tell her goodnight and escape to my bedroom before I do something I regret.

A couple hours later, I'm still tossing fretfully in my bed, unable to switch my mind or my body off enough to go asleep. My mouth is parched, thanks to the aftereffects of downing too many beers, so I pad out to the kitchen in my boxers to grab a drink of water, stalling on the spot as I see Summer, bent over, with her ass sticking up in the air, peering into the refrigerator. The light from the open door illuminates her stunning form, and my dick instantly turns rock hard. She's wearing a thin tank top and a flimsy thong, and her peachy ass cheeks are on full display, shattering my self-control in a nanosecond. All night I've denied the craving to touch her, and I can't resist any longer.

"Summer," I growl, stalking toward her like a predator hunting his prey.

She jerks upright, emitting a little shriek as she turns to face me. I slam her up against the refrigerator door, closing it, and my lips are on hers before she can mount any protest.

I ravish her mouth, pushing my tongue into her wet warmth as I grind my hips into hers, letting her feel what she does to me. She moans into my mouth, grabbing handfuls of my ass as she pulls me in closer. Blood thrums in my ears, and liquid lust races around my body while the devil in my ear taunts me to take her. To lay her out on the counter and fuck her senseless.

I slide my mouth along her cheek, tugging on her earlobe. "What the hell are you doing to me?" I whisper.

She palms my erection, and my dick jumps at her touch. "I think it's pretty obvious." I can hear the smile in her voice. Her tone turns breathless. "I want you to fuck me, Ryan. No second-guessing. Just do it. Right here. Right now."

A primal growl rips from the back of my throat as I lift her up. Her legs instantly wrap around my waist, and I carry her over to the counter, sitting her down.

"Fuck, that's cold." She laughs, tightening her ankles over my butt cheeks while bending down to kiss me.

My hands slip under her tank, moving up her flat stomach to palm her gorgeous tits. Her nipples instantly harden, and I roll them between my thumb and index finger as she writhes on the counter.

Yanking the top off in one fluid move, I lower my mouth to her breasts, lavishing them both with attention. My hands knead her delicate flesh, and my tongue laves at the taut peaks of her nipples until she's panting and begging me for more.

"Lie back," I command, my cock straining painfully against my boxers. She obeys immediately without question, and I strip her of her panties, nudging her thighs apart, as wide as they will go, until she's spread out before me in all her glorious nakedness. "You are so incredibly beautiful," I tell her, leaning over her bare body to kiss her. "Every single part of you. Inside and out."

Her eyes shine with happiness, and I kiss her mouth tenderly. "I am so fucking hot for you." My hand moves along the curve of her body, delighting in how responsive she is to my touch as I watch her arch into my hand.

"Me too," she rasps. "I want you, Ryan. Please, I need you."

I crouch down between her thighs, positioning her legs on my shoulders. Keeping one hand on her stomach to hold her in place, I lower my head to her pussy and dive in, swiping my tongue up and down her slit, tasting her glistening skin, before pushing my tongue into her channel and devouring her like I won't ever get to do it again. With my free hand, I press down on the sensitive bundle of nerves as I pump my tongue in and out of her. My finger swirls around her clit, and she explodes on my tongue, screaming and lifting her hips up, bucking against my mouth as her climax powers through her body.

Her limbs turn boneless, her body sated, and she glances at me with a dreamy look on her face. Precum leaks out of the tip of my neglected cock, and I want nothing more than to bury myself inside her, but the child-like, wondrous, happy expression on her face brings me back to earth with a bang.

She looks so young.

So innocent.

And I feel like the worst kind of predator.

Pain slices across my chest, constricting my breathing. I stumble back, burying my face in my hands. "Fuck." *What the hell am I doing?*

"Ryan?" Her questioning tone has me lifting my head. She scrambles off the counter, coming straight at me. "No! Don't do this!" Her hands land on my bare chest, her touch like hot coals, and I jerk sideways, away from her grasp. "Look at me!" She tries to grab my face, but I dart out of her reach. "Don't you dare say this was a mistake!"

"It *was* a mistake," I snap. "I shouldn't have done that. I'm sorry."

She glares at me with her hands planted on her hips. "It *wasn't* a mistake. We are two consenting adults giving in to our attraction to one another. There is nothing wrong with that." She drops to her knees in front of me, reaching up for my cock.

I race around the other side of the counter. "Don't fucking touch me, Summer. We can't do this."

She stands, shaking her head, pinning doleful eyes on me. "I want to kill your ex for what she did to you. Because you can spout the age gap and my brother at me all you like, but I know the real obstacle is your fear. Fear of feeling something. Fear of opening your heart and letting someone in again. So much fear you can't even give your body what it needs."

I both hate and love how observant she is. Hate she's peeled back my layers and seen what others rarely see. Hate how vulnerable I feel in front of her even though she's the one standing completely butt ass naked. But another side of me loves she sees me so easily. That she just gets me.

Her eyes lower to my aching cock. "I told you that first night I won't beg, and I meant it. And I won't get trapped in some back-and-forth drama with you. I've made my intentions clear, and I won't keep doing this." She grabs her tank and thong off the floor. "The ball's in your court, Ryan. But plan your move carefully, because the next move is your last one."

Holding her clothing clasped to her chest, she walks out of the kitchen, without uttering another word, leaving me rooted to the spot, utterly conflicted and confused.

CHAPTER 15
Summer

"I'M SORRY IF I hurt you," Ryan says as we walk from the car to the gym the following morning.

"I think you're hurting yourself more," I acknowledge, propped against the wall while Ryan unlocks the door.

"True," he quietly admits. "But I'm just trying to do the right thing here."

That pisses me off on several levels. "The right thing for whom?"

He steps foot into the building, inputting the code to deactivate the alarm, before responding. I saunter toward the front desk, dumping my bag on the counter.

"For you," he says, coming up behind me.

I snort, shaking my head. "At least have the decency to be honest. It's not for me or even for you. You're conforming to what society has conditioned you to conform to. Or you're doing it to appease my brother. Don't pretend you're doing it for me or for you."

"Believe what you want," he snaps, a muscle clenching in his jaw. "But one day, you'll thank me."

I flap my hands about, my anger increasing with every stupid word spewing from his gorgeous mouth. "Continue to wallow in your delusion if you want but I won't." We glare at one another, but the heat of arousal still simmers in the air. "Even now, you can't shield your desire for me, and I won't pretend I don't want you, but I meant what I said last night. I won't play this game."

"You think this is a game?" he shouts. "I'm not playing games, Summer. I'm trying to do right by you. I'm not the one for you. I'm not the one to help you explore your sexuality. Or be anything else. Why can't you accept that?"

I prod my finger in his chest, incensed. "Maybe because you say one thing but do another!"

"Well, that won't happen again." He works hard to rein in his anger and frustration. "I give you my word. I won't lay another finger on you. I'll be on my best behavior."

"So, that's it? That's your final answer?" I'm disappointed he isn't even prepared to think about it.

He nods. "It is. This is the way it has to be."

"Fine." I slant him a fake smile, plonking down in my chair and powering up the desktop PC.

"Good." He looks at me for a few seconds, but I purposely ignore him, concentrating on logging in as I try to bring my blood pressure back down. "For what it's worth, I'm sorry it has to be like this," he adds before walking off.

"Only because you're too chickenshit to give in to what you really want," I mumble under my breath once he's out of earshot.

I spend the rest of the day avoiding him. Only talking to him when my job demands it. I eat lunch at my desk, replying to Sean's earlier text and then updating Hannah on my plans for tonight. Although the gym remains open until ten p.m. on Saturdays, it's quieter after six, and there isn't a need for someone to man the front desk, which means I get off early today.

Sean strolls through the front doors at six on the button, just as I'm powering down the computer. I took a quick bathroom break a while ago to get changed into skinny, ripped jeans and an off-the-shoulder light sweater and to touch up my makeup, so I'm ready to get the hell out of here. I toe on my heels as I smile at my approaching date. "Hey, beautiful." He produces a single red rose from behind his back, handing it to me with a shy smile that's very endearing.

"Oh, wow, thank you!" I bring the flower to my nose, inhaling the familiar scent.

"You're welcome. Ready to go?"

"Give me a minute to tell my boss I'm outta here." I turn off the computer and zip up my bag, leaving it and the rose on the counter as I walk to Ryan's office. I knock on the closed door, and he calls me in. "I wanted to let you know I'm leaving now," I say in a polite tone.

"You're seriously going out with that guy?" He gestures toward the wall of cameras behind his desk, the screen of the lobby enlarged, and I shouldn't be surprised he was watching.

"It's none of your business." I turn to leave.

"I didn't have you pegged for one of those girls."

Slowly, I turn back around. "What girls?"

"The kind who manipulates when she doesn't get her own way. I turn you down, and you instantly revert to Plan B." He shakes his head, a look of disgust forming on his face.

I am so enraged I can barely speak. I want to rip his annoying head from his shoulders, but I won't give him the argument he so desperately craves. I'm anti-drama, and I won't indulge the fury, indignation, and frustration demanding I call him out on his shitty accusation, no matter how tempting. Instead, I adopt the moral high ground. "I don't have to explain myself to you, and I'm not going to. Goodnight, *boss*."

Holding my head up high, I walk calmly out of the room, down the hallway, and back out to the lobby. Forcing a cheery smile on my face, I grab my bag and my rose and hook my arm through Sean's. "Let's ditch this joint."

"Thanks for walking me home and for a great night," I tell Sean later that night, outside the apartment door, stifling a yawn. It's after three, and I'm officially pooped.

"I'm glad you enjoyed it," he says, moving his hand to my hip. He draws me in close. "I really want to see you again."

I cup his face. "I'd like that."

"Yeah?" Surprise is written all over his face. "I thought you'd make me work hard for date number two too."

I quietly laugh. "I had fun, and I enjoy your company, but I'm not looking to date anyone seriously, and I'm not interested in a relationship."

He kisses the tip of my nose. "Challenge accepted."

I snort. "It isn't a chall—"

My sentence is cut short when his mouth descends on my lips. We spent most of our time in the club making out, so the feel of his lips moving against mine isn't a huge surprise. And it's not unwelcome either. Sean is an amazing kisser. And he's been attentive and easy to talk to all night.

Last week, I initially thought he was a player, but now I'm getting to know him better, I realize my initial assessment was incorrect. Sean is definitely boyfriend-worthy, if that's what I was looking for. He's studying computer science. He's into acting. He comes from a small town not too far from Bridgeville, and he adores his family. He's handsome and funny, and he doesn't take himself too seriously. He also gets extra brownie points for his honesty, and his direct approach is very appealing. While I'm not in the market for a boyfriend, I've decided I'm going to just go with the flow and see where this takes me.

I circle my arms around his neck, drawing him in closer, and we stay locked in our embrace, kissing and kissing, until he finally breaks us apart. "I could kiss you all night long," he whispers over my mouth. "But I'll be a gentleman and go home before my wandering hands have other ideas." He winks, and I stretch up, pecking his lips one last time.

"I think you might be one of the good guys." I kiss his cheek before grabbing my bag off the floor.

"I think I'm already falling for you." He winds his hand through my hair, drawing me into his body again. He kisses me deeply before releasing me. "Sweet dreams, beautiful. I'll message you tomorrow."

"Goodnight, Sean." I wave him off, only entering the apartment when he's disappeared from sight.

I'm smiling to myself as I enter the darkened living room, dropping my keys and bag on the chair.

"Did you fuck him?"

I scream at Ryan's unexpected question, my heart rate elevating to coronary-inducing proportions as I scan the room for him. "You fucking scared the hell out of me!" I squint in the darkness to make out his form. As my eyes adjust, I see him sitting in the recliner chair, his back rigidly stiff. He turns on the lamp at his side, and we stare at one another in silence for a few beats. His gaze drifts to my lips, and he scowls at the sight of my mouth, glistening and swollen from Sean's kisses.

"Did you?" he asks, failing to mask his fear.

"Not that it's any of your business, but no."

His shoulders visibly relax, and then he's up on his feet, stalking toward me. "Can I have a do-over?" He stands right in front of me, leaving barely any space between our bodies.

"In what way?" I narrow my eyes, urging my pounding heart to remain calm.

"You're right," he whispers, reaching out to caress my cheek with the tip of his finger. "I am scared. And scarred from my past breakup. But no one has even attempted to breach my walls. Until you came along."

"And?" I arch a brow, determined I will not make this easy for him.

"And I want to stop fighting this." He gestures between us.

"What exactly are you saying?"

He takes hold of my hips, pulling me in flush with his body. "I can't make huge promises, Summer, because I don't want to commit to something and then let you down, but if your offer is still on the table, I'm in."

"Sex with no strings," I repeat, wanting to ensure we're both on the same page.

He nods. "Once we both agree we're exclusive for as long as we're sleeping together. And we have to keep this from your brother." Guilt furrows his brow as the words leave his mouth, and I know he's sacrificing a part of himself agreeing to this.

"And it ends as soon as one of us wants to stop," I supply. "No bad feelings or regrets. We agree to part ways with no ill feelings."

He palms my face. "I have no issue agreeing to that."

"And you won't turn around tomorrow and change your mind?" I inquire, needing to know he's not going to mess me around anymore.

"I promise I won't. I've thought of nothing else since last night, and when you left with Sean, I was going out of my mind thinking I'd missed my chance with you." He cups the back of my neck, his gaze boring into mine. "And I don't know why I'm so concerned about the age difference when it's clear you're the more mature one of the two of us." His lips kick up at the corner, and my heart swoons behind my ribcage.

I press my body into his, slipping my hands around his back and down to his delectable ass. "Not in every sense of the word," I whisper, gently rocking my hips against his so he catches my meaning.

"Perhaps we can both teach one another a few things," he whispers back, thrusting his solid erection into my lower stomach.

"When do lessons start?" I rasp in a breathy tone.

His pupils dilate and he licks his lips as his eyes drift to my mouth. "How about right now?"

I should probably tell him no. Not when I was just kissing another man outside the door. But Ryan has this hold over me, and I can't resist, so I raise no objection, shrieking as he lifts me up, urging my legs to move around his waist. I snake my arms around his neck as my legs hug his torso, and our mouths collide in a wild frenzy of lips and teeth and tongues, and Sean's kisses pale into insignificance in comparison. He cups my ass, keeping me upright, with my legs straddling his waist, while walking toward the hallway leading to the bedrooms.

He kisses me senseless, my head is spinning, and I'm wondering how the hell he can walk and kiss like that when he kicks open the door to his master suite, growling low at the base of his throat.

He flings me down on the bed, and then we're frantically tearing our clothes off, as if it's a race, our eyes never leaving one another as we shed our outer layers. I shunt up the bed before lowering onto my back, stretching my legs out wide in a welcoming gesture. Ryan pulls a bunch of condoms out of his drawer, tossing them on top of the bedside table. "This will be fast because I need to be inside you, baby."

"You won't hear any complaints from me," I confirm, my eyes glued to his long shaft as he fists one hand around himself and pumps his cock. I sit up, my tongue darting out to lick the bead of precum at his crown.

"Fuck," he hisses, his eyes rolling back in his head. "Lie back down, and spread your legs real wide."

I dutifully obey, and my body hums in anticipation as I watch him lower his face between my thighs. When his hot tongue touches my sensitive flesh, I emit the neediest moan, my body almost arching off the bed as intense pleasure courses through me. He licks me up and down, like I'm his favorite flavor of ice cream, and stars explode behind my eyelids. I cry out when his tongue invades my pussy, alternating between sliding inside me and swirling around my clit. My limbs are contorting in spasm-like motions, and I'm moaning like a woman possessed under his expert ministrations.

Damn, Ryan is so fucking skilled with his tongue, and I know he's ruining me for life. I get the sense no other guy will ever be able to match his skills in the bedroom.

He drives his tongue in and out of me with a faster pace before pressing his thumb down firmly on my clit, and I detonate, like a thousand fireworks exploding in the nighttime sky. My body shudders and shakes as the most intense orgasm grips me. Tears of pleasure leak out of the corners of my eyes as my body convulses with blissful sensation. Ryan stays with me through it all, milking every drop of my arousal, and then he's rolling a condom on and pushing inside me.

I clench around him, hugging his cock tightly as he eases in farther. My legs go around his waist, my ankles crossing over his firm buttocks, and then he's lifting me up so I'm sitting on him as he pounds into me with fierce determination.

His mouth suctions around my nipple, and I like this position. He plunges his cock deep inside me, and his fingers dig into my hip as he rocks me back and forth. He trails a line of hot kisses up my neck before claiming my mouth in a hungry kiss. "Fuck, you feel too damn good," he whispers, nipping at my upper lip. "Your pussy is so tight." He grips my hips firmly, ramming into me, and I throw my head back, giving in to the heavenly sensation.

Without warning, he pulls me off him, flipping me over onto my belly before I can protest. "Lift your ass, baby," he demands, pressing my head down onto the bed as he pulls up my legs until I'm kneeling, nudging my thighs farther apart. Then he slams back into me from behind, thrusting in and out as he holds me in place with one hand tight on my hip.

His other fingers roam the crease of my ass, and when he presses one finger into my hole, I shatter instantly as a powerful climax consumes me. He roars out his release, pulsing inside me in short, sharp, strokes, and we're both shuddering and moaning until we're fully sated.

I collapse on the bed, my trembling knees giving way, and Ryan drops behind me, curling his sweat-slickened body around me. "You okay, sweetheart?" he whispers in my ear, as his arm encircles my waist.

"I'm wonderful," I rasp, leaning back into him with my body as I clutch onto his muscular arm. "I think I could become addicted to sex."

His body rumbles with silent laughter. "I have zero issues with that." He presses a soft kiss to that sensitive spot just behind my ear, and a shiver works its way through me.

"Your touch does the most amazing things to me." I lean my head around, stretching my neck to kiss him.

"Ditto, babe." He kisses the tip of my nose. "And I haven't even begun touching you in all the places I want to." He kisses me deeply, his tongue sweeping against mine in languid strokes as I feel him hardening against my back. "You need another few minutes, or you're ready to go again?" he asks, quirking a brow.

I turn around in his arms, grinning. "Do you really need to ask me that?"

He laughs as his fingers glide down my body before curling back inside me. My eyes close, and I sigh in contentment. "My body is yours to do with as you please," I murmur, fully meaning every word.

"Buckle up, baby," he says, flipping me over onto my back and hovering over me. "Because the night is only getting started."

CHATPER 16
Ryan

WE ARE BOTH struggling to keep our eyes open the next afternoon as we drag our sleep-deprived bodies from the SUV in the parking lot at the gym. We're surviving on minimal sleep, thanks to our marathon fucking session. I lost count of how many times I was inside her or how many orgasms I gave her last night. All I know is it was one of the best nights of my life.

She joked she was addicted to sex. I'm terrified I'm addicted to *her*.

Glancing around to ensure the camera is angled over the other side of the lot, I reel Summer into my arms, leaning down to kiss her.

Now I've given myself permission to give in to our chemistry, I can't stop touching her. We held hands most of the journey from the apartment, and I couldn't stop looking over at her. She looks tired but happy, and I imagine it's how I look too. "I don't know how I'll get through the next nine hours without touching you," I honestly admit, hugging her.

"I'm sure we can steal a few sneaky kisses," she says, trailing her fingers along the downy hair at the base of my neck. Her touch ignites a fire in me every single time, and it's like every part of my body is hot-wired to my cock.

"Do you walk around with a permanent boner?" she asks, feeling my growing erection prodding the flesh of her stomach.

"Only since you appeared on the scene," I truthfully admit.

"That shouldn't make me proud, but it does." Her gratified grin does funny things to my insides, and I wonder how the fuck I'll avoid catching feelings.

"You should be proud, baby." I kiss her again. "It's a real talent. I only have to glance at you and I'm rock hard."

The gym is very busy for a Sunday, especially when I need to cover classes for one of our trainers who called in sick.

I'm back in my office, trying to grab a late lunch as I pore over last month's accounts, when Summer slips into the room, quickly locking the door behind her. I arch a brow in a silent question, and she hurries toward me with a naughty glint in her eye.

Rounding my desk, she stands behind me. Her small hands land on my shoulders, and a moan emits from my mouth when she kneads my tense flesh. Her velvety lips brush the bare skin at the nape of my neck as she continues massaging me, and a shiver tiptoes up and down my spine.

"I thought you looked stressed," she whispers in between peppering my neck with featherlight kisses. "But your shoulders are tied into knots, baby. You need to unwind," she adds, digging her fingers into the corded muscle on my shoulders.

"You have something in mind?" I ask, my voice thick with lust.

"I do, but I only have a ten-minute break, so I'll have to make this quick." Before I can ask, she spins me around in my chair, drops to her knees on the floor, and yanks my shorts and boxers down my thighs, freeing my hardening cock. "Sit back and enjoy, babe," she says before lowering her hot mouth over the head of my now throbbing dick. It's clear from the confident way she fists my cock at the base as she slides her mouth down my aching length she knows what she's doing.

I close my eyes as she works me over, taking me deep into her mouth and sucking me firmly. Her lips glide up and down my cock as she quickens the pace of her hand stroking my overheated flesh. A guttural moan rips from my throat when she gently grazes her teeth along my length, and precum leaks from my crown.

Suctioning her lips more firmly, she takes me all the way to the back of her throat as she picks up her pace, bobbing up and down, and a familiar tingle builds at the base of my spine. I open my eyes, reveling in the determination on her face as she sucks me off, and that's all it takes to lose control.

The orgasm rips through me without warning, and I shoot hot spurts of semen into her mouth before I've had time to even consider withdrawing. Summer stays with me, swallowing every drop of cum, and when she peers up at me with glassy eyes, glistening lips, and a satisfied, happy smile on her face, cracks splinter in the shell encasing my heart.

Tucking my cock back into my shorts, I pull her up into my lap and kiss her slowly, tasting myself on her lips as she kisses me back with the same longing. Very quickly, the kiss transforms, and we're devouring one another, our hands wandering as an intense need takes over. My cock thickens, and I need to be inside her. "How many minutes do you have left?" I ask, trailing a line of kisses down her neck.

"About four," she pants.

"I can make that work," I say, lifting her by the hips and spreading her, belly down, over my desk. "Are you on the pill?" I ask, yanking the yoga pants and her thong down her slim legs.

"I am, and I'm clean. I haven't slept with anyone but you."

The dormant Neanderthal gene in my DNA loves to hear that, and my cock needs no further incentive. "I'm clean too," I supply, driving into her in one quick move. I fuck her hard and fast over my desk, slamming in and out of her as I pull her ass back a little so I can slide my hand around her body and play with her clit. I up the ante, rubbing her tight bud quickly to match the thrusts of my cock, until we're both climaxing in record time.

I grab tissues from my desk drawer and clean her up before helping her fix her clothes. Smoothing her hair back into her ponytail, I slowly pull her into my arms for a hug. The feel of her slim body against mine brings all my protective instincts to the surface, and I hold her tightly as I press light kisses into her hair.

My heart expands, and I'm feeling things I haven't felt in a long time.

I know I'm in serious trouble with this girl, but I can't stop now.

I don't want to stop.

She already means so much to me.

"I better head back out before someone notices," she says into my chest, and I reluctantly let her go.

"Thanks, baby." I peck her lips tenderly. "I'm definitely less stressed now," I add with a smug wink.

"Glad to be of service," she teases, squeezing the cheeks of my ass before sliding out from our embrace. "But I better get back. My boss is a real stickler for timekeeping, and he can be a bit of a prick when he wants to be."

I quirk a brow as my lips fight a smile. "Is that right?" I smack her ass as she turns around to walk toward the door. "Better not delay so." My eyes stay glued to her shapely form as she sashays toward the door, pivoting at the last second to blow me a kiss.

I'm still grinning five hours later as I exit my office en route to the lobby although the sight of that idiot Sean leaning over the front desk, mooning at Summer, instantly wipes the errant grin from my face. "We're closed," I snap.

Straightening up, he frowns at me. "I was just going." He turns to Summer. "You know how to reach me if you change your mind."

"Goodnight, Sean," she says, smiling sympathetically as she powers off the computer.

Sean narrows his eyes at me on his way out the door. A rush of relief floods through me with his departure.

"You don't need to eyeball him like you want to murder him with your bare hands," Summer says, coming up alongside me and threading her fingers in mine. "I set him straight. He knows I'm not interested in any more dates."

"Good." I let go of her hand to activate the alarm, trying to shake my jealousy free. When the building is secured, I grab hold of her hand again, leading her out to the parking lot.

"I know how important trust and loyalty is to you, Ryan," she quietly admits while we walk. "And I would never promise you exclusivity and then sneak around with other guys behind your back. That's not who I am."

I slam to a halt, turning to face her. I gently cup her face. "I appreciate you reconfirming that, but I already know that, and I trust you." Truth. I know Summer isn't the type to say one thing and mean another. She's an open book, and I trust her to tell me when she wants our arrangement to end. A sharp pain stabs me in the chest at the thought of this finishing, but I ignore it, already feeling hugely conflicted over this girl.

Summer sleeps in my bedroom the next couple nights, but she's forced to return to her own room when her brother and Miley return from their London vacation, leaving me feeling lonely in my empty bed at night. She has a busy college schedule, and now that Miley is back, she's only working three short shifts a week, so we see little of one another in the weeks that pass.

On nights when Austin stays at Miley's, she's a firm fixture in my bed although we don't get much sleep. I can't keep my hands off her, and she's an eager student, readily agreeing to experiment with different positions and angles and excitedly embracing the sex toys I introduce her to.

For the first time in a long time, I'm having fun, enjoying life, and feeling happy. It's also forced me to assess how I've been living my life up to this point, and I can't deny how lonely and depressing my previous existence was.

I'm not the only one to notice the change.

"When are you going to tell me who she is?" Austin asks one morning, as we're eating breakfast together in the kitchen. Thankfully, Summer has already left for class and Miley stayed with a friend last night, so it's just the two of us alone with this awkward conversation.

"I don't know what you're talking about." I turn my back to him as I refill my coffee, trying to keep my burgeoning panic at bay.

"C'mon, man. You can't fool me. Even if I hadn't heard the sounds coming from your room the other night, I'd still know there's a woman on the scene because I can't remember when I last saw you this happy."

Fuck. I suspected Austin might have heard something when he turned up unexpectedly the other night. He'd had an argument with Miley in the middle of the night and had stormed back to the apartment. Summer had been energetically riding me at the time, and neither of us had been quiet. As soon as we'd heard him, Summer had fled to the en suite to hide, only creeping back into her room once the coast sounded clear. It was a close call and a timely reminder we need to be more circumspect.

Case in point.

"It's nothing serious." I casually shrug, hating how much those words make me feel like a liar. "Just a bit of fun."

"But it's the same woman?"

I could lie. I probably should. But it doesn't feel right to, so I merely nod.

Austin slaps me on the back. "Knew it. You're falling for her."

Panic jumps up and bites me, and I rear back. "I'm not," I bark. "It's just sex, and it won't ever be anything more, so drop it."

He holds up his palms. "Woah. Relax there, buddy. I won't mention it again." His eyes dart sideways, and his face lights up. "Oh, hey, Sum. I thought you'd already left."

"I had," she says, her voice sounding a little choked, and I mentally curse under my breath. I risk a quick glance at her, spotting the hurt she's not fast enough to hide, and I know she overheard our conversation. "But I realized I forgot one of my books a couple blocks away and turned around." She hurries past us. "Don't mind me. Continue your conversation."

Austin watches her scurry away with a frown on his face. "Does she seem upset to you?"

"No," I lie.

"I'll ask Miley to check in with her later. Find out if something's up," he mumbles, looking distracted as he rinses our plates in the sink.

"I'll grab my stuff and meet you downstairs at the car," I say, needing to get rid of him so I can talk to her.

I enter Summer's room without knocking, closing the door behind me as quietly as I can. She looks up from where she's sitting on the side of her bed, wearing every emotion on her face.

"Hey." I kneel in front of her. "I'm sorry you had to hear that, but it wasn't as brutal as it sounded. I said what he needed to hear."

Tossing her long wavy hair over her shoulders, she bites down on her lower lip, peering at me with earnest eyes. "You have nothing to apologize for. We agreed it was friends with benefits, so you spoke no word of a lie."

I take her hands in mine. "But?"

Her chest heaves as she stares at me. "It hurt hearing it spelled out like that," she honestly admits.

"Do you want to end this?" I whisper, silently praying her answer is no.

"No!" she blurts. "I don't want it to end, but I'm afraid I'm growing attached to you."

I'm already there.

I think it, but I don't say it. I've only known this girl a few months, only been sleeping with her for the past few weeks, and I'm already way too attached. But she doesn't need to know that. Whether or not I've caught feelings doesn't change the situation. I should let her go, but I need to work myself up to that.

"Are you sure you don't want to call it quits?" I ask again even as I'm cursing myself for pushing an agenda I *don't* support.

"Do you?" she whispers, and I detect the fear in her gaze.

I slowly shake my head. "While I don't enjoy all the sneaking around, I enjoy spending time with you, and this is the most fun I've had in ages. I'm not ready to end it yet."

A relieved sigh slips from her gorgeous lips. "Me either." She leans forward, resting her head on my shoulder, and I pull her down into my lap, cradling her against my chest.

"Good, because I want to take you out on a date," I blurt before I've had time to properly engage my brain.

Her eyes shimmer with excitement when she lifts her head to look at me. "I'd love that."

I kiss her quickly, my stomach churning unpleasantly as I wonder what the hell I'm doing.

My head and my heart are at war over this girl, and I've no clue who the victor will be.

CHAPTER 17
Summer

I CAN SEE Ryan from up here on the stage, and he is *not* a happy camper. I forgot that the director said we were rehearsing the kissing scene today. Otherwise, I would've met Ryan at the restaurant instead of agreeing he'd pick me up at the theater. I could tell he wasn't pleased when he heard they had cast me as Juliet against Sean's Romeo, but he articulated zero concerns. *Why would he?* It's not like we're boyfriend and girlfriend or that we have a right to demand anything of one another.

But it's obvious Ryan doesn't like it.

That shouldn't make me happy.

But it does.

I'm hoping Sean doesn't notice Ryan's scowl and put things together, because he's been pretty relentless in his attempts to convince me to go out on a second date with him, and I think he's smelling a rat. He's determined. I'll give him that. And very persuasive when he wants to be, but I've been persistent in declining his various offers.

I couldn't tell him I was seeing someone when I initially turned him down because that's not technically true.

I'm just sleeping with Ryan.

We're not dating.

Although, increasingly, the lines are becoming blurred. The fact he's seated in the auditorium, waiting for me, further proves that.

I was surprised when Ryan suggested a date, but I didn't hesitate to agree because I adore spending time with him, and I get as much out of our conversations as I do the amazing sex.

The longer this goes on, the more attached I become, and I can't deny I'm feeling something for him. I should probably cut him loose, but I can't make myself do it. And even though I feel guilty as hell because I'm sneaking around behind my brother's and my best friend's backs, I can't deny how much of a thrill it is to be conducting a secret, illicit affair with someone as incredible as Ryan.

"Want to grab something to eat?" Sean asks when the director calls it a night.

"I already have plans, but thanks for asking."

I hate the dejected look on his face. Hate I'm responsible for it. I'd love to propose we head out another time, as friends only, but I know he'd read more into it, and I don't want to mislead him.

"You'll never say yes, will you?" he asks, resignation clear in his tone.

"Not at the moment. I'm sorry, Sean. And it's like I said. You're great. This is nothing to do with you. It's all about me and where I'm at right now."

"The pathetic thing is I believe that," he says, shuffling awkwardly on his feet.

"It's not pathetic. It *is* the truth."

"I don't understand. We had a great first date, and you were into a second one. I don't get what changed overnight?" He runs a hand along the back of his neck, imploring me with his eyes.

"I just changed my mind." I grip the strap of my bag, praying he lets things go after this. I've started dreading rehearsals because I know he'll corner me at the end.

"I wish you hadn't, but I won't push it anymore. If you ever change your mind, let me know. I'd take you out in a heartbeat."

I lean up and kiss his cheek. "You're the best. And it's fun acting with you. I think it'll be easier for both of us if we just agree to be friends."

Ryan is waiting outside the theater when I exit after everyone has gone. "Hey." Butterflies scatter in my tummy as I look up at his handsome face. His piercing blue eyes penetrate mine as he lifts his hand, brushing his fingers across my cheek, leaving a trail of fiery tingles in his wake.

"Hey, babe." Dipping his head, he claims my lips in a sweet kiss. "You were fantastic up there. A real natural."

My heart soars at his compliment, and I lace my fingers in his as we walk. "Thank you. You'll come to the opening night, right?"

Lifting our conjoined hands, he presses a kiss to my knuckles. "I wouldn't miss it for the world."

We're tucked into the back of the quaint little Italian restaurant, pressed up against one another in a cozy booth, waiting for our food to arrive. Ryan has his arm wrapped around me, and my head is resting on his shoulder.

We're as comfortable with one another as if we've been together for years.

Unspoken words linger in the space between us, and while it's not awkward, it's heavy. Despite what we both agreed at the outset, I think it's safe to say we've both caught feelings, and I'm fearful things are about to turn messy. But I don't want to be a Debbie Downer tonight. Not when Ryan has brought me to this romantic restaurant and we can be ourselves without having to duck and dive to avoid discovery. This place is off the beaten track, so we figure we're safe enough to openly embrace without fear of being spotted.

"Is this where you take all the women you're hiding?" I joke, needing to lighten the atmosphere.

"You're the first woman I've brought here," he admits, running the tip of his finger up and down my bare arm, sending a cavalcade of shivers tumbling across my sensitive skin. "I don't date, remember."

"Yet here we are." I stare deep into his eyes, instantly getting lost in them.

"Yes. Here we are." His words are a whisper spoken over my mouth before he brushes his lips briefly against mine.

"What are we doing?"

"I'm fucked if I know."

I can't resist smiling. "You make me very happy."

"You make me happy too."

The waitress arrives then with our pasta, and we're both quiet until she's left. I twirl the spaghetti around my fork, mentally debating whether to open this topic up or just let it drop. But I've never been one to shy away from speaking my mind, and I'm not about to start now.

"Can I ask you something?" I inquire in between mouthfuls of the sinfully creamy pasta.

"Of course." He shovels a forkful of lasagna in his mouth, watching me warily despite his acquiescence.

"I know you said you didn't date because of what happened with your ex, but is there more to it? Because your sister and Slater are so happy. Your parents seem to have a great marriage, and so does your brother Caleb and his wife Terri. Aren't there enough positive examples to negate the bad experience you endured?"

"Why do you want to know?" he asks, placing his fork down, looking like he's swallowed something sour.

I shrug. "Because I'm nosy. Because I care about you. Because I can't understand how some woman hasn't ensnared you yet. Because I want you to be happy."

"I am happy."

I prod the crease in his brow. "That scowl suggests otherwise."

"Or I was until you started this line of questioning." He sighs, shoveling more food in his mouth and slowly chewing as he contemplates something.

I wait him out, eating my pasta as he deliberates.

"The truth is," he continues after a few minutes of silence. "I've never been into relationships or commitments. I've known since I was little. I've never seen myself getting married or having kids."

I put my silverware down. "Why?"

He runs a hand nervously through his hair. "Because relationships aren't always what they seem. And trusting another person, opening yourself up fully to another person, can come back to bite you." He eyeballs me, and I see a world of hurt hiding behind his eyes. "The people you love the most have the power to inflict the worst damage, and I don't want to open myself up to that kind of pain. I let my guard down one time, and it burned me, but Myndi also did me a favor, because she made me realize I'd been right all along."

"Sometimes we have to open ourselves up to risk experiencing the greatest joy of all," I muse, my heart heavy with sadness for all he's denying himself. "I've never had my heart broken, but I know it'll happen, and I won't deny myself intermittent moments of amazing happiness for fear I'll suffer pain down the line. I'd rather experience those fleeting happy moments than miss out on them altogether."

"Maybe you're a braver person than me. Or I'm just older and more embittered."

"Or scared of feeling too much?" I repeat.

He pushes his food away, draining his beer in one go. "If you're asking this because of you and me—"

"I'm not," I rush to reassure him, regretting opening this conversation because the mood is subdued now, and that's all my fault. "I told you I'm naturally curious, but I shouldn't have started this conversation. I don't want to make you sad or uncomfortable. I just … like you." I shrug, smiling as I grip onto his arm. "And I want to know what makes you tick."

"I think you have a fair idea of what makes me tick," he says, taking my hand and placing it on his crotch. I know what he's doing, and it makes me sad, but I want to redirect this conversation too, so I let him deflect with sex.

We're both quiet on the walk back to the apartment, and I fear my prying has driven a wedge between us. A wedge I'm desperate to eliminate before Ryan decides he's had enough and calls time on our arrangement. But, typically, my brother and Miley are in the living room when we return, putting paid to my plans to use my body to bring Ryan back around.

I wait a couple hours until all is quiet in Austin's room before tiptoeing into Ryan's bedroom. He's not asleep either. Lying on his side under the comforter, he looks as troubled as I feel. He whips his head around when I slide into bed beside him. "What are you doing?" he hisses. "You can't be in here."

I push him flat on his back and straddle him. "I need to feel you inside me. I need to make this right between us again. And I can be quiet."

He looks at me like I'm crazy. And I get it. I'm vocal in bed, but I'm determined to bite my tongue because I can't go asleep leaving things like this between us. I need to feel close to him.

"I very much doubt that, and you don't need to make anything right. We're fine."

"We're not." I whip my top up off my head, exposing my bare chest to him. "And it's my fault our date was ruined."

He cups the back of my head, pulling my face down close to his. "It wasn't ruined."

"I shouldn't have said anything. Sometimes I don't know when to shut my big mouth."

"Don't say that," he whispers, pressing tiny kisses to my face. "I love that about you, and I never want you to be anyone but yourself. You gave me a lot to think about is all." He cups my face, peering into my eyes. "You're changing me, Summer, and that scares me a lot."

"We can be scared together, because you're changing me too."

It's as close as we've come to admitting we have feelings outside the bedroom.

"I don't want to break your heart," he whispers with pain etched across his face. "And I'm terrified that's what I'll do."

"Don't be so cocky," I tease, wanting to defuse the heaviness that seems to have surrounded us tonight. I slide off him, shucking my panties off and tugging his sleep shorts down his body. "Maybe I'll be the one breaking your heart." I straddle him, stroking his hard length a couple times, brushing the tip over my aching pussy.

"I've no doubt," he rasps, gripping my hips and lowering me onto him. "But I'm too far gone to stop this now."

"Me too," I whisper as I rock against him. "So, let's agree to go with the flow and see where this takes us. We'll deal with the fallout when it happens."

"Sum!" Hannah squeals, jumping up and down in her chair when I arrive at the stadium for the football match on Friday night. "It feels like I haven't seen you in forever," she adds, grabbing me into a hug. "And that sucks, because this isn't how I imagined our freshman year of college."

Nor me. "I'm sorry I've been so busy lately. Between classes, working at the gym, and rehearsals, I have little free time." I didn't add Ryan to the mix because Hannah doesn't know about him, and I hate I'm keeping it from her, but I can't tell her, because she'll tell Jordan, and he hates Ryan, and I don't trust him not to blab to my brother. So, I'd no choice but to conceal it from her, which is the first time I haven't confided in her about stuff going on in my life. Guilt presses down on my chest. "Where's Jordan?" I look all around, but there's no sign of her boyfriend.

She gulps, and tears pool in her eyes. "He bailed to hang out with Sean and Dalton although he said he'd meet us at the club later."

"What's wrong?" I clasp her hands in mine.

She swipes at the tears leaking out of her eyes, sniffing. "I'm probably overreacting."

"To what?" I lower my voice, conscious we're in a packed stadium with prying ears all around.

She bites down on her lower lip. "He's been distant the last few weeks, preferring to hang out with the guys than spend time with me and he… he seems to have gone off sex. He's always tired, or it's late or there's some crappy excuse. I"—a shuddering breath rattles her chest, and her lip wobbles—"I think he wants to break up with me."

"He changed his plans to come to UD for *you*." I rub her hands, trying to reassure her, but a niggling worry presses at the back of my mind. It's been there since I had a long phone call with Justin last month.

He'd called me back the day after I hung up on him, and we'd had an honest conversation. Justin told me he has feelings for me, but he doesn't want to be tied to a long-distance relationship while he's in college, and I was glad we were on the same page. We agreed to be friends. That we'll hang out if we're both at home in Bridgeville, but we made no commitments outside of that, and the conversation considerably eased my mind.

Except when I quizzed him about Jordan, and he claimed he hadn't asked him to do anything regarding me. So, I don't understand where all the overprotectiveness has been coming from. Why Jordan took an instant dislike to Ryan. Why he seemed more than happy not to give my cell number to Sean at the start. I'd convinced myself he was just being a good friend, because I don't want to be thinking the things I'm thinking, but given what Han's just admitted, I'm scared I might be on the right track.

"I think he's regretting it," she says on a sob. "I think he regrets not going to Oregon with Justin."

"Have you spoken to him about it?"

She shakes her head. "I'm trying to pluck up the courage to have the conversation, but I'm terrified he's going to break it off. I love him so much, and the thought he might not feel it anymore is killing me."

"Which is why you need to talk to him, Han. You're torturing yourself not knowing. It could be completely innocent, and you're worrying yourself for nothing, but you won't know unless you talk to him."

The club is jam-packed by the time we arrive. We stopped to have dinner after the game and ended up chatting for hours. It felt good to spend that time with my bestie, but unease still claws at my insides, not helped by the fact the guys are smashed already and surrounded by girls fawning all over them. Hannah's face falls when she notices, and I loop my arm in hers, pushing the girls out of the way so we can reach their side. Sean acknowledges me with a sheepish smile while chatting to a cute girl with short blonde hair. Jordan kisses Hannah on the lips before dragging me into a bear hug. "Haven't seen you in ages," he slurs, tightening his hold on me. "Missed you."

Subtly, I extricate myself from his embrace, plastering a smile on my face. "Me too. But I'm here now." I nudge him in the ribs. "Get the drinks in."

He smacks a kiss off my cheek. "Anything for you."

Hannah is crestfallen, watching his retreating form as he heads toward the bar with Sean in tow. "See what I mean now?" She wraps her arms around herself. "He looked happy to see you, but he barely glanced at me." Her lower lip wobbles, and my heart aches for her.

I hug her close. "Do you want to go?"

She shakes her head. "No way in hell am I leaving him here with all these girls hanging around."

I nod in understanding, as my cell pings in my pocket. I check it discreetly, a wide grin appearing on my face as I read the text from Ryan.

I see you, gorgeous.

Without looking obvious, I scan the club, my heart jumping wildly when I spot him with some staff from the gym at the end of the bar. Miley's blonde curls bounce around her head as she sways her hips to the beat of the music, looking like she's lost in her own world. My brother is staring at her with a love-struck expression on his face, as if she's the only one in the room, and he looks suitably distracted.

My cell pings again.

Meet me in the disabled toilet out back.

I whip my head up after reading the text, licking my lips and narrowing my eyes as I zone in on Ryan. My pulse skyrockets, and heat floods my body as he levels a provocative look my way. I cast a glance over my shoulder, ensuring Hannah isn't looking, before I look back, blowing a kiss in his direction.

"I'm just going to the bathroom. Will you be okay here until Jordan returns?" I ask Han, feeling a little guilty for ditching her in favor of a bathroom hookup.

"I'll be fine." She kisses my cheek. "Go."

I fight my way through the crowded room, pushing through the double doors out into the hallway at the back. There's a spring in my step as I skip along the passageway, climbing the stairs to the upper level where the bathrooms are. Sneaking off like this with Miley and Austin in the vicinity is risky, but the thrill of being caught only adds to the allure.

I guess I'm a bit fucked up.

An arm wraps around my waist from behind, and I lean back into a warm body, a wide grin spreading across my lips. My hair is pushed aside, and someone presses a wet kiss against my neck. All the tiny hairs on my body stand on high alert because I instantly know this isn't Ryan. Removing the arm from around me, I stumble awkwardly, staring in shock at Jordan. I hoped I was wrong about him, but it seems my instincts were correct. "What the hell are you doing?" I splutter, just as I spy Ryan coming up the stairs. With a surreptitious shake of my head, I urge him to stay back. Although the immediate scowl on his face tells me he's unhappy, he moves into the corner, staying out of sight.

"Baby," Jordan slurs, taking a step toward me. "Come back here."

I place my hands on his chest, holding him at bay. He's trashed, so it doesn't take much effort to keep him at arm's length. "Jordan, stop."

"Come on, Summer. Don't pretend like you don't feel this thing between us."

"I don't, Jordan. You're my friend, but that's it. That's all there will ever be between us."

"I don't believe you. You're just saying that because of Hannah."

"I'm glad you've remembered your girlfriend," I say, struggling to keep my voice level. "The girl who's my best friend in the entire world. The girl who loves you to the moon and back. Have you forgotten all that?!"

"I can't help how I feel," he slurs, reaching for me again.

"Stop grabbing at me, Jordy. I don't want you to touch me."

"Please, Summer. Give us a chance."

I close my eyes, swallowing over the anguished lump in my throat. "Jordan, that'll never happen. Go back to Hannah. She'll be wondering where you are."

"I don't want her. I don't love her anymore."

My eyes meet Ryan's as my heart aches for my bestie. He's respecting my wishes, holding back in the shadows, but he's primed to intervene. I stare at Jordan, wondering if I've ever really known him at all. "If that's the truth, you need to tell her because you're hurting her. She knows something isn't right, and you owe it to her to be honest. But it's nothing to do with me. I don't have those feelings for you, Jordan."

"I came here for *you*," he pleads, slouching against the wall as he pins me with doleful eyes. "I love *you*."

"I'm sorry, but I don't love you, and I never will." I fold my arms across my chest as hurt slices across his face. "You need to tell Hannah the truth. If you don't, I will. I won't have you making a fool out of her, Jordan."

I see the moment his hurt transforms to a darker emotion. He darts forward, grabbing my arm before I can duck out of his reach. "Suck me off, then. It's the least you can do."

"What?! How the hell do you figure that?" I try to wrestle out of his hold, but he digs his nails into my arm, and I sense movement from the corner.

"You blew Justin. Now it's my turn."

"Fuck you, Jordan, and get your hands off me!" I fume, still trying to wriggle out of his death grip.

Ryan's livid face comes into view as he takes a step forward at the same time the door to the men's bathroom opens and Sean steps into the hallway, his eyes narrowed in anger. "I heard every word, Jordan, and I believe Summer asked you to let her go." He crosses his arms, glaring at his friend. "This isn't cool."

"I thought we were friends," I say, sadness dripping from my tone as Jordan finally releases my arm. "But no true friend would every treat me like this. Treat Hannah like this."

This will kill her.

I shake my head, swallowing back the bile swimming up my throat, as Sean pushes me back a little, shielding me with his body. Ryan has retreated to the corner, and I'm certain he hates staying hidden. I need to end this before he decides it doesn't matter and risks everything. "I won't tell her what you just said, but I *will* tell her the earlier stuff if you don't man up and come clean. She deserves better than this."

All the fight leaves Jordan, and he stares at me through bloodshot eyes for a couple minutes before nodding, and then he walks away with his shoulders hunched over and a dejected look on his face.

"Are you okay?" Sean asks, concern underscoring his tone.

I plant a fake smile on my face. "I'm fine. Just hurting for my friend."

He nods, as I place my hand on the door of the ladies' bathroom, indicating my intent. "Okay. I'll leave you to it. But if he hassles you again, you know where I am." He presses a kiss to my cheek before walking down the stairs.

I can't speak over the lump in my throat as I watch Ryan stride toward me. A sob breaks loose of my chest when he silently draws me into his arms, and I cling to him as I cry, understanding this will change everything between Hannah and me. And not in a good way.

CHAPTER 18
Ryan

SUMMER HAS BEEN distraught since earlier, and I'm trying my best to comfort her. Even though Miley and Austin are in the apartment tonight, there's no way I could leave her to sleep on her own. She's bundled in my arms as we cuddle in bed, having finally succumbed to sleep. I sensed Jordan was harboring feelings for Summer because his behavior wasn't normal, but hearing him tell her he loved her was still a shock. And I've never wanted to beat a guy as badly as I wanted to beat that douche when he told her to suck him off. He's lucky I wasn't drunk, or I doubt I'd have shown any restraint.

When this comes out, it will drive a wedge in her friendship with Hannah. She seems blind when it comes to Jordan, and I'm afraid she'll blame her best friend instead of pointing the finger squarely where it belongs—with him.

My protective instincts are in overdrive, and I want to shelter Summer from the incoming storm, but I know I can't. Feelings of helplessness add to the other turmoil in my head, further confusing me. All I know with certainty is that I'm not letting Summer go. Not when she'll need me to lean on in the difficult weeks ahead.

My alarm goes off a half hour earlier than usual, and I rouse the Sleeping Beauty in my arms. "Baby." I press a kiss to her temple, threading my fingers through her hair. I hate to disturb her when she looks like she's in a deep sleep, but she needs to go back to her room before Austin wakes. "You need to get up."

She snuggles into my body, and I close my eyes, savoring the warmth of her skin against mine. "This sucks," she murmurs into my bare chest, and a chuckle works its way through me.

"I won't disagree. But unless you want your brother to catch you in here, you need to leave. Now."

Yawning, she sits up, rubbing sleep from her eyes. Then she turns around, leaning down to press a delicate kiss to my mouth. "Parting is such sweet sorrow," she whispers against my lips, reciting one of Juliet's most famous lines, "that I shall say goodnight till it be morrow." Her smile is adoring as she kisses me one final time before tiptoeing out of my room.

I'm in a daze watching the closed door after she's left, because it's in this moment that reality finally dawns on me.

I'm in love with her.

I'm completely head over heels for Summer Petersen.

And that means I'm totally and utterly screwed.

"Thanks for agreeing to come with me," I tell Summer later that night as we leave the gym en route for my sister's house.

"It's no problem. I told Gabby previously I was happy to babysit and getting to spend more time with you is the icing on the cake."

My heart thuds in my chest, reminding me of my early morning admission.

All day, I've been walking around on autopilot, dazed and confused, wondering what the hell I'm going to do with the realization I'm in love. I found pathetic reasons to hunt her down during the working day—anything to spend even a few precious seconds in Summer's company.

I thought Austin was pussy-whipped with Miley, but I'm ten times worse.

I'm tempted to blurt out my feelings with the way she's looking at me, but thankfully, I still have some self-control.

"Thank you both so much," Gabby gushes as Slater tries to steer her out of the house. "I appreciate you stepping in at the last minute."

Our parents were supposed to be on babysitting duty, but Dad has a chest infection, and Gabby is worried about Daisy picking it up. She wouldn't even let Mom come alone in case she's carrying any germs. Some might say she's overreacting, but I can't fault her for the all-consuming way she loves her kids. Besides, I miss my niece and nephew, and it's nice to have this extra time with them. Although Daisy is asleep, we'll get to see her in the morning as we've already agreed to stay overnight so Gabby and Slate don't feel pressured to come home early.

"It's fine," Summer reassures her as Billy curls around her leg, gazing up at her like she's a Disney princess. "We had nothing planned, anyway."

Gabby sends me a knowing look before giving us both a hug and letting Slater drag her out the front door. Her son barely gives her a second look, because he's too enamored with my girl.

My girl.

Fuck.

We eat the dinner Gabby already prepared, and then we play a game of basketball before the light fades. "Pretty girl," Billy says, once we're back inside, batting his eyelashes at Summer. "Will you watch Avengers Finity with me?"

"Sure thing." Smiling, she raises her hand and he high fives her. "I love *Infinity War*, and I'm a big Avengers fan. The Cap is my favorite. Who's yours?"

He grabs hold of her hand, pulling her into the living room. "Iron Man is the best!" He jumps up and down. "I know! I know! Let's wear costumes!" He drags her in the opposite direction, and Summer giggles, shooting me a disarming smile.

"Go for it," I say, grinning back at her. "I'll set the movie up and make popcorn while you're gone."

I'm munching my way through the bowl of popcorn when Summer and the cute little guy return. "I'm Iron Man!" he proclaims in a gruff voice, puffing out his chest behind his costume and bounding into the room, displaying impressive arrogance like a true mini Tony Stark.

"And I'm Black Widow," Summer announces, in an assertive tone, striding into the room behind him in a figure-hugging black jumpsuit, holding two toy swords in her hands. She stands confidently beside my nephew, the two of them projecting superhero status, and I can't contain my laughter.

"You dare to laugh at me?" She quirks a brow. When Billy flips up his Iron Man mask, exchanging a devilish look with Summer, I'm on instant alert.

"What's going on?" I question with clear caution in my tone.

"Billy and I made a new rule," Summer says, winking at my nephew as a wicked smile graces her mouth. "You can only watch the movie if you're wearing a costume." She throws something at me. "You're up, champ. Go get dressed."

I inspect the flimsy red and blue silky material with trepidation, my mouth curling in disgust. "Oh, hell to the no."

"That's a bad word, Uncle Ryan," Billy says, wagging his finger at me. "Now be Spiderman, or I'll tell Mom you were cussing again."

The little blackmailing shit.

Still, I can't keep the smile off my face. There isn't much I won't do for my nephew, it seems, as I saunter out of the room with the offending costume in hand, subtly spanking Summer on the ass as I pass by her.

"What the actual fuck?" I question out loud to myself a few minutes later, all tangled up in the too-tight costume. How the fuck does Slate fit into this thing? I tug on the material, trying to stretch it out so it reaches my wrists and my ankles and isn't molded to my dick like a tight layer of foreskin. That's assuming it's Slater's because right now I'm questioning if this suit is even adult sized.

Little beads of sweat dot my brow as I finally get the damn thing on. I look in the mirror, laughing at the state of myself squeezed into the minuscule costume, deciding that Summer owes me at least a blow job for this.

The instant I step foot in the living room, shouting "I am Spiderman," because hey, when in Rome and all that shit, the room erupts in an explosion of laughter, and you'd swear there were twenty people in the room not two. Or one point five if you consider Billy's still a kid.

Summer drops to her knees, tears pouring out of her eyes, and she can't stop laughing long enough to speak. Billy is running around the room, giggling and squealing.

"Hey, it was your great idea," I say, strolling over to the couch and plopping down on it. The material scrunches up at my thighs, almost giving me a wedgie, and I squirm on the couch trying to get comfortable. Summer shrieks, almost convulsing with laughter, before jumping up and dashing out of the room. "Was it something I said?" I joke with Billy, and he giggles, snuggling up on the couch with me and snatching the popcorn.

I'm still cursing the damn costume a couple minutes later when Summer returns wearing a Wonder Woman outfit this time. If I thought the crotch of my Spiderman costume was tight before, it's nothing on how strained it is now I'm sporting the biggest boner known to man. Discreetly, I pull the throw off the back of the couch, covering my nether regions before Billy notices the giant bulge in my tighter than tight pants.

"Are you trying to kill me, woman?" I ask as Summer flops down on the other side of me. "Death by giant erection," I whisper in her ear, and she splutters, holding up a hand, trying to compose herself long enough to speak.

"Stop!" She titters, clutching her stomach as if she's in pain. "I've already had to change once because I peed my pants."

I just stare at her, and she cracks up in laughter again. "You seriously peed your pants?" I inquire, fighting a bout of laughter myself.

She punches me in the arm, but it's a feeble effort, and I barely feel a twinge. "It's your fault." She looks over me, snorting with laughter. "How the hell did you even get that thing on?"

"It wasn't without challenge, trust me." I wink at her, and she rests her head on my shoulder, her light laughter warming my insides.

"You look totally fuckable in that costume," I whisper in her ear. "I want you to wear it later when you're riding me."

"Do you think that's why Gabby and Slater have so many costumes upstairs? Do they play superhero in the bedroom?" she whispers, waggling her brows suggestively as my stomach sours.

My insides shrivel at the thought, and I scowl at her. "Thanks a bunch for that lovely visual of my sister. Now, I have a renewed urge to punch my brother-in-law in the face." I know Gabby and Slate usually dress up to go trick or treating with Billy at Halloween, and I'm sticking to that story as the most logical explanation.

Because, otherwise, I'm likely to land one on Slate the second he steps foot in the door.

"I think it's great they have such a healthy sex life. I hope I'm lucky enough to have that when I'm married."

I scrub my hands down my face as Billy, mercifully, presses play on the movie. "Can we please stop talking about my sister's sex life," I hiss. "You're making me ill."

A serious expression washes over her face. "I guess that's how Austin would feel if he knew the things you were doing to my body," she muses, and it in no way helps my current dilemma.

Thankfully, there's no more talk of sex during the movie, and the little guy keeps us entertained spouting most of Iron Man's lines before he's even spoken them on the screen. Think Billy's a bit obsessed. His eyes droop midway through the movie, and Summer and I share a conspiratorial look.

Billy only agrees to go to bed if the pretty girl reads him a bedtime story.

While Summer reads to him, I check on my little niece, beaming at her tiny little body, wrapped contentedly in a soft blanket in her crib. Her thumb is in her mouth, and she looks like a little angel. I bend down, placing a barely there kiss on her silky smooth cheek, my heart full of love.

Then I stand just outside Billy's door listening to Summer reading him a story, complete with animated voices and vivid expressions. As I watch her with my nephew, I can picture her with our kids, and that scary thought is enough to send me scurrying back downstairs.

I'm on my second beer when Summer reappears in the living room. I finally pried the nightmare costume off, and I'm only in sweats, with my upper torso and feet bare. My cock swells as she strides toward me with a wicked gleam in her eye. She's still wearing the red corset top, flimsy blue skirt, and gold knee-high boots, and my lust for her elevates to an all-time high when she climbs onto my lap, straddling me. "I'm not wearing any panties," she whispers, leaning down to claim my lips in a bruising kiss. I slide my hand under that excuse of a skirt, finding her wet and wanting. My fingers slide through her folds, and I pump them in and out of her while she pushes my sweats down to my hips, freeing my throbbing cock.

I grab her hips and position her strategically, and we both moan quietly as I situate myself inside her. She rocks on top of me, and I'm happy to let her set the pace. She bobs up and down on me, never losing eye contact, and my hand slips into the top of the corset top, my fingers finding a path to her hardened nipples. Her pussy hugs my cock as she continues to ride me, and my heart swells to bursting point while I hold her adoring gaze.

Her eyes shimmer with desire and something deeper, and I wonder if she's feeling it too. I move forward, claiming her lips, just as the tappity-tap of heels on the hallway floor brings me crashing down to Earth with a bang.

Our eyes pop wide, and she scrambles off me, hurriedly fixing her clothes and smoothing back her hair as I yank my sweats back up my body. I throw the blanket over us mere seconds before my sister and best friend step into the room.

Thank fuck, we hadn't switched the movie off.

"Hey." My sister's gaze bounces between me and Summer, and I pray she's not putting two and two together.

"You're home early." It's only just past eleven, and I wasn't expecting them home for at least another couple of hours.

"Yeah." She looks up at Slater with uncertainty in her eyes. "Our night was unexpectedly cut short."

I raise a brow in silent question. She gulps, knotting her hands in front of her. "Myndi's waters broke at the restaurant," she quietly adds.

"Oh, right." My chest tightens, like it always does at the mention of her name, but it's not as constricting as usual.

"That's exciting." Summer smiles at my sister, and I could kiss her for attempting to lighten the atmosphere. "I hope everything goes okay."

"Me too." Gabby chews on her lip as she scrutinizes my face with a furrowed brow. Her gaze flits to Summer, and her eyes pop out on stalks as she takes a proper look at her. "Is that my Wonder Woman costume?"

A slight blush stains Summer's cheeks, and it's the first time I've noticed even a hint of embarrassment on her face. Good to know she's not superhuman. "Yes, I hope that's okay. Billy wanted us to dress up for the movie."

Slater sends me a smug grin, and I know he's worked it out. Guess I'll be fessing up in the morning. I flip him the bird and mouth "shut the fuck up" behind the girl's backs.

"Of course," Gabby reassures her while her gaze bounces between us. It looks like she's debating with herself. Then the lines smooth out of her brow, and she says in a cheery voice, "I think I'll make coffee. Who wants some?"

CHAPTER 19
Ryan

"WHAT'S GOING ON with you and Summer?" Gabby asks me the following morning as we're eating breakfast in the kitchen. Summer has gone with Slater and Billy to walk Daisy in her stroller.

"What?" I splutter, almost spitting coffee all over the table.

"The room reeked of sex last night, and the telltale signs were all over both your faces," she calmly says, refilling my mug.

"Tell it straight why don'tcha, Tornado," I deadpan.

She's quiet as she reclaims her seat across from me. "Does Austin know?"

I shake my head, swallowing the thick lump in my throat. "He wouldn't approve."

"It's not his place to approve or disapprove."

"She's young."

"And you're immature." Gabby flashes me a grin. "I'd say it's a match made in heaven."

I poke my tongue out at her. "That's a little harsh, sis. I've grown up a lot the last couple years."

She slides her hand across the table, squeezing mine. "I know you have. I'm only teasing, but, honestly, I think Summer's perfect for you. She doesn't take herself too seriously, yet she's got a good head on her shoulders. And while she's young at heart, she's mature in all the ways that count."

"She is," I admit, unable to stop my big smile. "She's incredible."

Gabby's jaw slackens, and her eyes pop wide. "My God. You're in love with her."

No point lying. My sister is a persistent little minx when she wants to be, so it's easiest to come clean at the outset. I slowly nod, ignoring the nervous fluttering in my chest. "I am, but it can't go anywhere."

"Why the hell not?"

"Because I'm not destined for anything long-term."

"I'm fucking sick of hearing this bullshit, Ryan." She glares at me. "Why the hell don't you believe you're worthy of love? Why are you so against a loving home and a family like I have?"

"You know why."

"All I know is you felt this way long before Myndi screwed with your head, and I'm sick of your deflective bullshit. What made you so cynical? Especially when we had the perfect example of a loving marriage growing up!"

"Oh. please." I roll my eyes. "Don't tell me you bought into that charade."

Her eyes almost bug out of her head. "What the actual fuck, Ryan?" Realization creeps across her face. "This is something to do with Mom and Dad?" Her brow puckers in confusion.

"I'm not talking about this." I take a big gulp of my coffee, my chest burning with the knowledge I gleaned when I was seven.

"You damn well are." She glares at me again. "Our parents are as crazy in love now as they were when they met."

I snort. "It's bullshit. It always has been."

She leans across the table. "What are you talking about? Spit it out, Ryan, or I'm calling them right now."

"It's all lies!" I shout. "She cheated on him! Mom cheated on Dad!"

Gabby vehemently shakes her head. "No way, Ryan. There's no way she'd do something like that."

"I fucking saw her! All right!"

"What?!"

I rest my head in my hands, sighing. A sour taste coats the inside of my mouth as I pin my gaze on my sister and admit this for the first time. "I was seven when I saw her. I'd been out playing ball with Slate, and I came back early because I fell and cut my knee. She didn't hear me come in because she was shouting at some strange man. I edged toward the kitchen, frightened, and then I saw it. Saw them kissing." My jaw locks tight as the image replays in my mind as if I only witnessed it yesterday. It's ingrained in my mind, and I've never been able to look at Mom the same way since. I know she hates that she's not close with me like she is with Gabby, Caleb, and Dean. I hide my true feelings behind my humor, but my anger simmers behind the mask I wear in her presence, and I've come so close to telling my dad on so many occasions, but I've always held back out of fear.

Gabby slouches in her chair, looking deep in thought. She sits up straighter, a knowing look replacing her troubled expression. "I bet it was Mickey Delaney."

"Who the fuck is Mickey Delaney?" I ask, wondering why that name sounds vaguely familiar. "Wait. You don't mean the quarterback who used to play with the Patriots?"

She nods. "Yeah, I think so. Mom said he had a great sporting career." She pulls out her cell phone, and I'm thoroughly confused.

"What are you doing?" I stand.

"I'm getting Mom over here. You need to talk to her."

"No way. I'm leaving," I say, even though I already know my sister won't allow it. If she's risking the kids picking up germs by calling Mom over here, I know she won't let this drop.

"Sit the fuck back down," she hollers, rounding the table and jabbing her finger into my chest. "You're not leaving until you hear Mom tell you the story."

"What story?"

"The story of her first love. Mickey Delaney."

Summer, Slater, and the kids arrive back at the same time Mom pulls up to the house. Daisy is fast asleep in her stroller, and Summer offers to take Billy up to his room to play so we can talk. "Are you okay?" she mouths at me, and I shrug. Not gonna lie. I've no clue what Gabby knows only she's adamant that the scene I witnessed as a kid could not have been as it seemed. Summer doesn't know what's going on, but she's picked up the tension in the air.

"I'll fill you in later," I mouth back at her before Billy hauls her up to his room.

"What's going on?" Mom asks when she arrives, clasping my face, concern radiating from the back of her eyes. "Are you sick?"

"No, Mom." Gabby pulls her into a hug, before forcing her into a chair. "Ryan needs to hear about Mickey Delaney." She sighs sadly. "He has it in his head you cheated on Dad because he saw you kissing another man in the kitchen when he was seven."

Way to just put it out there Gabby.

"Oh my God." Mom clamps a hand over her mouth, tears pooling in her eyes as she stares at me, horror-struck. "Is that what you've thought all these years?"

I fold my arms across my body. "I know what I saw. You were kissing a man who wasn't my father."

"Oh, my poor boy. This is why, isn't it?" Tears roll down her face, and a heavy weight presses down on my chest. I might not have the best relationship with my mother, but I still hate to see her cry. "This is why you keep me at arm's length. Why you never let me in." She breaks down then, sobbing, and Gabby wraps her arms around her, offering soothing words as I stare at Slater, conflicted.

"Ryan," Mom sobs over Gabby's shoulder. "I have *never* cheated on your father. *Never*. I love him more than words can express. I can explain what you saw." She swipes at her tears, and Gabby releases her, sitting in the chair beside her.

Mom gestures for me to take the seat in front of her, and I silently sit down. I don't protest when she takes my hands in hers, leaning into me with earnest eyes. "I'm guessing you ran away after you saw that kiss?" I nod tersely. "Then you wouldn't have seen me push him away. Heard me tell him I loved your father and I would never go back to him."

"Who was he to you?" I choke out.

"Mickey Delaney was my first love. He lived four doors away from us when I was growing up. We were childhood sweethearts, inseparable, until he got a full ride to play ball at the University of Southern California. I didn't get a scholarship to join him, and my parents couldn't afford the tuition, so I went to UD where I met and fell in love with your father. Although it was a tough decision, I broke things off with Mickey before anything started with your dad."

Her chest heaves as she implores me with her eyes. "Mickey turned up at our house one time, completely out of the blue, after years, telling me he still loved me and begging me to leave your father for him. His most recent engagement had just ended, and he told me he couldn't move on, that no one else measured up."

She stares off into space, lost in thought for a few seconds, before she redirects her attention my way. "I told him no outright, then he kissed me. It startled me for a minute, and I didn't push him away straightaway, but as soon as I realized it, I did exactly that. I told him I loved your father, and I loved our family, and I would never betray him for any man. He got the message, and he left soon after that. He apologized for kissing me, and that was the last time I ever saw him. I swear it."

She squeezes my hands. "Please say you believe me." When I don't respond immediately, tears well in her eyes again. "Call your father! He knows all about that visit. He knows that he kissed me. If you don't believe me, maybe you'll believe it from him."

"That's the truth?" I croak. "And you've never cheated on Dad?"

"No!" she cries out, tears streaming down her face again. "I love all of you too much to ever risk ruining what we have. I'm so fortunate. I know that, and I'd do nothing to jeopardize it. I've never wanted to because I'm happy in my life."

"Mom." I'm fighting tears now. I can't believe I've been under a misconception all these years. That I've judged her so unfairly. I pull her into my arms, and then we're both crying. Gabby and Slate quietly leave the kitchen, and I cling to my mom, holding her in a way I've denied myself for years. "I'm so sorry, Mom."

"No, sweetheart." Mom eases back, cupping my face. "You have nothing to apologize for. I'm sorry you had to see that. Sorry you've thought that of me all this time. All these wasted years." She sobs, and I hate I've hurt her, hurt myself, for something that was never anything to begin with. "That's why you don't believe in love or marriage?"

I nod. "I always thought it was a lie. And if you could fool Dad for all those years, then I never wanted to marry. To leave myself open to that kind of betrayal. But I've been so wrong, and now I feel foolish."

She presses a kiss to my head, holding me close. "I can understand how it must've looked to a child. I wish you'd come to me or spoken to one of your siblings about it."

"I couldn't. I didn't want them to feel the way I did. To know your love wasn't true."

"Oh, Ryan." She presses kisses to my cheeks. "I love you so much, and it's always pained me that our relationship was strained. This explains everything."

"I'm sorry, Mom. I'm sorry I hurt you, and I love you too. More than I can say."

She palms my face. "Promise me you'll let go of these feelings and open your heart. I worry about you so much. I want you to find a nice girl and settle down, but you're so closed off. Don't let a misconception take something so precious away from you."

"Will you be okay?" Gabby asks me a few hours later at the front door. Summer is already in the car waiting for me, and Mom left a half hour ago.

"I just need to process everything."

She grabs me into a hug. "I love you, little big bro, and I want you to be happy." She keeps a hold of my arms as she stares into my face. "If you love Summer, tell her, and then make things right with Austin. It's only a matter of time before he realizes because you two can't disguise the way you feel about one another. I had my suspicions before we came home last night. Austin will figure it out, if he hasn't already, and it's better if he hears it from you first."

CHAPTER 20
Summer

RYAN'S BEEN VERY introspective since Sunday, not that I blame him. The truth has shaken his whole belief system to its core, and he's trying to process everything. I've been quiet too, because the situation with Hannah and Jordan is hovering over me like a bad smell, and I'm on tenterhooks waiting for him to talk to her.

Everything comes to a head Friday night, and it's a clusterfuck of epic proportions as I suspected it might be.

Ryan and I have only just gotten home from the gym when a loud pounding sounds on the front door. Ryan looks up from the stove where he's cooking dinner, sharing a puzzled look with me. "I'll get it." I move toward the hallway.

"Let me." He moves protectively in front of me.

"Open the fucking door, Summer," Hannah hollers, thumping on the door with her fists.

"Fuck," I whisper.

"You have done nothing wrong," Ryan reminds me, kissing my temple.

He opens the door and Hannah barrels inside, steam practically billowing out of her ears. "How could you do this to me?" she screeches, tears pumping out of her eyes. "You know how much I love him!"

"I haven't done anything, Han," I protest, closing the door before we air our dirty laundry to the neighbors. I'm grateful Austin and Miley are working the late shift and they're not around for this confrontation.

"The hell you haven't." She shoves me, and I stumble on my feet, my heart racing. I've never endured Hannah's anger before, and her vicious hostility surprises and upsets me.

"Touch Summer one more time," Ryan says, sliding in between us, "and I'll be escorting you outside. If you're not prepared to sit and listen to what she has to say, then I think it's best you leave now and return when you're calmer."

"She stole him from me," Hannah wails.

"Summer has done no such thing. I don't know what your boyfriend has told you, but she's been a loyal friend to you for years, and you owe her the benefit of the doubt."

I touch his arm, urging him back. I'm grateful for his support, and his quick defense only makes me love him more, but this is between my bestie and me, and we need to talk alone. He eyeballs me and I silently communicate the message. He nods. "I'll be in the kitchen if you need me."

"Thank you," I mouth. Hannah follows me into the living room, whimpering the whole time. I plonk down on the recliner chair and she sits on the couch. "I'm so sorry, Hannah. I know how much you love him, and I'm shocked over all this."

"Huh." She harrumphs, pulling a tissue out of her jeans pocket. "I'm sure you are. I bet you can't wait to hook up with him."

My eyes go out on stalks. "Are you for real right now?" She glares at me. "Jordan is nothing but a friend, and I've never, ever, given him any sign I felt any differently toward him. When he approached me last weekend at the club, I told him point-blank I wasn't interested, that I didn't share his feelings. I was the one who told him he had to tell you or I would."

"Why?" she spits out.

"Why?" My tone betrays my disbelief. "Because you deserved to know the truth, and you were already torturing yourself over things you couldn't explain."

"We could've gotten through this, but you had to interfere."

My mouth opens and closes like a fish out of water. I can't believe she's twisting this around. "I seriously have no words, Han. I know you're upset, but surely, you don't mean that. Why would you want to stay with a guy if he doesn't love you anymore?" I lean forward, resting my elbows on my knees. "You deserve so much better than that, and I didn't want to see him making a fool out of you. That's why I told him to tell you."

"Oh puh-lease." She sends daggers at me. "I know exactly why you told him that. You want him for yourself, and you can't wait to get me out of the way."

I wonder if some alien being has stolen my best friend and replaced her with a poor substitute because the woman sitting across from me now is a stranger. I get that she's hurt. I'm hurt for her. But that's no excuse for accusing me of shit she knows I'd never do.

"No. I don't."

"I don't believe you."

I shake my head sadly. "Even if I had feelings for Jordan, which I don't," I categorically state, "I would never choose him over you. Not in a million years. Your friendship is worth more."

Unlike you.

The thought flies into my mind, and even though I feel mean thinking it, I can't help remembering all the ways Hannah put our friendship to one side in favor of her relationship with Jordan. It never bothered me before, but considering her fake accusations, it enrages me now.

"You've a funny way of showing it."

"Do I?" I flap my hands in the air, losing the tenuous control of my emotions. "Time and time again, you've put your relationship with him above our friendship. When he changed his plans last minute to come to UD, I stepped aside so you two could get a place together even though it meant moving in here with my brother, which was something I wasn't keen on." Not that I can regret how things have turned out because Jordan's decision indirectly led me to Ryan.

"That doesn't mean you don't want him now." She's grasping at straws, and she knows it.

"For the last time, I've no interest in Jordan. Not now. Not ever." There's only one surefire way of getting through to her, and I blurt it out before I properly think it through. "Besides, I'm seeing someone else. Someone I'm crazy about."

She snorts, sending an incredulous look my way. "Who? The Invisible Man?"

I grind my teeth to the molars. I want to tell her, but with the way she's acting, I'm not sure I can trust her to keep my confidence. "I've kept it on the down low for a reason, but it's true."

"Sure it is." She snarls at me. "If that's the best you can do, you're even more pathetic than I thought." She rakes her gaze over me in a derisory manner, and a splinter cracks my heart in two. "I don't even know what he sees in you. You're not anything special."

"That's enough." Ryan's voice is laced with anger. He plants his hands on my shoulders, giving me a reassuring squeeze. "Summer and I have been seeing one another, and I'm every bit as crazy about her."

My eyes widen in shock at his admission, but it's happy shock. I reach up, taking his hand and smiling at him.

Hannah is momentarily speechless as she stares at both of us. Then her mouth twists into a hurtful grimace. "You've been fucking him all this time, and you didn't tell me?"

"I wanted to, but Jordan hates him, and I was afraid he'd cause trouble."

Her lower lip wobbles as the truth of my statement hits home. She stands abruptly, wrapping her arms around herself. "Jordan and I can fix this. But you need to stay away from him and stay away from me."

I rise, moving toward her. "Hannah. Please don't push me away. I'm your friend."

"You're no friend of mine." She brushes past me. "You think you know someone," she tosses over her shoulder before exiting the apartment, violently slamming the door shut behind her.

"Yeah," I whisper to myself, fighting tears. "I'm with you on that front."

CHAPTER 21
Ryan

SUMMER WAS UNCHARACTERISTICALLY quiet the rest of the weekend, and I'm sorely tempted to have a private word in Hannah's ear, but I doubt Summer would appreciate me interfering, so I leave it alone. I can't believe the nerve of that bitch to come here and throw that bullshit at Summer. *Who needs enemies with friends like that?*

Miley and Austin are at the movies Sunday night, and Derrick is covering the nighttime shift, so when we return to the apartment a little after six, I run a bath for Summer and then order takeout while she's, hopefully, relaxing. I have one of those sappy chick flicks paused on the screen when Summer materializes, bundled up in a fluffy robe with her damp hair tied into a messy bun on top of her head. A weird fluttering takes up residence in my chest as I walk to her, pulling her into my arms without hesitation.

Fuck, I'm turning into such a pussy.

But I honestly couldn't give two shits about it.

When she rests her head on my chest and sighs, I tighten my hold on her, lacing my fingers through her silken hair, wishing I could absorb her heartache and take away her pain.

Hannah is a shitty friend. I thought she might've cooled down by now and reached out to Summer to apologize for the way she treated her, but she has made no effort with her at all. If you ask me, Summer's better off without her.

The bell chimes, and I pry myself away from my girl to answer the door. I peck her lips lightly. "That's our takeout. Go sit, and I'll plate up."

When I return with our food and a couple beers, Summer is curled up on the couch, with her knees pulled into her chest, staring off into space. I set the food and drinks down on the coffee table and sit beside her. "Hey." I tilt her chin up with one finger. "She'll come around. She was just upset." I don't really believe that, but I know they've been friends since they were small kids and that her friendship means a lot to Summer, so I'm keeping my honest thoughts to myself.

"I don't know that she will, and I'm not sure I want her to."

I probe her gorgeous, sad eyes, reaching out to caress her cheek because I can't seem to go a minute without wanting to touch her. "Talk to me."

I lean back in the couch, pulling her into my side. She fists her hand in my shirt as she rests her head on my shoulder, and I could happily die right now, completely satisfied. Yup; I've most definitely traded in my Man Card. My heart elevates in my chest as I gaze adoringly at her.

Summer soothes something in me by her very presence, and I know I need to do right by her. Starting with telling her I'm in love with her and then breaking the news to her brother, if she's in agreement to make things official between us. But this isn't the time for that, so I bite my tongue as I wait for her to unburden herself, smoothing my hand up and down her back and holding her close.

"I've been doing a ton of soul searching since Friday night, and I don't think my friendship with Hannah is as close as I believed it was. It's like I had blinders on, because I didn't see how I always took second place to Jordan." She tips her head up, looking me directly in the eye. "And it's not that I expected to come first all the time. Not at all. But now and then would've been nice, except she always blew me off to spend time with him, and I never stopped to question it."

"I'm sorry." I kiss her temple.

"And I don't get how she can blame me for this. I've never said or done anything to lead Jordan to believe I had any romantic feelings for him, and I haven't betrayed her. Demanding he tells her the truth was my way of protecting my best friend from further pain but she has thrown even that back in my face."

She sits up straighter, leaning both her hands on my chest. "I was really upset yesterday, and, honestly, my emotions have been veering all over the place, but now, I'm just sad because I know that even if we patch things up, our friendship will never be the same. Or maybe it will be," she adds, her brows knitting together. "But that won't be enough, because I don't want a friend who isn't there for me when I need her or one who throws accusations my way when her life turns shitty."

"Just be true to yourself, Summer. Friendships are two-way streets, no different from any other relationships. There needs to be give and take and mutual trust and respect. If Hannah can't offer you that, then maybe she doesn't deserve a place in your life."

The working week is crazy, and I've barely seen Summer since Sunday night, except for brief stolen kisses as we pass each other in the apartment like ships in the night. All week, I've thought of nothing else but opening my heart and my life up to Summer, and I know I'm ready.

But I don't really know how she feels, and we need to have a heart to heart to see where things are going with us. I've been texting her all day, asking if she's free after rehearsal tonight to go for dinner, but I'm growing increasingly worried when I still haven't heard from her by the time my shift is over.

I head home to get changed, and then I plan to head over to the theater company to wait for her.

I'm turning my key in the lock, listening to the shouting coming from inside with growing trepidation. Stepping into the apartment, I close the door, toss my keys on the table in the hall, and walk into the living room.

Austin is pacing the floor, fisting tufts of his hair in his hands, shouting at Summer, while she stands stock-still with tears silently rolling down her face. She's wearing sweats and a ratty T-shirt, her face devoid of makeup, with her hair in a messy ponytail. She looks paler than normal, and something is clearly wrong. Miley is tugging on Austin's elbow, whispering in his ear, concern etched all over her face.

"What's going on?" I ask, stepping into the room.

Summer's lower lip wobbles as she looks at me with blatant fear in her eyes.

"Shall you tell him, or will I?" Austin yells, and Summer flinches at the harsh tone of his voice.

I instinctively move to Summer's side, wondering if he's figured out what's going on with us. "Stop shouting at her," I say, working hard to keep my voice calm.

"Don't tell me what to do with *my* sister!" Austin snaps, glaring at me.

"Austin." Miley's tone is firm. "Stop this. Your sister is upset enough as it is. All you're doing is making things worse. You need to calm down."

"I can't fucking calm down!" he screams. "And I'm upset too! She's eighteen years old, and this'll ruin her entire life!"

"That's not true," Summer says, sniffling as she wraps her arms around her shivering body.

Discreetly, I place my hand on her lower back. "Is someone going to tell me what's going on?" I'm guessing Austin hasn't figured it out as all my limbs are still intact, but I've no clue why he's so riled up.

"Some asshole has knocked her up!" he admits through gritted teeth, and I sway on my feet as my ears ring and my eyesight blurs.

"What?" My eyes dart to Summer's in shock. Her silent tears transform to full-blown sobs as she looks at me with these big, apologetic eyes. "You're pregnant," I whisper. "Seriously?"

"These things don't lie," Austin says, shoving something into my hand. Blinking to clear my foggy head, I stare at the three pregnancy tests with the clear blue line confirming she's pregnant. "Imagine coming home to find those on your little sister's bedside table," he fumes.

My mind is bouncing off the walls as panic joins the bile swimming up my throat. I know this baby is mine, but why didn't she tell me? And what the fuck are we going to do now?

"And she won't tell me who the father is." Steam is practically billowing out of Austin's ears, but I don't blame him. I remember how shocked I was when I discovered Gabby was pregnant at nineteen, and I almost punched Dylan's lights out.

I snap out of my daze, preparing to man up and tell him the truth when Summer pinches my arm, pinning me with anguished eyes as she answers her brother. "It's none of your business."

And that was so not the thing to say to him in the moment. "The fucking hell it isn't!" He paces again. "If it's one of those obnoxious, jumped-up frat boys, I will lose my fucking shit. I mean it, Summer."

"Austin, please calm down." Miley pleads, trying to grab her boyfriend and stall his frantic pacing.

"How the hell can I be calm?" Tears prick his eyes, and his voice cracks. "She's my little sister, and some asshole did this to her. She hasn't even begun to live her life." He shakes his head sadly, swiping at errant tears, and I feel like the biggest shithead.

"A baby isn't the end of the world, Austin," Summer quietly says. "And you know I adore kids."

"Adoring kids and raising one at your age isn't the same thing, and you know it! What about UD? And all your travel plans?"

"I can still do what I want. I'll just have to make adjustments and maybe push the time line out." She's shuffling nervously on her feet, avoiding looking at me as she talks in a soft but determined voice, and I know she's trying to put a brave face on it, but her fear is still palpable. I don't know how long she's known about it, but I'm guessing she only found out today because the girl I know, and love, wouldn't keep this hidden from me. I couldn't get a hold of her today, and I figure this is why. She was at home, by herself, trying to process this.

She doesn't even know I'm in love with her.

Or that I was planning on asking her to be my girlfriend for real.

Who knows what thoughts were going through her mind?

I may be confused and terrified too, but she needs me, and I won't let her down.

I'm done hiding.

Sliding my arm fully around her waist, I pull her securely into my side. Then I turn to my best friend and business partner with a fierce look on my face. "I'm the father. It's my baby."

Austin just stares at me in obvious shock. And it's like one of those cinematic moments. You know, where the screen seems to focus in on a scene and the surrounding environment fades out. Until an explosion happens, and everything comes back into focus in a nanosecond.

This is exactly like that because Austin just stares at me, and you could hear a pin drop in the room for a few seconds until an animalistic growl rips from the back of his throat, and he lunges at me, punching me square in the face.

Summer screams.

Miley shouts.

And I stagger back, a little dizzy, pressing my fingers to the trickle of blood leaking out of my throbbing nose.

Austin comes at me again, landing a punch in my gut and winding me so bad I drop to my knees, struggling to catch a breath. "You fucking asshole!" he roars, slamming his fist into the side of my head this time. "I told you to keep your filthy hands off her!" My head jerks sideways, and I stretch my hand out to stop myself from falling flat on the ground. My head is spinning, and my breathing still hasn't returned to normal, but I deflect his next hit as Miley yanks on his arm, trying to pull him away from me.

Summer crouches down in front of me, crying. "I'm sorry."

"Don't fucking say sorry to him!" Austin yells, wrestling to get free of Miley's hold. "He took advantage of you, and now you're paying the price!"

I see the switch flick in Summer. Jumping up, she dries her eyes, storming over to her brother, pushing her face up in his. "Ryan did *not* take advantage of me! He tried to do the right thing, and he kept pushing me away, but I pushed back harder every time until he caved." She fists hers hands on her hips. "Our relationship is one hundred percent consensual."

I stagger to my feet. "I love her," I tell him, hating that she's hearing this for the first time like this. "And while I'm shocked about the baby, because I didn't know, I won't leave her to deal with this alone." I turn my head to Summer. "I'll be with you every step of the way, if that's what you want."

"You love me?" is her wide-eyed response.

I ignore Austin and Miley, focusing on the only person in this room who matters. Or, the only two people who matter, I correct myself, as my eyes lower to her flat stomach. "Come here." I hold out my hand for her to walk to me because I'm afraid to move a muscle in case Austin goes for me again.

She walks toward me with fresh tears in her eyes. I reel her into my arms, kissing her forehead. "I love you so much. I was going to tell you tonight, and if you agreed, I was planning on speaking to your brother after that."

"I love you too," she whispers through her tears, and a hint of a smile ghosts over her lips. "And I only found out about the baby this morning. I don't even know how far along I am. I was planning on telling you tonight, but Austin went into my room while I was in the shower, discovered the tests I'd stupidly left out in plain sight, and then this whole shit show started."

I urge her head toward my chest, and she obliges, circling her arms around my waist. I hold her tight, pressing kisses into her hair. "It'll be okay. I know we've a lot to talk about, but we're in this together, right?"

She sniffles, nodding her head, and hugging me tighter.

I risk a look up at her brother. The anger has not left his face, and he's glaring at me like he wants to rip my torso apart with his bare hands and remove all the vital organs from my body until I'm no longer breathing. "I know you're pissed but—"

"Don't even talk to me right now, James. I mean it. I can't stand to look at your face."

"I'll look after her. Love her and the baby and make sure they want for nothing."

Austin snorts. "*Maybe* your intentions are honest, but you have no fucking clue how to be there for any girl let alone a baby. At the first sign of trouble, you'll run a million miles away."

"That's not fucking fair," I spit out.

"Isn't it?" He arches a brow. "Look what happened with Myndi and how much of a basket case you've been since then."

"This is not the same thing, and Summer means the world to me."

"Doesn't mean you'll stick around for her."

I rub a tense spot between my brows, eager to end this conversation because he's pushing buttons I don't want pushed. "You know what, I don't have to explain myself to you." I straighten up, keeping a firm hold on Summer. "Summer and I have things to discuss in private."

Austin opens his mouth to say something, but Summer pins him with a look the devil himself would be proud of. "I think you've said enough for one night, Austin." Then she sighs, and her features relax a little. "I know you love me and you're just worried, but you've got to step away from this and let me and Ryan figure it out." She moves to his side, tentatively opening her arms for a hug.

He pulls her into his arms, squeezing his eyes closed as he hugs her close. "I'm sorry for shouting, but this has come out of left field." Opening his eyes, he bores a hole in the side of my skull as he speaks to his sister. "This is not what I wanted for you, Summer." He pauses for a couple beats. "And Ryan is not who I'd choose for you," he cruelly adds, digging the knife in further. "I hope you know what you're doing."

CHAPTER 22
Summer

"ARE YOU FEELING okay," Ryan asks once we've sequestered ourselves in his bedroom, away from the wrath of my brother. "Have you been sick or anything, because you look a little pale?" He leans his back against the headrest, opening his arms for me.

I crawl into his embrace, instantly feeling less agitated as his strong arms go around me. "I've been sick a few times this week," I admit. "At first, I thought it was just a passing bug, but this morning, the sickness was terrible. I couldn't stop throwing up, and it was only then I realized my period was a couple days late. I went to the pharmacy and grabbed some tests and, well, you know the rest."

"It's my fault. I should've insisted we use condoms, but it felt so good to be inside you with nothing between us."

I cradle his face in my hands. "We both agreed, and I'm on the pill, so it should've been safe. I've no clue how this even happened." A little burst of laughter emits from my mouth. "I'm like one of those naïve virgins you read about in books. A few months after popping my cherry, I end up knocked up." I shake my head, because it almost feels fictional even though I know that's not true. No form of contraceptive is one hundred percent reliable, and we should've been taking extra precautions. And it's not like I'm the first eighteen-year-old to ever get pregnant.

"Don't say that." He kisses me softly. "You're nothing like that."

Although I don't want to, I shuck out of his arms, sitting up beside him. I can't have a serious conversation while I'm sprawled on top of him. "Can we get serious?" He nods, threading his fingers through mine. "How do you really feel about this?"

His chest heaves, and he scrubs his free hand back and forth over the scruff on his chin as he considers my question. Then he turns on his side, still keeping our hands connected, and peers directly into my eyes, letting me see everything he's feeling. "I think I'm still in shock, but I'm not unhappy about it. I love you, Summer, and I want to plan a future with you. I'd already decided that before I heard the baby news." He smiles, but it's a little off. "But I won't lie and say I'm not scared, because I'm terrified what your brother just said out there is true. I've only had one serious relationship in my life, and that ended up a complete mess. I want to care for you and the baby, but I've never done this before. I want to be who you need me to be, but I'm scared of failing you."

His honesty and vulnerability are exactly what I need to hear, and I'm so glad he was truthful. I press my lips to the corner of his mouth. "I love you, Ryan James, and I already love this baby." I take his hand, placing it over the smooth planes of my stomach. "And while I didn't plan on having kids this young, I can't be unhappy about it. It's a little baby." My grin expands. "A little miracle from heaven. A little piece of you and a little piece of me." Tears well in my eyes, but this time they're happy tears. "Once you are with me in this, we'll figure it out as we go along. That's all I ask of you, Ryan. Just be with me. Work through the highs and lows with me."

He rubs his hand back and forth across my stomach. "I can do that."

I sense he's holding back. "Please say what's on your mind."

He looks up at me, gulping. "You're so young, Summer. I can't help feeling selfish for wanting you, and now, everything you dreamed of for your future has changed in an instant, and I feel responsible for that."

"Stop." I press a kiss to his lips. "We made this baby together. You didn't force me into anything, and plans can be adapted."

"I'll take on the bulk of the childcare so you can continue with your studies," he says, still rubbing my belly. "Derrick has already taken on more managerial responsibility, so him and Austin can manage the daytime between them, and I can cover at night once you get home from school."

"I can drop the theater and cut out a couple of optional electives," I add, excitement mingling with the blood flowing in my veins. "And I'm sure my mom will help as much as she can."

Ryan's face turns a sickly shade of green, and I can't help giggling.

"Oh, boy. I'd totally forgotten about telling my family. If you think that was bad with Austin…" Oh shit. He has no idea what he's in for with Dad and my other brothers. He pulls out his cell. "What are you doing?"

"Looking for a store in Newark that sells full body armor."

"Good thinking," I immediately agree, giggling again, because there's no denying he'll need it.

We make the drive to Bridgeville early Sunday morning and I have never seen Ryan look so nervous. His knee jerks off the floor the entire trip, and he's gripping the steering wheel so tight it's a wonder he has any blood flowing to his fingers.

"You're sure Austin has said nothing to them?" he asks me as we breach the town perimeter.

"He promised he hasn't said a word. He knows he owes me for the way he reacted last week." I pat his hand. "Try not to worry. I already told Mom you were my boyfriend, so at least that's not a shock, and I should be able to get her on our side quick. She'll help me protect you."

"Not funny, Summer," he grits out as little beads of sweat form on his brow.

"At least they already know you," I supply, trying to help ease his anxiety. "That helps."

He snorts. "I'm not sure if that's a good thing or a bad thing."

"It's a good thing," I reassure him. "They know you're a good guy."

He looks skeptical. "I hope you're right."

Ryan looks like he's about to vomit as he pulls the SUV to a halt outside my parent's farmhouse. I fix my off-the-shoulder sweater, slip on my heels, and slick gloss on my lips. I tried harder with my appearance today, deliberately wearing more makeup than usual and wearing a smart sweater with skinny jeans and heels. Ryan's not the only one who's nervous, and looking good helps my confidence. Plus, I wanted to convey maturity with my look, so I avoided my usual Converse and casual clothes.

Ryan opens my door, helping me out. I place my hands on his shoulders and stretch up to kiss him. "I love you, and no matter what happens here today, it's you, me, and the baby that matters. They're bound to be shocked, but I know my family, and they'll support us. It might take a little while to process, but they'll be okay with this. Trust me."

He rests his forehead on mine. "I do, baby. I really do. I just don't want to mess anything up. I want them to see I'll love and protect you both. That I won't let you down."

I press my body into his, angling my head and pulling his mouth to mine for a slower, longer, deeper kiss.

"Ahem." A loud throat clearing has us pulling away, and I look up at my brother Charlie, meeting his scowl with a wide grin.

"Big brother, Charlie. How are you?" I go on an immediate charm offensive as I walk up the steps toward him. Ryan grabs the gifts for my parents from the back seat, following behind me.

"Seriously, Summer?" Charlie grumbles as he pulls me into a bear hug. "I know I warned you off the horny frat boys, but he's almost old enough to be your dad."

"Don't talk crap, man," Ryan retorts, narrowing his eyes at my brother. "I was only eight when she was born."

"Not a medical improbability," Charlie argues, and I jump in before this thing escalates.

"Don't be an old fuddy-duddy." I thump him in the arm. "Age is irrelevant. I'm an adult. Ryan's an adult." I snake my arm around Ryan's waist. "We love each other, and there's no law that says we can't be in a relationship."

Charlie's jaw hangs open, and his eyes pop wide at the mention of love. I close his mouth with a carefully placed finger under his chin while ushering Ryan into the house. "That fish out of water look is *not* attractive on you."

"Is that my princess?" Dad calls out as our footsteps echo along the hardwood floors.

"Hey, Daddy." I bound into the kitchen, wrapping my arms around my dad from behind.

"Hello again, Ryan," Mom says, welcoming him with a warm smile.

"It's nice to see you again, Mrs. Petersen," Ryan politely replies, handing her the large box of chocolates from that expensive handmade place she loves. "These are for you."

"You shouldn't have." She kisses his cheek, accepting the gift. "My lips thank you. My hips not so much," she teases, setting the box down on the counter and looping her arm through his.

"And this is for you, sir," Ryan says, looking my father square in the eye as he hands over the gift-slash-bribe.

Dad pulls his glasses down from his head, inspecting the label on the special edition bottle of whiskey Ryan picked up for him. "Very nice, son." He pats Ryan on the shoulder. "We'll sample that after dinner," he adds with a wink.

Ryan grimaces. "I'll take a rain check. I'm driving."

"I can drive back," I say with a shrug.

"Only if it's not late. I don't want you driving in the dark."

My heart swells with love like it has all week as Ryan fussed over me, running me nightly baths, driving me to and from classes and the theater, cooking me dinner. He even got up earlier than necessary to fix me a proper breakfast. And he came with me to the Ob-gyn, where my pregnancy was officially confirmed, asking questions while I sat there in a bit of a daze.

Mom smiles at me, and I grin back just as my other brother Marc steps into the kitchen. "Marky Mark!" I rush to my brother, throwing myself into his arms. "I didn't know you'd be here!"

"I flew home for the weekend, especially to see you," he says, enveloping me in his arms. "It's been too long, Sum."

It's been months since we were together. Marc recently got a promotion at the investment banking firm he works for in New York, and he's been working flat out with hardly any free time.

"I'm glad you're here." I slip out of his arms, casting a glance over my shoulder at Ryan. He's sweating bullets, and I feel for him. I grab his hand, pulling him over to Marc as he's the only one in the family he hasn't met before. "This is my boyfriend, Ryan." Marc's expression is carefully impassive as he gives Ryan the once-over. "Be nice to him," I plead. "He's important."

Marc quirks a brow in question, amusement teasing the corners of his mouth.

"They're in *love*," Charlie cuts in, teasing, as he swipes a bread roll from the basket in the center of the table.

"Well, I think it's wonderful," Mom says, pulling out a chair for Ryan. "And Austin's known Ryan a long time, so he's hardly a stranger."

Ryan helps me into the seat before claiming another chair beside me. Mom just beams at him like he hung the stars in the night sky. I had a feeling she'd be easy to win over, but I'm still not entirely sure how she'll take the baby news. Even though it might not be a good idea, we're waiting until after we've eaten to tell them about my pregnancy.

Hopefully, everyone will keep their food down.

"Speaking of Austin, why isn't he here?" Marc asks.

"He's working," Ryan supplies. "We rarely get to take time off at the same time." It's not a lie, per se, but the truth is, Austin has barely spoken to Ryan all week and things are tense at home and at their co-owned place of work.

Ryan has tried talking to him, but he refuses to listen to a word he has to say. The tension is unbearable, and I've tried talking to Austin too, but he's furious with Ryan, and nothing I say makes a difference. Miley asked me to back down, telling me she's working on bringing him around, and I've faith she can succeed where we've failed.

She has been amazingly supportive since the news broke, and nonjudgmental, and it only makes me love her more. If Austin doesn't marry her, I might just turn gay for her.

"Hmm." Charlie bites off the crust of his roll, slowly chewing as he watches me and Ryan. "What does Austin think of your relationship?"

Ryan's shoulders stiffen, and I reach for his hand, squeezing it in what I hope is a comforting gesture. "Austin's being a complete ass," I honestly admit. "Although that's partly our fault because we didn't tell him we were seeing one another until it got serious."

"It's my fault," Ryan cuts in. "I should've told him from the outset."

"Austin can blow smoke up my ass," Mom declares, and my body rumbles with laughter as Ryan gawps at her. "I haven't set eyes on his girl yet, and they're together seven months!" she exclaims. "He's in no position to criticize." She squeezes Ryan's shoulders. "Don't you worry about my stubborn eldest son. He'll calm down soon. He just doesn't enjoy being kept in the dark about anything."

"Truth," I add, nodding. "We planned this surprise party for his sixteenth birthday, and he got so mad," I tell Ryan, chuckling. "All he did was grumble all night we hadn't invited the right people, hadn't ordered the right food. Yada yada." I grab two rolls from the basket, handing one to Ryan.

"And it was all for the sake of complaining," Mom agrees, setting a plate piled high with food in front of Ryan. "Because he loved every minute of that party. He just hated the fact he knew nothing about it beforehand."

Thankfully, the conversation moves off us, and my brothers don't grill Ryan *too* much, while we all tuck into the gorgeous dinner Mom prepared, and it's going better than I expected. However, Ryan is still stiff as a brick beside me, and now we've finished eating, I want to get this over and done with.

I squeeze his hand, and he squeezes back, and we look at one another, silently communicating with our eyes. We argued on the way here over who would be the one to announce our news.

Ryan wanted to do it.

He feels it's his responsibility.

But this is my family, and I want to be the one to tell them.

We eventually compromised, agreeing I'd tell my family today, and he'll break the news to the rest of his family next weekend when we are at his parents' house for dinner.

We already told Gabby and Slater, because we needed advice on what to ask at our Ob-gyn appointment, and Ryan's sister was the perfect person to confide in. They were wonderful too, and very supportive, offering their congratulations and help in whatever way they can.

I clear my throat. "So, I have news I'd like to share." My gaze roams the table. Charlie's eyes have already narrowed in suspicion, but the rest of them look curious.

Rip the Band-Aid, Summer.

This is even harder than I imagined, and I gulp over the clump of nerves clogging my throat. Ryan squeezes my hand again, sliding his free arm around my shoulders in a blatant show of support. "I'm pregnant," I blurt before my nerve fails me.

"Oh, my fucking God." That's Charlie. "I knew it!" He all but growls at Ryan.

"Are you suddenly psychic?" I question, raising a brow.

"I wish," he snaps. "Then I could've predicted this and warned Austin to keep this douche away from you."

"He's not a douche! And I won't sit here and listen to you hating on him. We have done nothing wrong!"

"Except forget to use condoms it seems," Charlie continues.

"I'm on the damn pill!" I yell as Ryan pulls me closer into his side. "And unplanned accidental pregnancies happen to lots of women!"

"You're still a kid!" Charlie bites back.

Tears stab my eyes as my brother pins Ryan with a hateful expression. "Stop it! Just stop." Tears leak out of my eyes, and a dense weight settles on my chest.

"I know you're upset," Ryan says, ignoring protocol and pulling me down onto his lap. His arms wrap around me, taking the edge off my anxiety. "But you've no right to speak to your sister like that. And if you won't keep a civil tongue, we'll be leaving because I'm not having Summer upset. The stress isn't good for her or the baby."

"What are your intentions toward my daughter, Mr. James," Dad asks, leaning his elbows on the table. Clear shock is visible on his weather-beaten face, and I lose control of my tenuous emotions. I hate thinking I've disappointed him.

I bury my face in Ryan's neck, trying to stifle my sobs. Damn pregnancy hormones already have me in an emotional tailspin.

"I love Summer, and I plan to raise this child with her. I've already looked around for an apartment for the three of us, and my work situation is flexible, so I'll be able to mind the baby while Summer continues her undergraduate program. The gym is doing well, and I can provide for both of them." He straightens his spine. "I assure you I'm going nowhere."

"And what about long-term?" Dad asks.

"We're not together that long, but I already know Summer is the woman I want to spend the rest of my life with," he says, earning a shocked gasp from me. We haven't once discussed marriage, and I can't say it's crossed my mind because I'm still trying to come to terms with the baby bomb.

He drops a loving kiss to the top of my head. "But I know Summer is young, and I don't want to clip her wings, so your daughter will call the shots. I'm happy to go along with whatever she wants because I just want her to be happy."

I completely break down then, sobbing hysterical, happy tears.

"Sweetheart." Concern is laced in Ryan's tone as he gently lifts my head up. "Don't cry."

"Happy tears," I mumble, sniveling as I wipe my hand across my snotty nose and under my red eyes.

"Attractive, Sum," Marc says, speaking up for the first time. "It must be love if Ryan is still here," he quips, and I appreciate he's trying to reduce the thick tension in the air.

Ryan hands me a tissue from the supply he's started keeping in his jeans pocket for this very reason. "Your sister is always beautiful to me, inside and out. She's the most amazing person I've ever had the privilege to know."

That sets me off again, and everyone looks at me with a hefty dose of concern. I bat my hands in the air, half laughing, half crying. "It's just my hormones. Ignore me."

Silence descends for a few beats, and I stare at Ryan, trying to gauge his mood. He looks more relaxed now we have distributed the news.

"Very well," Dad says, reaching across and shaking Ryan's hand. "All I ask is that you take care of my daughter and our grandchild and you've assured me you will." His voice sounds a little choked and I'm struggling to hold my tears at bay again.

Seriously, pregnancy hormones are no joke.

"How far along are you?" Mom asks, genuine concern stretched across her face.

"The doctor thinks about four weeks," Ryan answers when he spots my trembling lower lip. "Although we won't know for sure until our hospital appointment."

"So, a May or June baby then, most likely," Mom muses. "That timing is great. You'll just be finishing freshman year, and if you like, you can come home for the summer, or the first few weeks, at least."

"Thanks, Mom. We haven't thought that far ahead yet, but we appreciate the offer."

"Anything you need, honey. You only have to ask."

"Let's all join hands around the campfire and sing *Kumbaya*, why don't we," Charlie grits out. "And pretend that it's fucking fine that my eighteen-year-old sister got knocked up by a pedo."

"That is enough, Charles," Mom demands, her jaw tightening. "And you will apologize to Ryan for that comment."

"The hell I will." He stands abruptly, slamming his chair back, and it knocks to the ground. Rounding the table, he looks down at me. "This shouldn't have happened to you, Summer. You had such big plans."

"A baby is God's blessing," Mom says, trying to be helpful, but it's the worst thing to tell Charlie.

"A baby will ruin her fucking life, Mom!"

"My sister had a baby at nineteen," Ryan supplies, and I'm in awe of how calmly he's speaking after the horrible comment my brother just made. "And she discovered her boyfriend was dying at the same time. I remember feeling similar things, but the truth is, my nephew Billy is the best thing to happen to my sister, and our family wouldn't be the same without him. I get that this is a shock, and it's not what I would've wanted for Summer either, but I won't sit here and say I'm unhappy because I know Summer will make a fantastic mother, and a smart woman once told me things happen for a reason, and I fully buy into that now."

I remember telling him that, not realizing how prophetic it would be. And as Ryan smiles at me—a sincere, confident, happy smile—I see the truth of his statement written all over his face.

CHAPTER 23
Ryan

"I THOUGHT AUSTIN was the biggest drama queen in your family," I joke as we make the trip back home later that evening, "but Charlie is a piece of work." He stormed off after my comment about Gabby and didn't return, not even to say goodbye to his pregnant sister. I feel bad for Summer that two of her three brothers are acting like idiots. And, it's like I said, I understand it, to a point. But you only need to look at her to see how emotional she is. Surely, they could set aside their feelings about me to support their little sister. That's what I did, when I was in their shoes, and I processed everything in the background in my own time.

"Honestly, Charlie's always been prone to dramatics, so his reaction isn't that unexpected. He'll stew for a few days and then snap out of his head, call me up, and beg for forgiveness. It's Austin I'm most disappointed with, because he's still keeping you at arm's length."

"It's only been a week. It'll all work out." I say what she needs to hear because she's been under enough stress today, but I don't know if Austin will ever forgive me.

Another couple weeks pass by, and Austin is still cold-shouldering me. It's making working together an absolute misery, and I've decided we're having it out today whether he likes it or not. I can't continue like this, and if he won't meet me halfway, we need to have a serious discussion over what to do with our business. Whether he buys me out or I buy him out. I don't want it to come to that, but I'm not prepared to put up with this stress every day for the rest of my life, and business partners can't run a company together if they're barely talking.

I call him to my office on the pretext of reviewing the new marketing plan the PR firm emailed over. He's wearing the same intolerant look that's been on his face for the last three weeks when he drops into the chair in front of my desk, folding his arms sternly across his chest. I get up and lock the door so we're not interrupted. He straightens up, eyeing me warily, instantly realizing I've hijacked this meeting.

"I want to talk about Summer."

"Well, I don't," he predictably barks back.

"You've made that perfectly clear. But the longer this goes unsaid, the more it hurts Summer. And this is *really* hurting her, Austin. She's crying most every night because we're not speaking. We need to work this out because we both love her."

He grinds his teeth, flashing me a dark look. "I asked one thing of you, James. One Goddamned thing. Not to lay a finger on her, and you just couldn't help yourself," he snarls.

I lean forward with my elbows on the desk, slanting him an earnest look. "I tried to stay away from her, I swear it. And I did at the start, but I couldn't stop myself from falling for her. Your sister is an amazing person and so easy to love."

"How do I know you won't let her down?" he asks, crossing one leg over his knee.

"Because I give you my word. I'm in this for the long haul, Austin, and I told your father that." His brows climb to his hairline. "I'd marry Summer tomorrow, but I'm respectful of her age and her dreams, and I've already told her she's setting the agenda."

He taps his fingers off the arm of the chair. "Do you mean that? You want to marry her?"

"I do." I wet my dry lips. "Although I haven't mentioned it to her, as I don't want to freak her out, and she's enough on her plate."

I stare absently at the wall as I work out how to best explain it. I eyeball Austin. "When I was with Myndi, I thought I was in love, but I know now it wasn't real love because the way I feel about your sister, after only a couple months, is ten thousand times more than I felt for my ex."

I get up, walk around, and prop my butt against the edge of the desk, shooting him an earnest look. "I'm so fucking sorry I didn't tell you sooner. There were good reasons, but I still should've told you."

"I get so mad every time I think about you two sneaking around and lying behind my back." His nostrils flare. "And I can't even think about that night I heard her in your room. I'll have nightmares for the rest of my life." A shudder works its way through him, and he squeezes his eyes tight.

"I can relate. I've heard Slate with Gabby occasionally, and it turns me into a raging bull. Every damn time, I want to drag his ass out and beat him bloody."

Austin's eyes blink open, and his lips twitch. "Man, you've no idea how many ways I've imagined killing you."

"Wow. Thanks for that, buddy."

He sighs, dragging a hand through his hair. "Look, I know I've been stubborn about this."

That's putting it mildly.

"But the betrayal stung, you know. And I'm worried about Summer. This is a lot of responsibility on her young shoulders."

"She's tougher and stronger than you and Charlie seem to think." I'm getting fed up of their bullshit in that regard.

"I know. I just don't want to see her life getting derailed."

"If you talk to her, you'll see she doesn't feel like that. We've discussed this at length. Summer was born to be a mom. She's amazing with kids, and she'll be a natural. And I'll do my utmost to give her everything her heart desires."

Austin stares at me, and then he stands, slapping me on the back in an unexpected move. "See you do."

"Are we good?"

He nods. "Yeah, and, look, I'm sorry for the things I said about you. That was a low blow, and I take it back."

"What about the ass kicking I let you give me?" I inquire, raising a brow.

"Let, my ass," he mumbles, and I give him that one. "Fucked if I'm ever apologizing for that. You deserved it, and you know it."

"I'm so happy you and Austin made up. My heart is singing a symphony," Summer croons later that night when we're lying in bed.

"You know what part of my body's rocking a symphony, babe?" I angle my hips into her side, stabbing her with my erection.

"You are almost as insatiable as me," she jokes, instantly whipping her nightie up over her head.

I slide my hands up her stomach, cupping her fuller breasts. "There's no almost about it. Fuck, babe. I love your bigger tits. If this is what you're like at seven weeks pregnant they'll be like giant melons by the time you're ready to deliver the little munchkin." I nuzzle my face into her breasts, loving the feel of her smooth, silky skin against the stubble on my chin.

"I knew you only wanted me for my body." She smirks as she climbs on top of me, lowering herself perfectly over my hard length.

We both groan, but before she moves, I flip her underneath me, leaning down to suck on her lower lip. "I want to make love to you."

"Show me what you got, stud," she says, pushing her hips up as her hands claw at my bare ass. "But don't go too slow. I need it hard."

"Your wish is my command." I alternate between driving into her in long, slow, seductive strokes and slapping her with my cock as I slam in and out at a vicious pace. Sweat glides down my back as I lift her legs up over my shoulder when she urges me to go faster and harder. I pound into her, quickly losing control, loving the feel of her insides tightly gripping my cock, and the way she tilts her hips up to meet my every thrust.

I gently cover her mouth with my hand when her orgasm hits, stifling her loud moans. After I've released inside her, we both collapse in a sweaty heap of tangled limbs. "Baby, you really need to learn to be quieter, at least until Austin moves out properly, because he's already imagining ways to murder me, and your cries of pleasure are not helping my cause."

"Well, stop fucking me so thoroughly then," she says, matter-of-factly. "It was nice of him to let us take this place," she adds, quickly changing the subject.

"He spends most of his time at Miley's anyway, but, yeah, it saves us having to look for another place." We've already decided we're converting Austin's bedroom into the nursery, and Summer has been scouring Pinterest looking at boards and color schemes and other shit.

"Ryan."

I jerk my head to the side at the noticeable change in her tone, instantly on alert. "Yeah?"

"Are you happy?"

Such a basic question, but if you'd asked me before I met Summer the answer would've been complicated. But not now. Now the answer is simple. I wrap my arms around her, kissing her deeply. "I'm happier than I've ever been. I love you." I slide my lips down her body, stopping to kiss her belly. "And I love you too, little munchkin."

I should've known my happiness would be short-lived.

"This is a fucking nightmare," I tell Austin when we finally get a minute alone. For the last few hours, we've been locked in our conference room at the gym with the local cops and our attorney. They have arrested one of our trainers, Matthias, on suspicion of sexually assaulting a female client, on the premises, one night late last week. We're co-operating as best we can.

"You think he did it?" Austin asks, as we stroll down the hallway toward our adjoining offices.

"I've had to speak to him a couple times about being too 'handsy' with some clients, not that that means he's guilty." I rub a tense spot between my brows. "I don't know."

"I thought they were dating, and I've a feeling there's more to this than meets the eye."

"Maybe. Still doesn't change things. We need to discuss how to handle it. We want none of our female clients thinking they're unsafe here."

"We'll have to fire him," Austin says, in sync with my train of thought, following me into my office.

"I know." I grab my cell off my desk where I'd left it. "Which'll suck if he's innocent." I punch in my code and the sight of dozens of missed calls and texts from Summer and Miley has alarm bells blaring in my ears. "Fuck."

"What?" Austin picks up on the anxiety in my tone, as I speed dial Summer.

"I've a bunch of missed calls from your sister and your girlfriend." Austin races out of the room before I've even finished my statement, returning a few seconds later with his cell in hand, while I listen to Summer's automated response.

I swipe my finger over the last text from Miley, and all the blood drains from my face.

"We need to get to the hospital," Austin says, with his cell pressed to his ear, but I'm already one step ahead of him, keys in hand, grabbing my jacket from the back of my chair.

I toss the keys to him. "You drive. I'm likely to crash." I call Derrick while we're dashing from the building, explaining it's a medical emergency, asking him to offer our apologies to the men waiting for us in the conference room and to manage the gym in our absence.

"Do your messages say anything specific?" I ask Austin as we climb into the SUV.

"No. Just that Summer was in the hospital and you needed to get there ASAP." He wastes no time flooring it out of the parking lot.

I cradle my head in my hands as he drives, offering prayers even though I haven't prayed since I was a kid. I've a horrible feeling that history is repeating itself, and my stomach churns so violently I think I might puke. Summer's only eight weeks pregnant, and we haven't even seen our baby on the ultrasound. Just hearing his or her little heartbeat at the Ob-gyn's office that time was enough to cement my love for my unborn child. If anything happens to Summer or our little munchkin, I'll die.

"Hang in there, man." Austin lands a hand briefly on my back. "We don't know what it is yet, and Summer will need us to be strong."

Neither of us articulate our thoughts, but I know we're both thinking the same thing.

We race through the hospital corridors toward the maternity section, and Miley jumps up to greet us the second we burst through the double doors. She runs toward Austin, sobbing, and something inherent dies inside me. I slam to a halt, air whooshing through my ears, my heart pounding in my chest. Miley flings herself into Austin's arms, tears pumping out of her eyes.

"Miley," I croak. "Is Summer—" I lose my voice, and my chest heaves painfully.

"She's okay," Miley sobs. "But she lost the baby."

I stagger backward, my spine slamming into the wall, but I barely feel it. The most intense pressure weighs down on my chest, and I'm struggling to breathe. I squeeze my eyes shut, trying to hold my tears in, but I'm fighting a losing battle, and tears roll down my face as the enormity of the situation hits me full force.

Austin grabs me to him, his shoulders shaking with emotion. My mind churns, my emotions veering all over the place. The pain in my heart is unbearable.

This is all my fault. I knew at the outset; I would hurt Summer, but I still selfishly claimed her.

She'll probably hate me now.

Although I'll take it.

I'll take all the pain if it means she comes out of this intact.

CHAPTER 24
Summer

THE DOOR CREAKS as it opens, and Ryan enters the room. His eyes are bloodshot and red-rimmed, and he looks how I feel. "Ryan!" I cry, sitting up in the bed and opening my arms for him. He enfolds me in his strong embrace, and the dam breaks.

I was trying to be brave, fighting tears as Miley burst out crying when the doctor confirmed I'd had a miscarriage. But I can't hold it in any longer, and I sob on Ryan's shoulder, soaking his shirt. His body shudders under my embrace, and I'm not surprised when I pull back and see his damp cheeks. "Our baby is gone," I wail, and the pain in my heart is so intense I wonder if this is what it feels like right before you have a heart attack.

"I'm so sorry, sweetheart." Ryan cradles me in his arms. "I'm so, so, sorry I let you down."

"I was so scared," I whisper, sobbing as tears continue to pour from my eyes. "I called you nonstop, but when I couldn't reach you or Austin, I called Miley. She hadn't left for her folks' place yet, so she came straight to campus and brought me here." Thanksgiving is only a few days away, and Miley was planning on spending it with her parents.

"Thank God, she was there for you, and I'll never forgive myself that you went through this alone. We had an emergency at the gym, and we were locked in meetings all morning. I'd stupidly left my cell in my office." He squeezes me tight, pressing a fierce kiss to my temple. "I'm sorry, Summer. I'm so incredibly sorry."

"It's okay." I run my fingers through his hair. "It's not your fault." Spasms cramp my stomach, and I wince, drawing deep breaths.

"What's wrong?" Ryan's entire body has tensed up.

"Cramping," I pant, breathing heavily, trying my best to ignore the slicing pain twisting my insides into painful knots. I draw long breaths, in and out, just like the nurse showed me. "Doctor said it's normal," I add, watching the layer of panic intensify on his face. The pain passes a couple minutes later although I know it's only a temporary reprieve. "I'm fine now." I cup one side of his face, hating to see him hurting so much.

A muscle clenches in his jaw. "What happened? And what did the doctor say?"

"I went to the bathroom after my first class because I had terrible cramps, and it worried me. When I noticed blood on my panties, I completely panicked, and I couldn't stop shaking and crying. It took three attempts to place the first call to you my fingers were trembling so badly."

I curl my fingers into his hair, biting down on my lower lip. Gently, he removes my teeth before it breaks skin.

"When I got here, they hooked me up to an ultrasound, and I knew instantly the baby was gone because I couldn't hear his heartbeat." Sobs overtake me again, and I collapse into Ryan's chest, fisting his shirt as piercing cries ring out in the sterile room. He rubs a hand up and down my back until my cries die out. I'm exhausted, clinging to him, in a weird alert-dazed state. My voice is monotone as I continue explaining. "The doctor said, unfortunately, lots of women experience miscarriages with their first pregnancy. I'm going into surgery soon to have a D and C so they can remove…" I burst out crying again, unable to verbalize it.

"Fuck, Summer. I'm so sorry." Ryan is crying again too. I know because I feel his wet tears hitting the side of my forehead.

The doctor chooses that moment to enter the room, offering us sympathetic looks. Ryan introduces himself, still keeping me locked in his embrace. "Is there any internal damage to Summer?" he asks with concern etched across his face. "She'll be able to have more kids, right?"

The doctor clutches the clipboard in his hand to his chest. "There's no internal damage, and Summer will most likely have no issue conceiving or bringing a pregnancy to full term in the future. In situations like this, we always run a set of routine tests to determine there are no genetic defaults or issues. Ninety-nine percent of the time, we find no explanation. The rate of miscarriage is much higher with first-time pregnancies."

He tilts his head to the side. "I know that's not much comfort, but provided nothing shows up in the tests, you should have normal pregnancies in the future," he says before advising that a nursing team will be with me shortly to bring me to the operating room. "I'm sorry for your loss," he adds before exiting the room.

Ryan and I cling wordlessly to one another until it's time for me to go to surgery. He kisses me on the lips before I leave promising he'll be here waiting when I get out.

The days after are some of the hardest of my life. I'm sad, and I can't stop crying. I can barely summon the strength to get out of bed. I've never felt this way before, and I don't know how to handle it. Both our families rally around, dropping by to offer support, but, honestly, I just want to be alone with Ryan. To mourn our loss together.

Austin and Derrick take control of the gym, ensuring Ryan is always with me. The doctor advised me to stay home and rest for at least three days, and I'm under strict instructions not to do anything strenuous. So, we spend our days cuddling on the couch watching back-to-back movies or binge-watching the latest Netflix shows.

After my crying jaunt in the hospital, and those first couple days back home, I'm unbelievably numb now. Maybe I cried myself out. Used up eighteen years' worth of tears in one go.

Now, I feel empty inside.

Hollow in more ways than one.

Without even realizing it, my hand keeps gravitating to my barren stomach. When I notice Ryan noticing, and the familiar anguish washing over his face, I remove my hand, but it keeps happening, like an invisible force wants to remind me of my loss at every conceivable moment.

Both of us lie awake for hours at night, pretending to one another that we're asleep as we suffer in silence. We haven't had sex. The doctor advised abstaining for a few days, but I've zero desire to have sex, anyway. It's as if my life force died the instant my baby's did.

The news reaches Hannah, and she drops by laden down with flowers and apologies. I'm grateful she's extended an olive branch but too numb to do more than acknowledge her gesture.

I can't fault Ryan for how well he's cared for me these past few days, but when the day comes for him to return to work, I silently admit to feeling relieved.

Things are… different between us.

I don't know how other couples deal with traumatic events, but we're struggling to find the right words to communicate. I don't want to keep talking about it, because it's too painful, but going on with our lives and having casual conversations about mundane things seems like an insult to our little munchkin's memory.

The grief only intensifies after we hold a small memorial service in the graveyard back home. We have no remains to bury, but we installed a little headstone and had a priest say a few prayers. Both our families attended, but I was numb during the whole thing, and my body felt like a block of ice in Ryan's arms.

We all go back to our farmhouse after the service, and I'm not surprised to see my parents getting on so well with Ryan's parents—both sets of grandparents bonding over their loss.

"Can I talk to you for a minute?" Charlie asks, looming over me as I sit on the couch, tucked under Ryan's protective arm.

"Sure." My voice is devoid of emotion.

"In private." His eyes dart to Ryan.

"Whatever you want to say to Summer will be said in front of me or not at all," Ryan says, holding me tighter to his side. "I won't have you upsetting her."

"That's the last thing I want," Charlie meekly replies. "And you can come. I guess you need to hear it too."

We go upstairs to my old bedroom. I sit on the bed with Ryan beside me. Charlie crouches down in front of me. "I owe you a big apology," he says, reaching out and taking my hands. "I'm so sorry for all the hurtful things I said the day you told us about your pregnancy. I planned to come to the city to apologize, because I knew I was out of line, but I never had time to before…"

"Before I lost the baby," I confirm.

"I'm so sorry, Summer."

"Are you?" I question, but there's no malice in my tone. You'd have to feel something to invoke such strong emotion, and I feel dead inside. "You didn't want me to have this baby, anyway."

"Of course, I'm sorry! And I didn't want for this to happen." Air expels from his mouth in frustration. "I don't blame you for thinking that, but I hate you're hurting. I'm so sorry you lost your baby. I genuinely am." He stands, offering his hand to Ryan. "And I'm sorry I was so judgmental. I never should've said the things I said."

"Forget about it," Ryan says, accepting his handshake.

"I forgive you," I whisper to my brother, because I don't want to be estranged from him any longer.

Life is too short.

I've just learned that lesson the hard way.

I lean my head on Ryan's shoulder, suddenly drained. He doesn't hesitate to hold me tight, and I siphon some of his warmth and his strength hoping it'll help get me through the weeks, and months ahead.

Time ceases to have much meaning. I get up, eat breakfast, go to my classes and rehearsal, do my shifts at the gym, and attend study sessions in the library, jam-packing my day so I collapse into bed at night, exhausted, hoping tonight will be the night I stop dreaming about things that have been stolen from me. But no matter how far I push myself, nothing works. I still toss and turn most nights, snatching an hour's sleep here and there, but it's never enough.

I'm yawning as I stand in front of the mirror staring at my pallid reflection. I look like shit. There are massive bags under my eyes, my lips are dry and cracked, and my skin lacks vitality. I'm like a shell of a person, and I know I can't continue like this.

"Are you okay?" Ryan asks from his position in the doorway. He's holding onto the top of the door, offering a nice view of his impressive biceps and chest, and an inkling of desire stirs in my loins for the first time in weeks.

"I think we'll be adding that to your epitaph too," I joke, in reference to how many times he asks me that question. I pad toward him in my towel, beads of moisture still clinging to my skin from the shower, and I rest my head on his chest, circling my arms around his waist. "I'm tired of feeling sad all the time," I admit, and it's the first real honesty I've given him since the day in the hospital. I've struggled to talk to him about my feelings which is most unlike me, but then I've never dealt with anything like this before. He's shut himself off as well, and I realize, in this moment, that I don't want to lose him too.

"Me too," he quietly says, enfolding his massive arms around me.

"Let's take the day off," I suggest, looking up at him with pleading eyes. "Let's make love and then go out and do something together."

He weaves his fingers through my hair, slanting me an apologetic look. "I can show up late, but I can't take the full day off. We're firing Matthias today and our attorney is attending the meeting. It's important I'm there." My heart sinks when I recognize he's no clue of the importance of the date. "I'm sorry, baby. What about tomorrow? We can spend the day together before we both head home for the Christmas break."

"Sure." I plaster a fake smile on my face and wriggle out of his grasp, but he hauls me back instantly.

"We can still go back to bed for a couple hours." His eyes darken with lust as his hand climbs up my bare thigh, his fingers sweeping across my pussy. The look he pins me with is hot as fuck, but the urge has already deserted me, blanketed by a fresh layer of sadness.

"I can't miss two days of classes," I lie, reaching up to peck his lips. "Rain check later tonight?" I uphold my cheery expression, feeling like pure shit when a dejected look appears on his face.

"No problem, babe." He moves past me, switching the shower on. "Have a good day."

As I pull the door shut behind me, I can't help wondering if it's metaphorical.

CHAPTER 25
Ryan

"FUCK, FUCK, FUCK!" I exclaim, banging my head against the wall when it finally clicks with me.

"What the hell, man?" Austin asks, his brow furrowing.

"Summer asked me to take the day off today, and I'm a dumbass because I didn't realize why until now." Austin looks as confused as me. "It's one month today since we lost the baby," I explain.

"Shit."

I'm sick to my stomach. "I can't believe I forgot. I feel like a complete shit."

"Hey, don't be too hard on yourself, man." Austin clamps a hand on my shoulder. "I know this has been rough for you too."

A lump the size of a bus wedges in my throat, as I nod. I'm trying so hard to stay strong for Summer, but I'm cut up on the inside too. Everything I never realized I wanted was in arm's reach until it was snatched away. Guilt churns with sorrow in my gut every day, and it's a miracle I can get out of bed most mornings.

There's no handbook when something like this happens, and I feel like I'm drowning in a pool of failure. Summer and I grow more distant every day. Sure, she sleeps in my arms, but she may as well be invisible. I hate that her light has faded, and I feel wholly responsible. I want to erase her sadness and openly love her, but I'm struggling with the how. We haven't had sex, or shared intimacy other than hugs or kisses, since she miscarried, and I miss feeling close to her. I don't know if I should be the one to initiate it or just wait until she's ready. So, I take care of her in other ways, hoping it demonstrates how much I still love her.

It elated me this morning when she suggested we make love, but her subsequent rejection tore more strips off my fragile heart. Now I know why she reconsidered.

Before we lost the baby, Summer would've told me outright the significance of today. But that's another closeness we've lost. We don't talk like we used to, and I'm scared I'm losing her.

Maybe she's no longer interested.

I hate even thinking this, but the truth is there's nothing tying her to me now.

Perhaps she's realized that.

Perhaps she's realized that she'd rather be with a guy her own age. Someone with considerably less baggage.

But I don't know, because we haven't properly talked since the miscarriage.

Partly that's my fault, because of the crippling guilt.

"Hey, where'd you go?" Austin asks, pinning me with worried eyes.

"I need to make it up to her," I say, plonking my butt in the seat and lifting the phone. "And I think I have just enough time to organize it."

A few hours later, I'm standing outside the theater waiting for Summer to exit the building. I couldn't stomach watching her rehearse with Sean, so I'd rather stay out here in the biting cold than watch his hands, or his lips, anywhere near her.

She doesn't know I'm here. I spent the late afternoon lining things up. I've booked us a table at the little Italian we've grown fond of, and I've a simple bouquet of lilies waiting for her in the car. I thought we could visit the graveyard, but they've already closed, so I'll offer to take her this weekend instead, if she wants to go.

I pat the envelope in my inside coat pocket, allowing a sliver of hope to build inside me. I'm hoping the surprise trip to Venice will bring color to my girl's cheeks again. And I think the time away will do us the world of good.

We need to live our lives again.

We'll never forget our little munchkin, but we can't wallow in grief forever.

Summer wants to travel, and she's never been out of the U.S. so I'm hoping this trip will set our relationship on a new path and remind her of all she's got to look forward to. I've also found a great grief counselor who specializes in counseling couples who've lost children, and I hope she'll agree to go to a few sessions with me, because it's fair to say we need help. The counselor was my sister's idea, and I'm glad I called her earlier.

I rub my hands together, tugging the collar of my coat up higher as the door to the theater opens and people spill out. Summer is last out, and her loud peals of laughter tickle my eardrums from here. She's with Sean, and she's doubled over, in convulsions of laughter. Didn't realize he was such a comedian, my snarly inner voice spits, as my insides contort painfully.

I'd give anything to be the one to make her laugh, but the truth is, it's been weeks since I've seen her face light up like that.

There have been zero smiles around me.

Jealousy and anger batter me from all sides as I watch them laughing and chatting, lingering by the door, reluctant to leave.

It's the slap in the face I needed.

The reality check I've been fighting every second from the instant she came into my life.

Summer should be with someone like Sean.

Someone the same age with no cares or responsibilities.

Someone who can make her forget her grief.

Not someone who reminds her of it every minute of the day.

I've been deluding myself into thinking we could turn this around.

We can't. I see that now.

She hasn't spotted me yet, so I tuck my chin down, keeping my head low, and hightail it out of there.

We spend Christmas break at home with our respective families, and the time apart helps cement my belief I'm right to end this now before I hurt her anymore. My family notices I'm withdrawn, and they try to coax me into talking, but I don't want to discuss it with anyone. I know what I have to do, and once we return to the city, I set about sticking to my guns.

I'm pacing the living room waiting for Summer to return home from classes, just anxious to get this over with now. I've practiced what I want to say. I don't want to lie to her, but if I tell her the truth, I'm afraid she'll try to talk me out of it.

I'm even more afraid that she'll agree with me.

So, I know what I need to say to make this happen.

She'll probably hate me. Austin most definitely will. But, hopefully, in time, he'll realize I loved her enough to set her free.

"Fuck, it's cold out there," Summer says, bounding into the apartment, bundled up in a puffy jacket, woolly hat, and scarf, looking adorably cute. I want to grab her into my arms and never let her go. But I can't. For once, I need to act selflessly and let her live the life she deserves.

"Why don't you take a shower to warm up, and I'll have some hot chocolate ready when you get out?" I suggest, not wanting to jump straight into this the second she gets home.

"That sounds perfect," she agrees, approaching me with a little gleam in her eye. Quick as a flash, she cups my face, welding her ice-cold hands to my skin.

I jerk back out of her reach, my skin tingling as a shiver works its way through me. "Fucking hell, Summer. Your hands are like blocks of ice."

She giggles, and I want to change my mind. There's no doubt she's turned a corner recently. Showing me glimpses of the girl I fell in love with. It hasn't escaped my notice it's happened while we've largely been apart.

Which is why breaking up with her is the right thing.

"Go shower." I kiss her forehead even though I want to kiss her lips, heading toward the kitchen to make hot chocolate before I do something stupid.

Like drag her to the bedroom.

Or revert to selfish mode and kick my plan to the curb.

"Ohmigawd, this is so good," Summer says, moaning in a way that has my dick twitching in my boxers. "I nominate you chief hot chocolate maker," she proclaims, closing her eyes and groaning as she sips on the chocolaty goodness.

My dick now salutes her at full mast, and I subtly adjust myself in my jeans before she notices.

We flippantly watch TV as she sips her hot chocolate. With her makeup-free face, hair scraped back in a tight ponytail, and the slouchy sweater, pajama pants, and fluffy socks combo she's sporting, she looks every bit the young, innocent girl she should be. I hate that her involvement with me has dulled the edges off her shine, but she'll bounce back, once she has the freedom to spread her wings. Once I'm no longer blocking the light.

I can't delay this anymore.

Turning off the TV, I turn to face her, taking her hands in mine, hoping she can't feel how badly I'm trembling. "We need to talk."

"Annndddd nothing good ever comes of starting a conversation like that," she jokes, her lips tugging up until she sees the sober expression on my face. "Oh." Her smile disappears, her eyes growing wide. "Oh." Tears well in her eyes, and I already hate myself.

"You know how special you are to me, Summer, and I wanted so badly for things to work out between us, but they're not. It has strained things between us ever since we lost the baby and—" This is the hard part. The part that will devastate her. But I have to say it, because she needs to let me go. "I think it happened for a reason. To prove that we're not right for one another after all. That there's someone better out there for you than me."

"You can't honestly believe that," she whispers as a tear creeps out of the corner of one eye.

I'm suffocating inside.

Drowning in my own lies.

Yet I push on.

"I do. You're the one that taught me to believe in that, and don't say you don't believe it now because it's been your mantra right from the start."

"You misunderstand," she says, yanking her hands from my grip and swiping angrily at the tears sliding down her face. "I still believe things happen for a reason. You think I haven't thought of this in the weeks since we lost our child? Haven't raged at God, if there is one, asking him why he took something so precious from us? Why he took away something I never even realized I wanted that badly until it was dangled under my nose?" Her voice cracks, and I sit on my hands to stop myself from pulling her into my arms.

Our inner musings were so similar. What a shame we couldn't talk to one another about it.

"Because I've done all that soul searching, and I've made my peace with it." She leans into me, and the floral scent of her shower gel swirls around me, almost choking me with renewed pain. "The time wasn't right. That's all," she says, rubbing her finger back and forth across the locket I gave her for Christmas. "And I firmly believe our time will come again, maybe when we're in the right place to start a family." She cups my face. "I'm sorry I've been so shut off. That I've given you no attention. It doesn't mean I don't love you, because I do. There aren't adequate words to describe how very much."

It's so typical of Summer to assume all the blame, but I won't let her. She has done nothing wrong. I'm the one that's made all the mistakes, right from the start. "Don't," I croak, unable to hear anymore, removing her hands from mine. "Don't make this any harder than it already is."

Her lip wobbles, and her face falls, as she realizes I'm deadly serious. My heart is fracturing behind my rib cage, and I need to get this done and get out of here before I cave.

"Why?" she whispers.

I harden my heart and force the words from my mouth. "I'm just not feeling it anymore. I'm so sorry."

Her chest heaves, and she licks her lips, fighting to keep her composure. Neither of us speak for a few minutes, and it's the worst form of torture. "Okay," she quietly says. "The agreement was we'd end it when one of us wasn't into it anymore, and I'll uphold our deal."

That deal was thrown out the window a long time ago, but if that's how she needs to handle it, I won't disagree.

I stand, pulling the duffel bag I previously packed out from behind the couch. "I've checked into a hotel. You're welcome to stay here until a dorm room becomes available. I'll cover the rent and utilities and lodge money into your bank account to cover groceries."

"I don't want your money, and I don't want to stay here. I'll go," she says, springing up from the couch with fire in her eyes.

"No way." I fold my arms and stare her out. "We may not be together anymore, but I still care about you, and you are *not leaving*. I've made this decision, so it's only right I'm the one to go."

"This is your apartment, Ryan!"

"Don't fight me on this." I sling the bag over my shoulder. "It's yours for as long as you need it."

And because I'm a glutton for punishment, I take her in my arms for a goodbye hug, holding onto her firmly before she can pull away. "I'm so sorry, Summer," I whisper in her ear. "But you'll be fine."

And as I walk away from her without another word, with pain burning a hole straight through my heart, I remind myself I'm doing this for her.

So, she can have the life she deserves.

Find someone worthy of her.

Someone who doesn't ruin everything he touches.

CHAPTER 26
Ryan – Four Months Later

MY FINGERS CLUTCH the pen, hovering over the paperwork as I experience last-minute doubts about signing on the dotted line. Dropping the pen, I lean back in my chair, rubbing my hands down my face. I know making this official is the right thing to do, but I'm still reluctant to sign. Because, even though I haven't spoken to Summer since the day I broke her heart and mine, at least here I'm comforted by the knowledge I'm breathing the same air as her.

No one knows this, but I hung out around campus and the theater company in the weeks following our split, desperate to just see her beautiful face. She quit working at the gym and moved out of the apartment almost immediately, cutting herself out of my life.

I almost went crazy without her.

Hence why I sought her out.

I made sure she never saw me. Sticking to hiding behind corners and watching her from the shadows. Until I realized my behavior was borderline stalking, and I forced myself to go cold turkey.

But, at least here in Newark, I know she's within reach if I ever grow a pair of balls and acknowledge that I made the worst decision of my life the day I walked away from her. If I ever find the courage to fix it.

With that thought swirling through my mind, I snatch the pen up and sign my messy scrawl on the new contract paperwork. Moving to manage our new gym in Dover is the right move. It was that or let Austin buy me out of the business because we can't continue to work side by side when we barely talk anymore.

I knew when I ended things so callously with Summer that Austin would never forgive me. And he hasn't. I cannot fault him for that. I deserve the animosity he's shown me these past few months. I deserve to have lost one of the best friendships I've ever had. Because I promised him I'd take care of his little sister, and in his eyes, I abandoned her to her grief too soon after she lost our baby.

I want to come clean with him. To tell him I did it for her. To set her free. To admit that I'm heartbroken and lonely and so, so lost without her in my life.

But if I do that, he might just understand, might try to talk me around, and he might just convince me.

No, removing myself from Newark, from the temptation of having Summer so close, is the right thing to do.

Stuffing the paperwork back in the envelope, I leave it on my empty desk, grabbing the box with my belongings, and walk out the door telling no one goodbye.

I've only been at the Dover gym a week when Austin pays me an unexpected visit. "What's up?" I ask, closing the door to my office after he steps inside. We're both tense, standing across from one another, neither making a move to sit down.

"Look." He rubs a hand along the back of his neck. "I hate how things were left between us, and I want to talk to you about Summer."

"Is she okay? Has something happened?" I blurt, terror caging my heart in a vise grip.

"Calm down. She's fine. It's nothing like that."

"What then?" I fold my arms across my torso, my shoulders still rigid with stress.

"Let's sit." Austin walks to the small leather couch in the corner of the room, and I trail behind him.

We sit down, and I brace my arms on my thighs, waiting him out. I don't have to wait long. "I want to level with you," he says. "No bullshit. Just cards on the table." I nod, encouraging him to go on. "You've been utterly miserable since you broke up with her. She's putting a brave face on, but I know she's hurting too. I was so fucking angry with you I didn't realize it at first. But having some distance this past week gave me time to think about things, and it doesn't add up."

He stares at me, really stares at me, as if he can see into my messed-up head. "Why did you break up with Summer? And don't feed me the same bull you fed her."

To tell the truth or continue the lie? I lean back, sighing. May as well come clean. Maybe we'll be able to salvage our friendship from the ashes. "Because I believed letting her go was in her best interests. She was so sad all the time, and it was my fault. I felt like I was holding her back. Stopping her from fulfilling her dreams. And I never want to be that selfish."

"Do you still love her?"

Pain rattles my chest and my heart aches for the girl I lost. "More than ever," I quietly admit.

He twists around, eyeballing me. "Then fight for her, Goddamn it."

"What?" I splutter, sure I must be hearing things.

"Don't let her go, or you'll end up regretting it."

I arch a brow, wondering if I've wandered into some alternate realm. "I'm not who you'd choose for her, so why would you tell me to do that."

"You *are* who I choose for her. You two were good together, and you made her happy. It's not your fault she lost the baby."

Well, I guess we'll just have to agree to disagree on that. "It's probably too late," I say, looking down at the ground.

"It's not, but if you leave it much longer, it could well be."

I jerk my head back up. "Why d'you say that?"

"That punk Justin is sniffing around. He's asked her to transfer to Oregon State next year to be with him. He's a big deal to the Beavers, and I know he'll make it happen."

"So, you just want me to get back with Summer to stop her from moving across the country?" I surmise, anger bristling under my skin.

"Fuck, no!" Austin sits up straighter, scrubbing a hand over his chin. "Truth is, I've been a shitty friend and a shitty brother. And you might as well add a hypocrite to the mix. My background with chicks wasn't any cleaner than yours, but I still gave you crap. And—" He blows air out of his mouth. "And I'm so fucking sorry, man. Sorry for being a sanctimonious, stubborn prick. If I wasn't all up in my head, I would've realized the truth earlier, because you're good people, James, and I've always known that." He clamps his hand on my shoulder. "You're also my best friend, and I miss you. I'm sorry I fucked up. That I wasn't there for you more. But I'm here now, and I'm telling you to get your shit together and go get your girl." He drills me with a dark look. "Before that punk ass swoops in and steals her away from you."

"Okay, I've had enough," Slater says, slamming his beer bottle down on the table and powering off the TV.

"Hey, I was watching the game," I protest, even though I can barely concentrate on anything after my talk with Austin earlier.

"No, you fucking weren't." He glares at me. "You were staring at the screen, but you weren't watching a second of the game. You were lost in your own head again. Like you've been every single time I've seen you since you broke up with Summer, and I'm done with the bullshit." He leans forward on his elbows. "You have Gabby worried sick about you, and, honestly, you're freaking me out too. I've never seen you like this. Not even after Myndi."

"Because I've never loved and lost *the one* before," I blurt.

"Finally." He rolls his eyes to the ceiling.

"Finally, what?" I snap.

"Finally, some show of honest emotion."

I flip him the bird. "Screw you, asshole. We can't all be perfect and have the perfect fucking life."

"Sometimes, I seriously want to beat the shit out of you in the hope it'll knock sense into that thick skull of yours."

"Wow. You're really rolling out the hospitality."

The Dover move happened fast, and I haven't had time to find a place to live yet, so I'm staying with Slate and Gabby for a few weeks until I find my feet. After living in the apartment on my own for months, it's been nice surrounded by noise and people again.

"We should've had this conversation months ago. Hell, years ago." He moves over to the couch, dropping down beside me. "I, no, *we*, can't sit back and watch you self-destruct anymore. You need to talk about all the shit you keep locked up in your head. If you won't talk to me, at least talk to your sister. It's killing me seeing how upset she is for you."

"You don't play fair." I pout.

"I'll use whatever advantage I can, but it's no word of a lie. We're worried, and I'm not accepting the bullshit anymore. I'm your best buddy. Fuck, we're basically brothers. And you used to tell me everything. Now you shut me out, and I don't know what the fuck I did to deserve that."

"Slate, it's never been about anything you've done. If I tell you the truth, you'll definitely want to beat the shit out of me."

"I think you want to tell me. I think you need to for your sanity." He lays a hand on my shoulder. "You're the closest I have to a brother, Ryan, and I'd never judge you. You've been there for me. Let me be here for you."

"We're really going there? Doing the heavy shit?"

He nods, grinning. "It's been a while."

"We'll need more beer for this. Lots more beer." I waggle my empty bottle at him.

"I'll be back."

"And Slate?" I call out after him, looking over my shoulder. "Make sure Gabby isn't around. She can't hear this."

I settle back in my seat, closing my eyes as I wait for his return. He's right, not that I'll admit that out loud. But I need to purge this from my soul. And I want his advice on Summer. I don't want to lose her. Not if there's a chance she still has feelings for me. But I'm crippled, plagued by guilt and taunted by selfish thoughts, and I'm driving myself demented with all the back and forth.

Perhaps Slate can help me make sense of my head. Help me figure out where I go from here.

"The coast is clear," he says, when he re-enters the room with an ice bucket and a bunch of beers.

We pop the lid on a couple bottles, a comfortable silence descending for a few minutes. "I still love Summer, and I miss her so damn much. Every day I go without seeing her, another little piece of me dies," I admit, finding this easier to divulge than I expected.

"I know how that feels, and it sucks. Big time," Slate agrees.

"I remember telling you you were an idiot for letting Gabby go when she was pregnant because you believed it was the right thing for her, and I've basically done the exact same thing."

He doesn't hesitate. "Idiot." Slate fights a smile, and I flip him the bird again.

"I'm no good for her, man."

"Why?"

"Because I'm a total fuckup in relationships, and she lost the baby because of me." And though it almost killed me to break up with her, and it's killing me all over again, every day I wake up without her in my life, I'd do it all again if it's the best way of protecting her. Of letting her live a full and happy life.

"Dude." Slate's brow creases. "You can't honestly believe you're responsible for her losing the baby. It isn't anyone's fault. Miscarriages happen, and there isn't anything you could've done to prevent it."

"She was stressed, and mostly, that was because of me. Because Austin and Charlie didn't approve."

"Did the doctor say stress caused her miscarriage?" Slate demands in an angry tone.

I shrug, and that only angers him more. "Why the fuck do you do this to yourself? It's not your fault," he roars.

"Keep your fucking voice down, or this conversation's over!"

"Why are you shouldering the blame? Why?"

"Because it's not my first rodeo."

His eyes narrow. "Explain that."

I rub my throbbing temples, sighing. "The day everything turned to shit with Myndi, the day that bitch kissed me and posted it online, was also the day I discovered Myndi was pregnant with my baby."

Slater's jaw drops to the floor, and I don't think I've ever seen him so shocked. He urges me on with his eyes.

"I hadn't known. She was hysterical, crying and shouting, beating her fists at me. She refused to believe I was innocent, and she already had her bags packed. She went to her sister's place the next day, telling me she needed space. And I wanted to give it to her, but she'd just dropped a bomb, and my head was a fucking mess."

"Why didn't you say anything?"

"Because you and Gabby were planning your wedding, and I didn't want Gabby to get caught in the crossfire. I was still hoping Myndi and I could work things out."

"But you didn't. What happened?"

"I'd been sending her daily texts, and she was sending me back hate-filled replies. After ten days of that shit, I'd had enough, so I went to her sister's house, demanding she speak to me." I rub at the sudden tightness in my chest. "She was so angry and still worked up. Maybe it was pregnancy hormones, or her ex, Travis, ruined her faith in men, I don't know, but she was screaming and shouting at me, pushing me around, refusing to listen to the truth. And something snapped in me then. I gave up. I told her we were done, but I wanted to be involved with the pregnancy, and I'd help raise the baby."

I stare at the ceiling, hating to be reliving this, but feeling a little lighter at the same time. "Her sister threw me out of the house, saying I was stressing Myndi out and it wasn't good for the baby." I exhale heavily. "I went home and licked my wounds for a couple weeks, debating what to do."

I eyeball Slate before I admit this next bit 'cause he's gonna be pissed I went to my brother instead of him—even if he knows it makes sense because my eldest brother is a respected attorney. "I went to Dean and told him everything. I needed to know what my rights were, what I could legally do, because Myndi was refusing to answer my calls or texts, and I knew she was shutting me out."

Slate's jaw tightens, but he says nothing, just waits patiently for me to continue.

"A few days later, I got a text, a *fucking text*," I spit out, "from Myndi's sister saying she'd lost the baby. I was upset and angry, because she'd shut me out. She was already home from the hospital and everything."

A shuddering breath leaves my body. "I should've waited until I'd calmed down before charging over there, but you know how much of a hothead I used to be."

"Used to be?" Slate teases, and the faintest hint of a grin appears on my lips.

"It was, hands down, the most God-awful conversation I've ever had in my life. I won't rehash it all, but the gist of it was she told me, point-blank, that it was my fault she'd lost the baby. Because I cheated on her and then broke up with her, and the stress of it led to her miscarriage."

"What the actual fuck?" Slate snaps, his features contorting into an angry scowl. "The nerve of that bitch!"

"As long as I live, I'll never forget that conversation," I quietly admit, rubbing my tense jaw. "And I live with the guilt of it every day. And then, basically, the same thing happened with Summer, and it was at that point I really believed it."

I eyeball my best buddy. "I'm not the guy who gets the girl and the family. I'm the guy that messes everything up. The guy who ruins relationships. That's who I am, and it's why I walked away from Summer even knowing she's the only one for me."

The pain in my chest intensifies to the point I can barely breathe. "I've no interest in anyone else. I can't even look at another woman. All I ever see is Summer, but she'll never be mine, and I'm trying to come to terms with that."

I'm returning from walking Daisy in her stroller the following morning when I notice the strange car in the driveway. Slate greets me at the door, helping lift the stroller inside. "She's asleep," I whisper, so he knows to be quiet.

"I had nothing to do with this," he cryptically says, and my brow puckers in confusion.

"To do with what?" I whisper.

Just then, Gabby appears behind her husband, reaching for my hand and tugging me forward. "I overheard your conversation last night," she admits before thumping me in the arm. Unlike Summer's feeble attempts, my sister knows how to throw a punch and hurt.

"Ow."

"That's for not telling me," she says with tears in her eyes. Without warning, she throws herself into my arms. "I'm so sorry you went through that, Ryan, and it's not your fault. Either situation." She looks up at me, tears streaming down her face. "I hate you've believed that for years, and I'm so fucking pissed at Myndi for treating you like that."

"And that's why I never told you or Slate. I didn't want to come between your friendship."

"You're my brother. I love you, and I always want to be the shoulder you lean on. I need you to promise that you'll never shut me out again. I hate the thought you were dealing with that on your own."

She's sobbing, and I hate seeing her cry. I wrap her up in my arms, kissing the top of her head. "I promise I won't keep stuff from you again."

Sniffling, she straightens up, taking my hand and dragging me toward the living room. "Good. Now, just remember that, and don't be mad." She shoves me into the room on my own, pulling the door closed behind her.

Myndi stands in front of the fireplace, staring at me, her eyes red from crying, her skin damp with tears.

My guard goes up automatically. "Why are you here?" I glance around the room, wondering where her baby is. Gabby let it slip the other night she'd given birth to a little girl. But there's only the two of us here, so she must've left the baby at home with her fiancé.

"Because Gabby called and told me what you said."

"And?" Because that still doesn't explain it.

"It wasn't your fault, Ryan," she says, nervously approaching me. "And I've wanted to apologize to you for years, but you never let me speak."

"What does it matter now?"

"It matters because you've pushed that girl away because of me!"

I harrumph. "Don't flatter yourself, Myndi. Summer and me breaking up had nothing to do with you."

"It has everything to do with me, and you know it." She gets braver, moving directly in front of me. "I said horrible, hateful things to you after we broke up, Ryan, and you didn't deserve that. I don't want to offer excuses, but I felt betrayed, and I was heartbroken and hormonal, scared and angry, and it was easiest to lash out at you than admit I was the one in the wrong. That I was the reason we broke up, because of my trust issues. It was never anything you did."

Her eyes well up, and her gaze pleads with me. "You were an amazing boyfriend, Ryan, and I hate how we ended. You don't suck at relationships. You're at your best when you're in love. Although, I sense what we had doesn't even come close to what you share with Summer."

"It doesn't," I say, because there's still a small part of me that wants to inflict hurt in the way she did.

"I'm thrilled to hear that," she says, and my eyes pop wide at the genuine expression on her face. "I've hated myself over what I did to you. Gabby doesn't speak of you often, but I knew you'd reverted to your old ways, and I feared it was all my fault. You're an amazing person, Ryan, and I want you to experience the joy and happiness I have in my life, because no one deserves it more than you. You've a big heart, and you shouldn't deprive the world of that."

Tentatively, she reaches out, touching my arm. "I'm so sorry for the hurtful way I pushed you away. For doubting you. For hiding the pregnancy and miscarriage from you. It's unforgiveable. You should've been there, and I deprived you of that."

Big, fat tears roll down her cheeks. "But most of all, I'm sorry for saying it was your fault. I was stressed, yes, but that was all my doing. You were telling me the truth, and I refused to believe it. That's on me. Not you."

She squeezes my arm. "It was so wrong of me to blame you. I'm sure the stress wasn't good for me, but it's not the reason I lost our baby. It's never been your fault and I hate I planted that thought in your head. That it grew roots."

Her features soften. "I'm heartbroken that you and Summer lost your child. I cried when Gabby told me. No one should have to endure that twice, and my heart aches for you both."

I swipe at the errant tear that escapes my eye. "Thank you for saying that."

"Do you love her, Ryan?"

I should tell her to fuck off and mind her own business, but she's reached out to mend bridges, and I want to make my peace with this.

I'm sick of hating her.

Of feeling so guilty all the damn time.

It ends now.

"I love her so much it physically hurts."

"Then fight for her!" That old Myndi feistiness rises to the surface. "Don't do what I did. Don't push her away. Especially not out of some misguided notion I stupidly planted in your brain. I know I only met Summer briefly, but I knew by looking at her she was perfect for you. It's why I didn't hesitate when I asked if she was your girlfriend. You both looked like you fit together. Gabby gushes buckets about her, and that's the stamp of approval if I ever heard it. No one is ever good enough for her little big bro," she says, her smile expanding. "So, if Gabby is on Team Summer, then I know you've found a good one."

In a surprising move, she grabs me into a hug.

Even more surprising, I let her.

"Be happy, Ryan. That's all I want for you. You deserve it. If Summer is your happiness, don't lose her. Win back your girl."

CHAPTER 27
Summer

I WIPE MY sweaty brow as I return from the dance floor, grabbing the bottle of water from Hannah's outstretched hand, guzzling it back like I'll die if I don't rehydrate immediately. The club is packed with students on one last hooray before final exams start. I've been studying up a storm, and I'm confident I'm adequately prepared, so when a bunch of our classmates organized tonight, I jumped at the chance to go out after months spent in virtual hibernation.

"That guy is so checking you out," Hannah hollers in my ear.

"I'm not interested," I say without even looking in the direction she's pointing.

"You can't stay celibate forever."

"I've three words for you." I tip the empty bottle up, opening my mouth and trying to suck down the last few droplets of water. I pin my bestie with a smug look. "Pot. Kettle. Black."

"So original," Hannah drawls, slinging her arm over my shoulder. "I'm thinking about turning gay. You up for it, sister?"

I shake my head. "I'm strictly hetero, but you should go for it. That chick in the corner has been staring at your butt all night."

"What?" Hannah shrieks, her hands landing on her butt as she slings wide eyes over her shoulder.

"I'm just joking. Not about the gay thing though. I'd support you no matter what. You know that."

Marc came out over Christmas, confirming he's in a relationship with a man. My parents were pretty much floored, but when I thought about it, I wasn't all that surprised. Not that it makes any difference. I love my brother no matter who he loves. I just want him to be happy, and if being with another man does that for him, then I'm behind him one hundred percent.

Her eyes tear up, and she yanks me into a bone-crushing hug. "I know that. And I'm so glad you forgave me. You're an awesome human being, Summer May Petersen. The absolute best."

After Ryan broke up with me, I felt lost and alone until Hannah rode to the rescue. We hashed things out, and she apologized for the way she treated me. We got everything off our chests, worked through our issues, and came out with a stronger friendship at the end.

I don't doubt she has my back now and vice versa.

She kicked Jordan to the curb, and we both moved into a dorm together.

Neither one of us has been with a guy since then. We're both waiting to heal our hearts. Although, to be honest, I don't know that any guy will ever measure up to the guy I lost.

"Have you heard from Justin," she asks, dragging me with her to the bar.

I shake my head. "Not since I turned him down." Justin surprised me at spring break by turning up on my doorstep and begging me to transfer to Oregon State to be with him. Seems college life isn't all it's cracked up to be, and he was apparently missing me. Hearing what had happened with Ryan, and the miscarriage, freaked him out because he realized he could lose me. He wanted us to give things a proper go which isn't something we could do while separated by thousands of miles.

I was half-tempted, because everywhere I go in Newark, I look over my shoulder for Ryan. Silly, I know, but for a while there, I kept imagining I saw him. Perhaps it was my mind playing tricks on me or my heart just refuses to let him go. I've picked up the phone to call him so many times, but I never follow through. I went out on a limb for Ryan James before, and if there's ever any chance of us getting back together; he has to initiate it this time.

Hannah says I'm an eternal optimist, and maybe she's right.

Or I believe in true love. And I know that's what I shared with Ryan.

I've been seeing a therapist. I know, shock, horror. First time in my life I've had to see a shrink. But I've recently turned nineteen, and I feel like I should win some award for only having to seek one out now. She's helped me work through my feelings. The aftermath of my miscarriage is a bit of a fog as I ghosted through my life for a while there. If it wasn't for Ryan, I'm not sure I'd have found the will to even attempt to function.

Instead of talking to him, I internalized everything, shutting him out. I gave no consideration to his feelings, and I feel horrible about that now. But I wasn't being deliberately selfish. I just couldn't see past my own grief.

My head is clearer now, and I think that stuff he fed me the day he broke up with me was a crock of shit. I think he said what he knew would work. That I'd accept it and not fight for our relationship. And I'm sick I fell for it. But not enough to grovel at his feet to take me back.

If we are meant to be, we'll find our way back to one another. I still firmly believe in my mantra, and that's how I've gotten on with things since our split. I wouldn't call it living life to the fullest, but I've gotten a lot of my spark back.

I can't give my heart away again.

Not when Ryan still owns every piece.

Not until I know he doesn't want it for real.

"Are you sure you did the right thing turning him down?" Hannah asks as she battles her way through to the bar, yanking me out of my inner monologue.

"Yes. I don't love Justin, and moving to be closer to him wouldn't have made a blind bit of difference. I still love Ryan. Whether he loves me back doesn't change how I feel."

It's opening night at the theater, and a rush of butterflies has taken up residence in my stomach as I stand at the side of the stage with Sean, ready for the show to start. "You nervous?" he whispers.

"Definitely," I whisper back. "You?" I arch a brow.

"A little, but I like that I am. The day I don't feel nervous is the day I've become complacent, and complacency is never a good thing."

Sean and I have become great friends, and he was a wonderful support in those early weeks after my breakup. He's been happily dating Evangeline for the past six months and there's nothing but friendship between us now, but I'm cool with that.

I beam up at him. "I love that, and it's so true."

The music starts, and we're called into position behind the curtain. "Break a leg," Sean whispers, kissing my cheek.

"You too!"

The nervous fluttering in my belly subsides after a few scenes, and I'm thoroughly enjoying myself now. However, I can't stop sneaking surreptitious looks at the audience, wondering if he's out there somewhere. Which is silly. Because Ryan won't show. It's been months since I've seen him, and if he didn't show up to Austin and Miley's engagement party last week, he will hardly show up here. I hate that my breakup affected Austin and Ryan's friendship, but Miley said they are recently back on speaking terms, and working their issues out, which makes me happy.

My family is in the third row, and they give me a standing ovation when the play ends. Austin and Charlie let rip with loud whistles, and the biggest grin is planted on my face. The rapturous applause is ear-shattering, and when the whole auditorium stands to applaud, a surge of pride floods my chest. Sean and I hug, both on a complete high, and I'll miss rehearsing with him.

We've a couple more shows to put on, then there's a couple weeks before exams start, and then I'm heading back home for the summer.

I still haven't decided about Venice. The day I moved into our dorm, a letter arrived from Ryan with the tickets, explaining he'd purchased them before we split. He beseeched me to take the trip. To finally breach the skies over the US, and though I really want to go, going without him doesn't appeal. But the tickets expire at the end of the year, and during summer break is the best time to go, so I'll have to make my mind up soon.

I'm due to meet my family at a local restaurant to celebrate, but I'm still stuck at the theater, trying to get away from the party atmosphere backstage and the well-wishers. At last, the building empties out, and I wave goodbye to the final few stragglers as I make my way outside to wait for my Uber.

"Summer."

Goose bumps sprout up and down my arms, and butterflies scatter in my chest at the sound of his deep, dulcet tones.

He came! My heart rejoices as I spin around toward his voice.

Ryan steps out of the shadows, smiling as he walks toward me. He's wearing a black button-down shirt, rolled up to his elbows, highlighting his strong, tan arms. A glint of silver from the watch I gave him as a Christmas gift flashes in the darkness, warming my heart. I drink him in as he advances, trying not to ogle the way the dark denims hug his muscular thighs, or the way his shirt stretches across his defined chest and abs. His hair is a little shorter, but a few strands of dirty blond hair still sweep across his brow. His piercing blue eyes penetrate mine as he draws to a stop directly in front of me.

Tears glisten, unbidden, in my eyes, as I stretch my neck up to look at him. God, how I've missed him. I shove my hands in the pockets of my light jacket, resisting the urge to touch him.

Electricity crackles in the space between us as we stare silently at one another.

No measure of time apart will ever dilute the love I feel for this man.

"You look beautiful," he says, pinning me with a panty-melting smile.

"Thank you." I drag my lip between my teeth. "Did you see the show?"

He nods. "Told you I wouldn't miss it for the world." He reaches out, brushing his thumb along my cheek, eliciting a trail of fiery shivers. "You were magnificent. You belong on that stage, Summer."

My heart rejoices at his words, and his tender touch. "How've you been?"

"Lonely," he instantly replies, dropping his hand, and I feel like crying. "Missing you like crazy."

"Yeah?"

"Yes." He runs a hand nervously through his hair. "I know I've just ambushed you, but could we go someplace to talk? I've so much I need to tell you."

"My family's waiting for me at Gallagher's. Maybe another time?"

"Tomorrow then? I could pick you up first thing, and we could go for breakfast somewhere?"

"I've got a study session in the library in the morning. Exams are close." I shrug apologetically. "But I don't have plans for tomorrow night," I add as my Uber pulls up to the curb.

"Okay, great. I'll come pick you up."

"Okay, thanks."

Awkward silence descends, and I hate it, but that's the way it has to be until I hear what he has to say. "Okay, bye." I wiggle my fingers at him as I open the door to the car.

"Good night, Summer. I'll see you tomorrow."

His sultry voice does funny things to my insides and I'm a quivering mess as I slide in the backseat of the car, staring at Ryan through the window as we drive by.

"There's our Juliet!" My dad's loud voice carries over the noisy restaurant, and I swear heads turn in my direction.

"You say that like I've just stepped off a Broadway stage not the stage of a college theater company," I tease, hugging my dad from behind.

"You might as well have," Miley says, jumping up and squealing as she hugs me. "You were amazing. Like, you're seriously talented, Summer."

"Thank you. That's sweet of you to say."

"She clearly is," Charlie says. "Because that kiss seemed so real I almost believed it."

I slap the back of his head. "Stop stirring shit. Sean has a girlfriend, and we're strictly friends."

"If you say so." He waggles his brows, stuffing a piece of bread roll in his mouth. Hopefully, that'll shut him up for a few seconds.

"Well done, Summer." Austin pulls me into a hug. "I'm proud of you."

"Same here. I'm so glad I got vacation time to come. I would've kicked myself if I missed it," Marc interjects, waiting his turn for a hug.

"Thanks for coming," I say, stepping into his open arms. "Both of you." I smile over his shoulder at his partner, Eric, delighted Marc brought him to meet the family.

The dynamic at the table should be interesting.

"What the fuck are you doing here?" Charlie barks, glaring at someone over my shoulder. I don't need to turn around to know it's Ryan. And it's not my brother's hostile reaction either. I think Ryan could step into any room, in any place, in any country, and I'd know he was there. I'll always feel an invisible pull toward him.

"I didn't come to cause trouble," Ryan says, approaching the table cautiously. I notice Austin grinning, giving Ryan a none-too-subtle thumbs-up. Guess the bromance is back on. Slowly, I turn around, surprise evident on my face. "I'm sorry," he says to me. "I just can't wait until tomorrow. And I figured your family should probably hear what I have to say too."

"What the fuck is he talking about, Summer?" Charlie demands, putting himself all up in my face.

People at the tables closest to us perk their ears and tilt their heads up.

"Everyone, sit down," Mom hisses. "Let's not make a scene in public." She calls a passing waitress over, asking her to bring one more chair for Ryan.

He sits down beside me, and I look around the table at the silent, mostly stony faces of my family, thinking Ryan has monster balls for following me here. "You sure you want to do this now?" I whisper in his ear.

Reaching under the table, he covers my hand with his and squeezes, nodding at the same time. He clears his throat, twisting his body so he's looking me directly in the eye. "I lied to you."

It's a good opening line, ensuring he has my full attention. "About what?"

"I didn't want to break up with you, but I truly believed I was doing the right thing for you."

Charlie snorts, and I level him with a warning look. Mom clamps a hand down on his thigh, and I trust her to keep him in line.

Ryan ignores everyone but me, keeping his eyes locked only on mine. I sway a little in my seat. He always had the ability to melt me on the spot, and when he focuses his sole attention on me? I'm a goner.

"I've done a lot of soul searching. Talked with a therapist. And I've realized that I've let what other people think of me affect my actions. Especially when it comes to you. I knew the age gap concerned your family, and it's why I held back initially. It's also one reason I ended things with you in January." His hold on my hand tightens. "I was afraid being with me was holding you back. That you'd be better off with someone your own age. Someone who didn't come with the baggage I have. I thought the best way to prove my love was to set you free."

"That—" I can't not say something, but he shushes me with a carefully placed finger to my lips. I clench my jaw to stop myself from sucking his finger into my mouth like I want to. It's one thing I know he likes. One way I used to turn him on.

However, I doubt my brothers, or my dad, would appreciate seeing that.

"Please, sweetheart. Let me get this out." His Adam's apple bobs in his throat, and it shows how truly nervous he is.

"I won't interrupt. Go on," I urge.

"I felt like I failed you when you lost the baby. Because I wasn't there, and I knew you were under a lot of stress, and I blamed myself for that."

It's so hard to stay quiet. To hear the torment in his voice and do nothing to reassure him. But I promised I wouldn't interrupt, so I start a mental checklist of all the things I want to say to him later.

"I also blamed myself for my inability to comfort you appropriately in the aftermath. I wanted so much to help you, but I didn't know how, and I was hurting. It was my little munchkin too," he whispers, tears filling his eyes. My fingers automatically curl around the locket I never take off. Ryan gave it to me for Christmas and it has the initials S, LM, and R intertwined in three interconnecting hearts. I don't even remove it to shower, and during the long months of our separation, it has given me some measure of solace.

"You have always been so vibrant," he continues, "so full of life, and you weren't in those weeks, and I hated myself for what I'd done to you. It felt like I dulled your light, and I never wanted to do that." Emotion slashes across his face, and I want to hug him so badly.

So, I do.

Screw my family and what they think.

I fling my arms around him, resting my head on his chest, listening to the wild thumping of his heart. We cling to one another, and no one at the table utters a word. Ryan pulls back a few minutes later, still keeping his arms loosely around my back, and I keep my hands planted on his waist. "I made a mistake, Summer."

He caresses my cheek, his eyes burning brightly. "I love you. I've always loved you. I never stopped. Not for a second. And if you still feel anything for me, I'm begging you for another chance. Let me prove to you we belong together. Let me love you the way you deserve, and I promise you won't regret it."

I don't realize I'm crying until tears drop off the edge of my chin, trickling down my neck. Some girls wouldn't back down, even in the face of such a romantic declaration, making the guy work harder to win back her love.

But I'm not like other girls.

I've always marched to my own beat.

And I won't torment either of us any longer.

"Ryan," I choke out, my throat clogged with so much emotion. I cup his face. "I've loved you from the minute I met you, and my feelings have never changed. I still love you every bit as much. Maybe more after you risked the lion's den to pour out your heart," I tease, giggling. "You don't need to beg for another chance. I want that too." I take his hand, placing it on my chest, in the place where my heart beats in sync with his. "My heart still belongs to you. You own every part like you own me body and soul."

We move at the same time, our lips meeting in a tender kiss suffused with every emotion we're feeling. Vaguely, I hear the restaurant break out in a round of applause, and I wouldn't be surprised if a video popped up online at some point later.

But I don't care about anyone else.

All I care about is the man kissing me like I'm the only oxygen he needs. And, as we cling to one another, kissing like we're in our own little cocoon, I know I was right to believe in our love.

I had faith we'd find our way back to one another, and now we have.

EPILOGUE 1
Ryan – Three years later

"I'M SO PROUD of you, baby." I pocket my keys and wrap my arms around Summer from behind. She tosses her graduation cap onto the counter, leaning back against me.

"I can't believe I've graduated." Her voice is giddy with excitement as she turns around, circling her arms around my neck. "And I can't believe we're going traveling in two days!" Her squeal of joy does twisty things to my insides. I love seeing her so happy.

"Believe it, babe." I kiss the tip of her nose, surveying the boxes littering our apartment and the half-packed suitcases open on the living room floor. We bought this place when we got back together, and we're renting it out for the next year while we're overseas. "It's happening."

"You're the absolute best boyfriend in the whole wide world," she says, pressing her hot body into me. "And I'm the luckiest girl in the whole wide world."

"Hey." I swat her ass. "Stop stealing my lines."

Her eyes fill up. "I love you, Ryan. Thank you for making all my dreams come true."

This girl.

She gets me in the feels every damn time.

"Waking up with you every day by my side is a dream come true for me. I'd do anything for you, Summer. I want you to be happy."

I remember the dark days, when we lost the baby, and the way her light dimmed. I've made it my mission since then to ensure her light shines brightly. We'll never forget our little munchkin, and not a day goes by where our little angel in heaven isn't on my mind.

But life has to go on. And I look forward to giving Summer plenty more babies. But she's only twenty-two, and even though I'm feeling broody as my thirtieth birthday approaches, I can wait a little longer before taking our relationship to the next stage.

She hugs me close, and her heart beats strongly against my chest. "I never thought it was possible to feel so happy," she whispers into my ear, her warm breath tickling me and stirring my desire. "And I know it's because I get to share my life with you."

I hold her tight, knowing I will never let her go. She's mine. For now and always. "Ditto, babe." I kiss her deeply, and every kiss is like the first time we kissed. Even after years together, I still lust after her so much. "Why don't you take a shower while I put the champagne on ice?" I suggest.

"Only if you join me." She looks up at me through hooded eyes that blatantly transmit her longing.

"I thought that's a given." I smirk, swatting her butt and shoving her toward our master bedroom. "I won't be long."

I set the champagne in a bucket of ice, grab two glasses from the cupboard, and remove the chocolate-covered strawberries from the refrigerator before walking toward our room, shedding my clothes as I go.

Steam swirls around the en suite bathroom, masking my view of my girl, but I can hear her. Singing to herself like she usually does in the shower. Summer has a fabulous voice, and I could listen to her sweet tones all day long.

I slide the door open and join her, pulling her back into my chest and brushing her wet hair to one side so I can kiss her neck. She stops singing, and a little whimper emits from her mouth as I press my hard cock against her ass while my hand slides around to her stomach, my fingers inching lower.

She's filled out a little more, sporting shapely curves in all the right places, and it only makes me love her body even more. "You still turn me on so much, Summer," I rasp, nipping at her earlobe as my fingers sweep over her pussy.

"Same for me, babe," she murmurs, angling her head so she can kiss me. My tongue plunges into her mouth the same time I slide two fingers inside her, and her pleasurable moan has precum leaking from the tip of my cock.

We continue kissing, our tongues dancing wildly as our desire elevates, while I pump my fingers in and out of her, using my thumb to swirl circles around her clit. I know when she's close, because she bites down on my lip, her breathing is ragged, and she's riding my hand with wild abandon. "Come for me, babe," I say, pinching her clit, and she detonates in my arms, screaming out my name as she orgasms.

She reaches around, takes hold of my aching cock, and starts leisurely stroking it from root to tip, just how I like it. But I'm impatient today. And I just want to be inside her. "Hands on the wall and ass in the air, baby," I command, moving us both a little more directly under the water.

Summer places her hands on the tile wall and tilts her peach of an ass up. I rub my fingers from her pussy up along the crack of her ass and she sucks in a sharp breath. "This is gonna be hard and fast, baby, because I can't wait a second longer." Gripping her hips, I position my cock at her entrance and ease inside her. This is one of my most favorite things. Taking my time inching into her, feeling her walls grip my cock, her hips jerking with need, as she demands I give her all of me.

As soon as I'm fully seated, I pull back out and then slam back into her, over and over, hitting the top of her pussy with my cock, ensuring she feels every part of me. Releasing one hand from her hip, I move it down to her clit, rubbing her swollen nub as I ramp up the pace of my thrusting, pounding in and out of her as warm water cascades over both of us.

My orgasm hits out of nowhere, tingling sensations darting up my spine as my balls tighten up, and I release inside her, shouting her name as we both fall apart together.

After, I bundle her up in a towel and carry her into our bedroom where we make love and drink champagne until the early hours.

The next year is, hands down, the best year of my life. We planned our itinerary carefully, and it paid off as we travel between continents enjoying the best of different cultures.

We visit the pyramids in Egypt, the Colosseum in Rome, the Eiffel Tower in Paris, go up on the London Eye, and kiss the Blarney Stone in Ireland on the first leg of our journey. We can't resist returning to Venice, enjoying another romantic sojourn in the historic city. Venice will always have a special place in our hearts because it was our first foreign trip together, and it's the city where we fell in love with one another all over again.

From there, we travel to Asia, visiting the bustling city of Hong Kong, walking the Great Wall of China, and the Cu Chi tunnels in Vietnam, gawping in awe at the Borobudur Temple in Indonesia, and sampling the wonderful cuisine in Thailand.

In between exploring, I do a couple hours work a day, managing the business finances, acquisitions, and expansion plans and working on our new franchise business model while Austin holds the fort back home. We have weekly conference calls to discuss key decisions, and the business is going from strength to strength. We now have ten gyms in Delaware and Philadelphia, and with our franchise plans, we have the ambition to grow it to fifty locations within the next five years.

I'm lucky I run a business that allows me to take a year off and that I have a business partner who loves his sister so much he was willing to take on the bulk of the responsibility while I'm traveling. I had returned the favor, somewhat, when Miley and Austin had their first child last year, running things single-handedly while he took three months off to be with his new family.

Once Summer and I got back together, Austin and Miley agreed to take over the Dover gym while I moved back to managing the original Newark one so I could be close to Summer while she finished her studies at UD. Now, we have managers running each location, and Austin and I recently set up a small operations office in Milford.

When we return from our year abroad, we plan to sell the apartment and buy a house in Lewes, and I'll work out of the operations office while spending time on the road traveling to the various gyms.

But I need to make things official first, and I can't wait any longer. I've been dying to make Summer my wife for years, but she was too young, and the timing wasn't right.

Eight months into our trip, we relocate to Australia, and I propose to Summer on the steps outside the Sydney Opera House. I'm a basket of nerves, but she says yes before I've even finished speaking, flinging herself at me with tears of joy rolling down her face.

We spend three more months touring Australia and New Zealand before flying to South America on the last leg of our trip. Hiking the Inca trail to Machu Picchu was at the top of Summer's list, and we kept the best for last.

By the time we return home, we're exhausted but happy, and I'm looking forward to starting this next stage of our lives.

"Now, don't be mad," I say to Summer as we exit our flight, heading into the airport terminal. "But I have a surprise."

"What kind of surprise?" she asks, hooking her hand in mine.

"I sold our apartment and bought us a house."

She slams to a halt, her mouth trailing the ground. "What the what?"

I pull her into my arms, walking us over to the side of the hallway, out of the way of the throngs rushing through the airport. "I wanted us to come back to a fresh start, so I've been looking for houses online, and I found a few that looked promising. Austin helped me sell the apartment, meeting the realtor and sending me the paperwork to sign, and Gabby and Slate helped me find the new place. It's in Lewes, like we discussed. I paid a deposit, but I haven't completed the paperwork yet in case you don't like it." I peer into her eyes. "Are you mad?"

"I haven't decided," she says, her lips fighting a smile. "I'll reserve judgment until I see the place."

♥

"I freaking love it!" Summer exclaims, twirling around on the wide lawn at the rear of the property. We have our own apple orchard, a small vegetable patch, neat, and pretty flowerbeds, and it comes equipped with a small children's playground. The house itself is a modern build, and it's in walk-in condition although I know Summer will want to put her own stamp on it. With four bedrooms, four bathrooms, a study, a dining room, a large living room, and a massive homey kitchen, it's the ideal family home. I had a good feeling about it when I first saw it listed online, and Gabby and Slate loved it when they visited.

If we go ahead with the purchase, we'll only be five minutes from their place and only twenty minutes from Austin and Miley.

Summer jumps into my arms, wrapping her legs around my waist. She peppers kisses all over my face. "It's absolutely perfect, and I am definitely not mad. Thank you, babe." She plants an excitable kiss on my lips, and it quickly grows heated.

A throat clearing reminds me we're not alone, and I reluctantly place my fiancée's feet back on the ground.

"Does that mean you want to go ahead with the purchase?" Mrs. Johnson, the realtor selling the property, inquires with a warm smile.

"Absolutely," Summer says, clapping her hands before she leans into my side, clinging to my arm.

I circle my arm around Summer's back as I face Mrs. Johnson. "How quickly can we close the deal and move in?"

EPILOGUE 2
Summer – Six years later

"IT'S TIME TO sing Happy Birthday to Harper," I holler out the kitchen window, where everyone is congregating to enjoy the glorious summer sunshine. Our youngest is two today and both families are here to help us celebrate.

We're a lively bunch now with more kids than I can count. Gabby and Slate's eldest son Billy is fourteen and getting more grown up by the day. He towers over Gabby and me, and he's already pushing six feet. Daisy is ten, and they also have Jayden who's eight and Olivia who's six. Caleb and Terri's two are fourteen and twelve, respectively. Ryan's eldest nieces, Mia and Tia, are turning eighteen soon, but neither of them is here today as they are on a cruise with their mother and her third husband. Dean is here with his wife Alice though. They found out after they got married, and were struggling to conceive, that Alice can't have children, which was a huge blow to them, but they got through it, and they love having their nieces and nephews to stay, especially now Dean's girls are grown up and heading to college in New York in September.

On my side, Miley and Austin are here with their two kids. Landon is almost eight and Lillian is five. Marc and Eric couldn't come because of work commitments, as they both still live in New York, but they mailed an extravagant gift for Harper, which she loved. Charlie is here with his wife, Evita, and their twin four-year-old sons. Charlie is running the farm full-time on his own since my dad passed away three years ago. He had a massive heart attack, and it was a huge shock. We were all so upset because it was so sudden, and we never got a chance to say goodbye.

Mom still hasn't gotten over it, and I don't know if she ever will. I cast a glance over my shoulder, watching her chatting with Miley, noticing how much she seems to have aged since Dad died. They spent almost forty-five years together, and they were soul mates in every sense of the word, so it's really hit her hard.

We've offered Mom the opportunity to come live here if she wants. We got permission to build a small two-bed bungalow on the grounds of our property, so she'd have her own space. She turned us down, citing her inability to leave the farmhouse, and I understand it. She spent her entire married life there, and all her memories are tied to that house. Still, she knows the offer is there should she ever want to avail of it.

"The cake monster is here!!!!" Brayden proclaims, bursting through the door into the kitchen. He's our eldest. He's five, and he was a honeymoon baby. Ryan and I got married a couple months after we came home, settling for a small ceremony with family and a few close friends.

I discovered I was pregnant the day the local elementary school offered me a teaching position, but, thankfully, they were good about it. I still teach there although it's only on a part-time basis as I want to be around for my kids as much as possible in their early years.

We're incredibly lucky Ryan and Austin's business is doing so well. They have fifty gyms now in eight states with sixty percent franchised and forty percent directly owned. I'm very proud of them, and it's given us a very comfortable lifestyle. I don't have to work at all, but I like the few hours I do three days a week, and it helps me keep my identity outside of my important role in the house.

"Calm down, Bray," Ryan says, chuckling as our son races around the kitchen with his cousins, screaming and shouting. He's closest to Olivia and Lillian, which isn't surprising because they're all the same age and they've grown up together.

Austin and Slate wrangle the kids into chairs, and Harper bangs on the table with her plastic spoon, gurgling and laughing and trying to wriggle out of her highchair.

While Brayden is dark like me, Harper is the spitting image of her dad with her blonde hair and big blue eyes. She will definitely break hearts one day. Although she may look like her dad, her personality is all me. She's into all kinds of mischief, she loves singing and dancing, and she never stops babbling, having an amazing vocabulary for someone so young.

Slater is already teasing Ryan over what a handful she'll be in her teenage years. They are lucky with Billy. He's mature for his age, and he doesn't give them too much to worry about. At least, not yet.

Brayden is the opposite. He looks like me but has more of Ryan's personality. He's so adorable with his little sister, and so protective, just like his dad.

"Say cheese," Lucy, my mother-in-law says, ushering everyone around the table for a group photo. Since my father-in-law, Paul, retired last year, they have both taken up new hobbies, and she's glued to her Nikon like you wouldn't believe. They now spend half the year in Florida, but they returned last month to spend the summer in Delaware.

"Cheezzz," Harper says, clapping her hands and bouncing so enthusiastically in her chair I worry she'll bounce right out.

"No more Coke for her," Ryan whispers in my ear as we pose for the photo.

"Don't be ridiculous." I shake my head. "I wouldn't give a two-year-old Coke." He bites down on his lip, averting his eyes, his guilty expression giving the game away. "Ryan! Seriously?"

"It's her birthday, and I only gave her a teeny drop."

I roll my eyes, but I can't stay mad at him, because he's such an amazing father and very hands-on. The kids adore him. I joke it's like having three kids because he sometimes acts like he has the maturity of a three-year-old, but I wouldn't change him for the world. I find it ironic I'm the strict one and he's the big softie.

Ryan starts everyone off singing Happy Birthday, and I record the moment on my iPhone, zooming in on Harper's delighted little face as she sings along, not yet knowing all the words and oblivious to the fact it's her we're singing the song for. She blows out her candles, and we cut the cake, enjoying five minutes of peace while the kids stuff their faces.

After we've cleaned up the kitchen, we ask Billy to keep an eye on the little ones outside in the backyard while we usher the adults to the living room. Ryan refills wine glasses before sitting in the last vacant seat, pulling me down onto his lap. "We have news," I say, unable to keep it in any longer.

"Oh, shit," Charlie splutters. "Hearing those words coming from your mouth still sends the fear of God into me."

"No ageist remarks," I warn him, patting Ryan's chest. "My old man still gets testy."

"Less of the old," Ryan retorts, squeezing my waist. Pinning my brother with a smug look, he adds. "And Groucho Marx said you're only as old as the woman you feel so I'll be eternally youthful."

"We might be related by marriage now," Charlie replies with an equally smug expression. "But I can still beat your ass."

"Okay, enough, you two." Charlie and Ryan have this twisted relationship where they constantly banter and wind one another up, but it's amicable all the same. However, I know if I don't put a stop to this now, they'll derail our announcement.

"Sorry, babe." Ryan pecks my lips, and smiling, I lean my head on his shoulder. He places his hands carefully on my stomach, a wide grin stretching across his face as he skims his eyes over our family. "We're pregnant again. Baby's due in six months."

The room erupts in a cacophony of congratulations, and I'm manhandled by each person as I'm pulled into happy hugs.

There was a time when I worried I wouldn't be able to get pregnant, and when I fell pregnant so easily with Brayden, I was ecstatic but terrified too. Every twinge, every pain, sent me running to the doctor's office, afraid something was wrong. Ryan was the same. He'd told me what happened with Myndi when we got back together, and while he let go of his guilt and self-blame a long time ago, old fears resurfaced when I was pregnant, and he was every bit as worried as I was.

But we worried for nothing, because both my pregnancies were easy sailing, and I'm determined to be uber relaxed this time.

I run my fingers over the locket at the base of my throat, always remembering our little angel in heaven. Ryan had Brayden's initial engraved on it after he was born, and the same after Harper arrived, so I know he'll do the same with this new little one. Brayden knows he has a sibling in heaven, and we took him with us on our annual graveyard visit this year. Harper is too young to understand, but we'll tell her when she's old enough.

"You okay?" Ryan asks, pulling me back down onto his lap.

I plant my hands on his shoulder, pressing a featherlight kiss to his lips. "I'm perfect. I was just thinking about our little one in heaven," I truthfully admit.

"Me too." He runs his finger over mine on the locket, staring deep into my eyes. "I love you so much, Summer. Thank you for this amazing life."

"You don't have to thank me. We were meant to be, Ryan. It's always been written in the stars."

"I'm glad you broke through my walls. Obliterated my concerns, because if I hadn't opened my heart, hadn't let myself feel all the things I was feeling for you, I would've missed out on all this."

My heart is full of love for this man. "It worked both ways, babe. You showed me something I didn't realize I was looking for, and you showed me how to love. You're the best husband and the best father. But above everything, you're my best friend."

Our relationship has taught me many things, but the most important lesson learned is that you should never close yourself off to love. That love comes in many guises, and forms. And people will have opinions. Some supportive. Some not so much. But all that matters are the two people in the relationship. Whether others approve doesn't matter once you're in it together.

We're lucky both our families came around.

And I've gotten to live my dreams with my dream man by my side.

It doesn't get any better than this.

THE END

If you enjoyed *No Feelings Involved*, please consider supporting the author by adding a review to Amazon.

If you would like to read Gabby and Slater's love story, check out *When Forever Changes*, available now in e-book and paperback format. FREE to read in Kindle Unlimited. Turn the page to read a sample.

Subscribe to my newsletter to claim a free e-book and receive early news on all sales and new releases. Paste this link into your browser: http://siobhandavis.co.uk/free-stuff/kennedy-boys-freebie/

AMAZON TOP 25 BESTSELLER

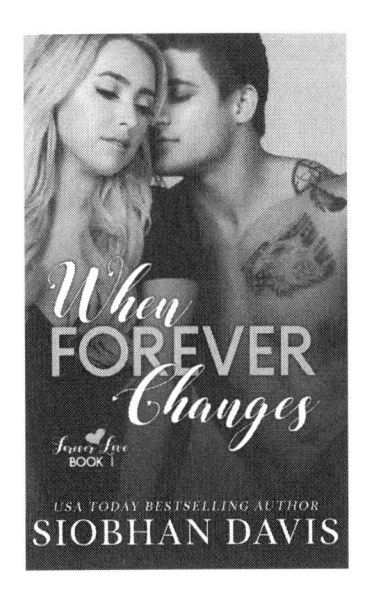

Gabby

Looking back, I should have seen the signs. Perhaps I did, but I subconsciously chose to ignore them.

From the time I was ten, when I first met Dylan, I knew he was my forever guy. Back then, I couldn't put words to what I was feeling, but, as the years progressed, I came to recognize it for what it was—soul-deep love. The kind only very few people ever get to experience.

Dylan was more than just my best friend, my childhood sweetheart, my lover. He was my soul mate. We were carved from the same whole—destined to be together forever.

Until he changed.

And I believed I was no longer good enough.

Until he shattered me so completely, it felt like I ceased to exist.

And I'd never experienced such heart-crushing pain.

Until he leveled me a second time, and I truly wanted to die.

But I had to stay strong because I wasn't alone in this cruel twist of fate.

I look to the sky, pleading with the stars, begging someone to tell me what I should do because I don't know how to deal with this. I don't know how to cope when my forever has changed, and I can't help wondering if I had seen the signs earlier, if I'd pushed him, would it have been enough to save us?

Or had fate already decided to alter our forever?

Turn the page to read a sample.

WHEN FOREVER CHANGES – SAMPLE

CHAPTER ONE
Gabby

Start of sophomore year in college

"A BUNCH OF us are heading to the frat party later. Want to come with?" Myndi asks as we make our way out of the building on Friday after our last class of the day.

"Thanks for the invite, but I've already got plans."

She smiles knowingly at me, her green eyes twinkling. "Let me guess? With a certain hot, rich, tech nerd who worships the ground you walk on?"

I grin. "Yep. It's our four-year anniversary, so Dylan is taking me out to dinner to celebrate."

"Aw, he's so romantic. You've definitely got yourself a good one, Gabby."

"I know. I'm really lucky to have found my person. I can't ever imagine my life without him in it."

Sticking her fingers in her mouth, she makes a gagging sound. Late afternoon sun glints off the red undertones in her hair, highlighting her natural beauty. Myndi's genuine personality and laid-back manner completes the perfect package. Travis was a damn fool for cheating on her. But it's most definitely his loss.

And my bestie has had no shortage of offers since we returned to campus from summer break a couple weeks ago.

"Too cheesy?" I'm still grinning as I say it. Nothing can put a dent in my good mood today. Not even the mammoth assignment Prof Brown just handed us.

"Definitely, but you own that, girl, and feel proud! Dylan's the catch of the century, and if you weren't my bestest friend in the entire universe, I might feel jealous."

I loop my arm in hers as we walk through campus. Glorious sunshine beats down on us, and it feels good to be alive. "Your Prince Charming is out there too, waiting to be claimed." I had thought Travis might be the one, but after the shit he pulled, it's clear I was mistaken. "I still can't believe Travis cheated on you with that skank. He was so devoted last year."

My bestie shrugs, but she can't disguise the flash of hurt glimmering in her eyes. "Neither can I, but I guess I never really knew him at all. Everything he said to me was a bare-faced lie."

"Let's schedule a girl's night for next week," I suggest. "Just you and me. We can grab dinner and a movie or hang out at my place. I'll kick Dylan out for the night."

Myndi and I met our first week of freshman year, and we've been pretty much joined at the hip since then. We're both studying nursing, so we spend every day together, and when she started dating Travis last year, double dates became a regular occurrence.

Travis and Dylan were close, until Travis did the unthinkable over the summer and Myndi kicked him to the curb. Now, Dylan refuses to return Travis's calls, and I admire his loyalty to my friend—as if I need additional reasons to adore my long-term boyfriend and childhood sweetheart.

"That'd be great, but I don't want to kick Dylan out of his own condo. We'll just ban him to the bedroom and commandeer the living room."

"Sounds like a plan."

A shrill whistle pierces my eardrums, and I look up as my name is called. My brother, Ryan, waves from across the street. He's in his running gear, and, judging by the hair plastered to his forehead, I'm guessing he's on the return route of his daily jog. He sprints across the road with a certain look on his face. One I've seen way too many times to count.

"Good evening, ladies," he says, all but ignoring me as he grins seductively at my friend. Very slowly, he peruses the length of her body, licking his lips and folding his muscular arms across his torso. Myndi's chest visibly heaves as she returns the eye-fuck, and I know it's time to stop this train wreck from happening.

I punch Ryan in the arm.

Hard.

"Ow!" Rubbing his arm, he scowls at me. "What the fuck was that for?"

"Quit with the sleazy 'come fuck me' looks. Myndi is my best friend so that means she's off limits to the likes of you." I prod my finger in his solid chest to drill my point home. And it's not the first time I've had to issue a warning. He's been after her since last year. Although he'd never make a move on any girl in a relationship, now that Myndi and Travis are no more, he seems to have made it a mission to get her underneath him.

As much as I love my brother, and I truly *adore* him, he's a complete manwhore, leaving a trail of broken hearts all over campus. If I thought his intentions were serious, and that Myndi was into it, I wouldn't stand in their way, but I don't want to see her hurt. And I don't want things to become awkward. Even though Ryan, Slater, and their crew are seniors, we still hang with them a lot, and if Ryan treated Myndi like one of his "girls," things would definitely get messy.

"You're lucky you're my favorite sister," he grumbles, shoving my finger away.

I purse my lips and narrow my eyes. "I'm your *only* sister."

"Exactly." He smirks, and I roll my eyes.

"Myndi has just had a bad breakup and the last thing she needs is Mr. One-night Stand hitting on her."

He slams a hand over his chest, feigning upset. "You slay me, little sis. Such cruel words."

"Don't even try to deny it. There's a running roll call of your conquests on the wall in the girls' restroom." A sour taste fills my mouth. "And that is *not* something I should ever have to see." I'm not confirming it's a list of the hottest guys on campus with each girl rating their skills on a scale of one to ten. Or the fact he and Slater are more than holding their own at the top of the list. Ugh. A sister does not need to know this stuff.

He puffs out his chest, and his lips curl up at the corners. "Can't help it if the ladies love what I'm offering." He shoots us a smug grin. "It's all in the James' genes. You'd know it if you hadn't attached yourself to Woods when you were still in diapers."

I smack his chest this time. "I was fifteen when Dylan and I first started going out. Asshat."

"Does Woods know you get off on beating up defenseless men?" He grabs his chin between his thumb and forefinger. "Or is that the standard he's used to?"

I fist my hands into knots, working hard to quell the urge to thump him again. "Ugh. You are so freaking annoying. Thank God, it's your last year here."

Quick as a flash, he grabs me into a headlock, messing up my hair. "Don't be mean, Tornado. You know you'll miss your favorite brother."

Ryan started calling me Tornado when I was about five after my propensity to race around the place, blowing in and out of rooms like a tornado. I've always had an abundance of restless energy, and it's why you'll rarely find me lounging around doing nothing. I like to keep active. The only exception is sleep. I love my bed and enjoy sleeping late, but once I'm up and out in the world, I'm always on the go.

I aim a punch toward his gut, but he snatches my wrist and effortlessly lifts me up, throwing me over his shoulder. I hate being the smallest in my family and the fact all three of my brothers use that to their advantage when it suits them.

"Put me down, Randy Ryan," I yell, balling my hands into fists and pummeling his back. Ryan hates that name, and I love throwing it out to piss him off. The girls in high school gave him the label, and it stuck, much to his disgust. Especially when Sexy Slater rubbed his much cooler nickname in his face. My brother's best friend was a permanent fixture around our house growing up, so I've spent years listening to them winding one another up. Slater's practically a surrogate James.

Especially in the last year.

A pang of sorrow slams into me, but Ryan derails my emotions when he swats my butt, dragging me back into the moment. "Hitting is not nice, Gabby. Mom and Dad would be so disappointed to realize their little baby girl is a wannabe Katie Taylor."

"Neither is screwing girls, making them fall in love with you, and then ignoring them, but you don't see me running to the folks like a big blabbermouth." I wriggle aggressively in his hold, and he relents, finally letting me down. I move to punch him in the gut again, but I'm only messing around. When he holds his hands up in a defensive stanch, I grab his face and smack a loud kiss on his cheek instead. "Love you, little big bro."

I'm the youngest in our family, and Ryan is the youngest of my big brothers, and we're the closest in age so, naturally, we formed the closest bond. When I was a kid, I used to call him little big bro, and it's kinda stuck over the years.

He slings his arm around my shoulder, kissing my temple. "Love you too, little sis. Always."

"You two are legit crazy," Myndi says, and I hear the amusement in her tone. "How the hell did anyone survive living in a house with the two of you?"

"We mostly just ignored them," a familiar deep masculine voice says from behind. I brush knotty strands of blonde hair back off my face and grin at my pseudo-brother.

"Sup, bruh?" Ryan greets Slater with a loud slap on the shoulder.

"I'm heading to Lil Bob for a workout before the party tonight."

My eyes drift over Slater, noticing the new tatt on his left arm and the rippling biceps stretching tight under his formfitting shirt. Slater has always enjoyed working out, but since his Mom passed six months ago, he's become a little obsessed. He's a permanent fixture at the sports facility the students have christened "Lil Bob." I guess it's part of his coping mechanism, and I'll never criticize him for that. Just thinking about his mom brings tears to my eyes, so I can only imagine how he must feel.

Noticing my lingering gaze, he arches a brow, and I blurt the first words to land in my brain. "You cut your lovely hair."

His lips curl up at one corner. "Not since the last time we met. Your observational skills suck, Belle."

Slater is the only one to call me that. I was obsessed with *Beauty and the Beast* when I was little, and Slater used to tease me saying I wanted to be Belle for access to the library. But he was only partly right. I did daydream about being Belle, but I was no different than any young girl my age, and I wanted to be her for the *prince*. Not the books! Anyway, the name stuck, and Slater has called me Belle ever since. Ryan prefers Tornado, Mom insists on using my full name, and Dad always calls me Buttercup. Most everyone else calls me Gabby. Dylan and I have pet names for one another, chosen when we were kids before either of us fully realized what we would become.

Some girls might hate being known by so many names, but it's always made me feel special.

I stick out my tongue, and Slater laughs.

"I swear your haircut must have its own Twitter profile by now," Ryan supplies, mock scowling. "If I see one more tweet about how hot Slater Evans is with his buzz cut, I'm gonna puke." He punches Slate in the shoulder. "It's good to know at least one girl is immune to your charms."

Myndi is watching all the back and forth with amusement, and I half-expect her to whip out a bucket of popcorn and settle in to watch the show.

Reaching up on tiptoes, I run my hand over Slater's shaved head. "Wow, it's so soft." He flashes me a blinding grin, showcasing his perfectly white, perfectly straight teeth. "Maybe I can convince Dylan to follow in your footsteps." Slater's smile fades, and his Adam's apple jumps in his throat.

"Dylan would look so hot with that haircut," Myndi agrees.

"I'm gonna head," Slater says, eyeballing Ryan. "See you back at the house." He gives me and Myndi a quick wave. "Catch you later."

"You coming to the party?" Ryan asks, his gaze bouncing between me and Myndi.

"I'll be there," she confirms with a smile, and they share a look. I have a feeling that train wreck is gonna happen whether I stage an intervention or not.

"I'm not sure. I don't know if Dylan has something planned for after dinner."

Myndi smirks, her mind clearly gone to the gutter, and Ryan frowns a little. Guess he doesn't like the idea of his sister having sex any more than I like thinking about him and his hordes of female admirers.

I kiss Ryan on the cheek before looping my arm through Myndi's again. "I'll text you later," I say, starting to walk away. "Have fun and stay safe!" I practically have to drag Myndi away, watching with resignation as she glances over her shoulder, shooting him a final drawn-out look. "You like him."

Her smile disappears, and she chews on the corner of her lip in an obvious tell.

"It's okay if you do," I rush to reassure her. I've never understood the apparent taboo of getting with your friend's brother or vice versa. It's not like there's any shared DNA or blood relation, so who cares?

You should be free to love who you love without barriers.

"You're both adults, and you can do what you want. I just don't want you to get hurt, and Ryan's not exactly boyfriend material."

"I know that, and I'm not looking for a replacement boyfriend. I want to focus on my studies this year, and boys will only get in the way, but that doesn't mean I can't have fun. I don't want my vajayjay to shrivel up and die from lack of use."

I grin. "That would never happen around here, and you should do what feels right. I'm a judgment free zone, but you've got to promise it won't come between us. If Ryan fucks things up, I don't want it to affect our friendship because you mean too much to me."

She squeezes my arm. "I would never let anything come between us. Especially not the weaker sex."

We both burst out laughing at our own private joke, and as we make our way through campus, I hope she's right.

***

End of Sample. Available to purchase now in ebook and paperback format. FREE to read in Kindle Unlimited.

ABOUT THE AUTHOR

USA Today bestselling author **Siobhan Davis** writes emotionally intense young adult and new adult fiction with swoon-worthy romance, complex characters, and tons of unexpected plot twists and turns that will have you flipping the pages beyond bedtime! She is the author of the bestselling *True Calling*, *Saven*, and *Kennedy Boys* series.

Siobhan's family will tell you she's a little bit obsessive when it comes to reading and writing, and they aren't wrong. She can rarely be found without her trusty Kindle, a paperback book, or her laptop somewhere close at hand.

Prior to becoming a full-time writer, Siobhan forged a successful corporate career in human resource management.

She resides in the Garden County of Ireland with her husband and two sons.

You can connect with Siobhan in the following ways:
Author Website: www.siobhandavis.com
Author Blog: My YA NA Book Obsession
Facebook: AuthorSiobhanDavis
Twitter: @siobhandavis
Google+: SiobhanDavisAuthor
Email: siobhan@siobhandavis.com

BOOKS BY SIOBHAN DAVIS

TRUE CALLING SERIES
Young Adult Science Fiction/Dystopian Romance

True Calling
Lovestruck
Beyond Reach
Light of a Thousand Stars
Destiny Rising
Short Story Collection
True Calling Series Collection

SAVEN SERIES
Young Adult Science Fiction/Paranormal Romance

Saven Deception
Logan
Saven Disclosure
Saven Denial
Saven Defiance
Axton
Saven Deliverance
Saven: The Complete Series

KENNEDY BOYS SERIES
Upper Young Adult/New Adult Contemporary Romance

Finding Kyler
Losing Kyler
Keeping Kyler
The Irish Getaway
Loving Kalvin
Saving Brad
Seducing Kaden

Forgiving Keven
*Releasing Keanu^*
Adoring Keaton*
Reforming Kent*

STANDALONES
New Adult Contemporary Romance

Inseparable
Incognito
When Forever Changes
Only Ever You
No Feelings Involved
*Say I'm The One^*

Reverse Harem Contemporary Romance

Surviving Amber Springs

ALINTHIA SERIES
Upper YA/NA Paranormal Romance/Reverse Harem

The Lost Savior
The Secret Heir
The Warrior Princess
*The Chosen One^*
The Rightful Heir*

^Releasing 2019
* Coming 2020.

Visit www.siobhandavis.com for all future release dates. Please note release dates are subject to change based on reader demand and the author's schedule. Subscribing to the author's newsletter or following her on Facebook is the best way to stay updated with planned new releases.

Made in the USA
Columbia, SC
30 April 2022